girls in search of cover

part 1

girls
in
search
of
cover
part 1

PAMELA MARIVA MSHANA

Published in San Bernardino, California, by Seven Visions Entertainment & Consulting, LLC. For information about special discounts for bulk purchases, please contact Seven Visions Entertainment & Consulting, LLC at (909) 572- or 0646 or sevenvisions.EnC@gmail.com

Scripture quotations marked NKJV are from the New King James Version®. Copyright©1982 by Thomas Nelson, Inc. Used by permission. All rights reserved.

Publisher's Note: This book is a work of fiction. Names, characters, places, and incidents either are products of the author's imagination or are used fictitiously. Any resemblance to actual events or locales or persons, living or dead, is entirely coincidental. Please be advised that this book contains adult content.

Any third-party information (websites, blogs, phone numbers, etc.) in this book are offered as a resource. They are not intended in any way to be or imply an endorsement by Seven Visions Entertainment & Consulting, LLC or the author, nor do they vouch for the content of these sites for the life of this book.

Library of Congress Cataloging-in-Publication Data

Names: Mshana, Pamela Mariva, author
Title: girls in search of cover, part 1: a novel / Pamela Mshana.
Description: San Bernardino, California: Seven Visions Entertainment & Consulting, LLC, [2022] | Summary: "When a young girl and her brother are relocated to her mother's hometown in Bovina, Mississippi—a deeply religious backwater where they all move in with Carmia's grandmother, Ma Evans. The girl's life is made difficult by Mother Johns, a conniving church leader with a dark hatred for Ma Evans, who convinces the community that Ma Evans entire bloodline is cursed. Carmia is sexually abused and becomes an outcast. Will the voices of her ancestors (spiritual cloud of witnesses) be enough for her to overcome a legacy marred by sexual trauma." –Provided by the publisher.
Identifiers: Library of Congress Control Number: 2022908752 (print)
ISBN paperback: 979-8-9858623-0-0
ISBN ebook 979-8-9858623-1-7
Subjects: BISAC: FICTION | African American & Black / Christian | FICTION / Family Life | LCGFT: Novels.

Printed in the United States of America

To my beloved Patricia and Mariva, the ladies divinely
designed to be my mother and daughter

AND

Abused, hurting girls and boys around the world.
I pray you find healing and peace.

"As for your nativity, on the day you were born your navel cord was not cut, nor were you washed in water to cleanse you; you were not rubbed with salt nor swathed in swaddling clothes. No eye pitied you, to do any of these things for you, to have compassion on you; but you were thrown out into the open field when you yourself were loathed on the day that you were born. And when I passed by you and saw you struggling in your blood, I said to you in your blood, 'Live!' Yes, I said to you in your blood, 'Live!' I made you thrive like a plant in the field: and you grew, matured, and became very beautiful. Your breasts were formed, your hair grew, but you were naked and bare..."

EZEKIEL 16: 4–7 (NKJV)

1

Going Home

LAUREN EVANS-PULLEN WANTED TO CURSE GOD AND DIE, BUT she had two kids depending on her. She gripped the steering wheel in despair as she floored the gas pedal driving down the highway. Like Job, her life was crumbling around her. That Bible story was one of the few scriptures she still remembered from childhood. At least Job had a happy ending, she thought. Her troubles were just beginning. She loathed her hades-inspired life that was chasing her back home, a place she thought she had escaped as a teenager. Everything was revving and racing. Not her car, her mind. And each mile she drove took her closer to Ma, who she knew would not tolerate her curse-God-and-die energy. So she shooed those thoughts away.

It was a late September morning in 1992. The sky hinted of blue even though the radio weather broadcaster foretold of rain. Laura worried about making it home before the roads turned muddy. The back areas of Vicksburg, Mississippi, weren't places where anyone who knew better wanted to be caught driving in the rain. It was a sure thing to get a wheel stuck in a mud hole just as mushy as quicksand. She turned the radio station, catching the tail end of Whitney Houston singing, "Where Do Broken Hearts Go?"

Shoot. Whitney don't have no broken heart, about to star in a movie with Kevin Costner. "Lucky B. Wish I could even pretend to be his lover wth his fine self," she mumbled. *"Where do broken..."* she grinned and sang.

Laura watched the sun peep in and out of view, mingling with gray clouds. She noticed an abandoned building that used to be the Goody's Department Store where she played hide-and-seek as a child—back when the local kids of all shades were still young enough to play together. The building now reeked of mildew and was under renovation. It bore a sign, *Mann & Sons Privately Owned Prison.* Her stomach tightened, knots moved from side to side, felt like they were spreading throughout her body. She fidgeted in the car, finding no comfortable position. She sighed.

Getting closer to these controlling people around here makes my insides itch.

She was thirty-one years old, only nineteen when she'd left the area. She eyed her two children in the rearview mirror as they slept in the backseat. Carmia had just turned ten, and Carl was eleven. She smiled.

Beautiful children, my only real accomplishment.

She glanced at them again. *Angels, only surface deep.* She knew her children loved each other, but keeping their hands to themselves and not thinking more grown of themselves than they ought wasn't their strength. They had a way of injecting themselves too frequently, too deeply, into grown folks' conversations. Laura was proud of her kids, spoiled them, but didn't entertain any Pollyanna thoughts about them or anything else for that matter.

She had left home for stealing another woman's fiancé but married another man she thought was a better catch. All she wanted now was to erase the memory of her husband from her mind and her kids' minds.

Said I'd never be like Ma, but it's her face in my mirror.

She rolled down the window. The humid air sucked her breath away and frizzed up her feathered brown hair with golden highlights. Her light skin warmed satisfyingly. Her sweat left moist patterns in the shape of her butt on the vinyl where her skirt stuck to the seat.

Reddish-brown dirt and tall green grass all around was a beautiful view to most people, but the sight of it made her nauseous.

I hate this place, roads that lead to nowhere and nothingness—full of deception and sadness. But a heck of a lot better than the one we left. She wiped her tears. *Come on, Laura. Put on your happy face instead of your I-don't-give-a-crap face.*

Her children needed her to get them through the death of their father and the reasons that led up to it. She looked ahead. She tried to convince herself she could live in her hometown again for her kids' sake.

When in Rome, pucker up and kiss butt as the Romans do. She wanted to keep them safe—or at least safer than they were in Alabama.

Ma will help me. Just gotta get to Ma, and things will be better.

She inhaled deeply, but the smell of cow dung filled the air even though they were a quarter of a mile away from the milk farm. She huffed the breath out, spat outside, and rolled up the window. Carmia repositioned herself in her seat and leaned against Carl's shoulder. The back passenger wheel bounced into a medium-sized crater and boomeranged out just strong enough to wake the children. Laura pulled her skirt down to cover her tattoo of a crowned lion and lioness standing side by side. Beneath the drawing read: *J & L rule the jungle.*

That loser, a king? She rubbed the tattoo with her skirt as if she could blot it out. *Will my kids forgive me for sleeping with the devil— baking demon DNA into their flesh?* She was shaky. *I need a fix. Got to figure out where to score.*

Bang.

A gunshot. She ducked slightly behind the wheel.

"Y'all get on the floor." The kids scurried to their knees. Carmia covered her head.

A few men passed by on foot, then a few more. Angry faces. She knew their expressions wore the pain of death—unnatural deaths that happened to black men in the South. She had seen these angry faces so many times in her youth.

Shoot, what have I gotten us into? She wondered if she should turn back to Alabama.

"I just have to get to Ma," she whispered to herself.

Carl rose to the seat, shaky, but he masked his fear. Carmia followed. Laura looked back quickly and saw her son pick a booger out of his nose and wiped it onto his sister's sleeve.

"Mommy, Carl is nasty," Carmia complained then climbed into the front seat with stiff legs.

No good man! She was glad her daughter was too young to have her father's seed growing inside of her. She watched the sullen ten-year-old clean the corner of her eyes, look around, and pout at her surroundings. Laura reminded herself to breathe, to put on a happy face.

Trying to sell my children a pipe dream.

The area wasn't just country but country poor. Nothing like the city world they loved. She knew her daughter would be slow to warm up to their new home, and gunshots weren't helping. All that was too much, so she focused on lesser problems.

"Y'all have to behave, I told you...more now than ever. Carl, stop putting boogers on your sister. Don't lie; I saw you. And Carmia, you stop whining like a baby."

The crowd forced Laura to drive ten miles per hour. Carl curiously rolled down the window. "Nosiness will get you killed." She rolled the window back up, leaving only a crack for her to hear what was going on—more and more of her former black neighbors and some people she didn't recognize hurried by them. Carmia removed her seat belt and got onto the floor of the passenger side as if that might keep her safe from bullets.

Between the crowd's mumblings, she heard someone mention her. "Who's that in that fancy car? Was them black folk in a brand-new Toyota Supra?"

A woman standing in front of the driver's side screamed to the man next to her, "What if it's ours been shot? Oh Lord, up yonder they saying the boy is dead." She was hysterical. Laura slammed on the brakes to miss hitting the woman and threw her family into a tumbling stop. *Dummy, act like she got bumpers.* The woman didn't seem to care that she was interrupting traffic.

"All we know is somebody got shot. Who is what we gonna go see. Now calm down," the man said.

"Oh, Lord, don't let it be ours," the hysterical woman yelled. The couple ran even faster.

They were all moving like a herd protecting its young, just like her, but they were in her way. In the distance, a mass of townsfolk surrounded what she imagined was a figure lying in the road, and many more people were on their way to the site where the dead person lay.

Can't get caught up in this mess. Gotta get to Ma.

The dead body and all the ruckus were blocking her quickest road home, so she had to go the long way. Dust kicked up from the tires and mixed with the crowd's anger as she turned left onto Mills Street, avoiding the human swarm and the nastiness of the South.

Man, I'm home, and this place with all its crap is better than where we came from.

After driving a quarter of a mile, she made a right turn down Maple Drive. The feel of that street alone put distance between them and the commotion. She always thought it was the nicest street around because of the way the tree branches on each side reached the center and touched each other—a type of heavenly covering.

Maple Drive brings me peace, even if just for a pinch of a mile.

She sighed and smiled at how being home had already changed her vernacular—a pinch of a mile. She made a quick left onto Hunter Street and slowly drove past Frederick Douglass Elementary School.

Still small and rundown, but it kinda makes me happy.

It represented simpler times before grown-up things happened. The building was white but looked beige, trimmed in faded medium blue, with poorly sketched pictures of African-American inventors on almost every door. The dodge ball walls, four square, and hopscotch lines were drawn with popping colors of yellows, reds, and greens. Laura envisioned herself years ago sliding down the yellow slide into a pile of leaves. It had to be around 1971. She remembered Mark, her first crush at ten years old. He'd always magically appear in the leaves just as she hit them. They'd smile face-to-face and start all over again. It was as if she could see herself holding hands with her best friend Kantrel as they walked home from school.

These memories faded as Carl asked, "Mom, is this a school?"

"Yes. Y'all gonna go to school where Mommy did years ago."

Carmia raised herself, peered out the window at the old school, and said, "Ugh," as she slid down into her seat. Carl reached around the front passenger seat and rubbed another booger onto Carmia's shirt, and she cried. Laura slapped him, then froze. Tears welled in Carl's eyes, but he refused to let them fall. She wanted to take it back. She stretched her arm behind her seat, attempting to wipe his cheeks dry. Carl flinched away from the hand that hoped to make things better. Laura hated herself at that moment. Too much going on—making more hurtful mistakes with her children while on the way to try to correct others.

What's wrong with me? Ain't never slapped my kids. This area, this hellhole, already getting to me.

She felt the weight of a stack of faults on her shoulders. A man was crossing the street, but she noticed him late. She swerved and skidded, almost hitting him. He raised his hand, probably about to give her the finger but moved on.

She pulled to the side of the road and parked. Her muffled cry was due to her effort to hold it in, but her heart forsook her mind, and she showed her kids the full extent of her pain—unsteady nerves and inadequacies. Her convulsion in tears stopped both of her children's tears.

"I hate my life," she said, bawling.

Carmia moved close to Laura and hugged her. She couldn't bear the sight of her daughter's sore body. Laura hyperventilated.

All this pain.

She hugged Carmia almost too tightly—wanting to comfort her soul. She cried on, seemingly softening Carl toward her.

All three were in tears. Carl hugged his mother too.

"I'm sorry, Mommy." He looked at Carmia. "I'm sorry. I shouldn't have put boogers on you."

Then the kids wiped Laura's face, a routine they had done many times before.

I suck as a mother.

She fluttered in a breath, hiccup-cried, then dried their faces too.

She and the kids put their seat belts on, and she drove down the unnamed route she had to follow to get to Ma. The dirt road began to weave into the familiar, bumpy, weed-decorated trails she remembered walking down as a child to get to school. Every kind of berry grew there right along with the weeds. Blueberries, raspberries, strawberries. Her mouth watered for the freshness of these fruits, but she was determined to get to Ma's before she changed her mind altogether. She stayed on the path whose end was an area of Bovina called Oak Ridge, a small location in the heart of Mississippi not too far from Vicksburg and Jackson. She braced herself as she got farther away from what she considered civilization because in the light of a city like Vicksburg, Bovina wasn't much, and Oak Ridge was the least in Bovina.

Almost home now.

Laura tried to escape this area for its boredom, backwardness, and lack of bravery, but there she was again, caught in Bovina's web. She shook her head at her former black neighbors who made up this community—six generations removed from slavery but still wearing fortified chains of the event upon their souls. Some lived on former plantations, descendants of sharecroppers, working with pride the jobs that were the residue of that history: log men, maids, and cooks. She remembered how Ma had begun prepping her to do the same. Submit to those servant jobs. Her mother's grooming of her for those jobs was the real reason for her abandonment. She'd have nothing to do with the subservient role blacks still played in Bovina. She had done greater things—assistant manager of JCPenney department store in Huntsville, Alabama.

Laura watched her past community happily walking to and fro with their shabby work clothes on, then she spotted Darnell—whistling as he emptied trash cans into the garbage truck. She smirked at the sight of him hooting while he worked.

They're dumb for not wanting more. Not gonna let my kids get caught up in that life, so help me, God.

The rest of the way to Ma's house, everyone was silent in his or her thoughts. Laura remembered her mother's smell—yams and butter. Ummm, ummm, good eating. Yams were her favorite; she could picture the deep-orange sliced delights smothered in butter, vanilla, and sugar.

Much farther up the hill were sporadic, spacious rows of pretty white houses—important looking. Laura didn't want the kids to focus on those houses. Homes only whites could own. Those homes looked like mansions manicured by heaven, but Laura knew their decoration was due to the careful hands of black yard workers. She remembered how she used to help nurture them when she was a youth: irises, cross vines, wisteria, creepers, lavender, and periwinkle. At six, she should have been playing with tea sets like her white counterparts in the house where she worked, but she was picking roses for ten cents an hour. She used to steal some of the roses for her bedroom, grabbing a little piece of heaven for herself.

Carmia's face showed the sight of such beautiful houses was filling her mind with an unrealistic anticipation for what their new home would be.

Ma's house ain't nothing like that, child. Roll your tongue back in.

Laura drove on. The vision of the lovely homes began to turn into miniature dollhouses then specks until they vanished altogether from their sight. The sun was warmer now, even though the sky still threatened rain. She drove for several minutes, turning corners through dark patches of greenery, browns, and cotton whites.

Begged to go into them cotton fields to make a little money. That desire cured the minute the palms of my hands ripped like frayed cloth.

She looked at the cotton fields, shook her head, then saw Ma's place. She trembled inside.

She slowed the car down, her heart throbbing faster, then she stopped in front of Ma's house. It was even shabbier than she remembered. She kept the car running but shifted the gear into park at the end of the long dirt driveway. After trying so hard to get there, she wasn't ready yet. She looked at her mother's house, a former plantation, now nothing more than a rundown shack. She saw it with fresh eyes.

In its heyday must've been the talk of the town, perfect green grass and gardens that made the houses we passed on the hill look small.

Ma's house had large front windows overlooking the outside. Although they didn't shield the family from the townsfolks' prying eyes, the windows were great for displaying Christmas trees when Laura managed to get one as a child. She remembered going under the house, playing with friendly rabbits, and sometimes hiding to get away from the world. She could keep herself a secret and her things, too, anything just as important to her as herself, like the one red satin glove that belonged to her mother before she was born. She imagined all sorts of fancy or wild occasions that might have made her mother wear them.

When she asked her mother about those before-she-was-born days, Ma told her to mind her business. Although thin and curvaceous now, Laura had been a chubby youth, had to squeeze through the mangled wood entrance that wasn't an entrance but a hole in the house's platform worn by time and the weather. She squirmed on the driver's seat, imagining the stickers that would sometimes pinch themselves into her butt.

"Five, four, three, two, one, and breathe," she used to say when she first got settled, got away from whatever in the adult world was ailing her.

Ma taught her that therapy to keep her from breaking into fits of anger, sadness—even too much joy. Ma had called her her overly expressive child.

I wonder if my notebooks of poems are still under there in my tin box.

She remembered the taste of the clay dirt she breathed in under the house. Laura felt a warm satisfaction run across her entire body just looking at her hiding place, a faint hope that she could go back to safer days. If not for her allergies, she would have sniffed it all in.

"We're home, children," Laura said with a bright, airy tone.

Although Ma's house had once been a plantation and some black folks resented her for living in it, she admired Ma for staying there despite the backlash. It was the rebel in her that enjoyed doing anything that made her neighbors balk. It was their expression of freedom, their fight to be themselves, to be unlike the overly religious folks around them. They enjoyed owning a place where, in the old days, blacks could only serve.

She grinned widely as her eyes found Ma, her heart still thumping hard inside her chest. Ma sat in her rocking chair on the porch—might've been nodding. It took a while before she noticed a car had eased to the bottom of the driveway.

Breathe, Laura, breathe.

Ma grabbed her cane, struggling to stand as though her limbs had gone to sleep, her half-leg moved with prosthetic help. Ma leaned forward, squinting like that might make her see them better. She was a vision Laura longed for so deeply. Ma was making her way down the porch when Laura recognized she walked with a bigger limp than years before; she moved closer to them, still a little unsure about who they were. Then her eyes settled on Laura, and she hurried even closer.

She's sure of my face now.

Then Ma laid eyes on her grandbabies and smiled as wide as the skyline, revealing a dark front tooth and an overly white one. She looked at Laura a second time and to each of the kids again. Then Ma stood with her arms open to the kids with a greedy desire for hugs. Carmia sat like her stomach was sour. The kids mumbled disappointment to each other, and Laura threatened to pinch each one to shush them before her mother came near.

I don't feel bad either. They made me do it.

Laura nudged them out of the car as she sat watching. Carmia and Carl walked hesitantly into Ma's massive body and received hugs. It seemed she forgot to release them, so they looked back at Laura while being smothered.

Laura had wanted nothing more than to get to Ma, but now she was completely frozen. Fear had come over her.

I see she wants her grandchildren, but after the way I left, does she want me too? Does she want all the trouble my return to this area will bring?

Laura made herself get out of the car, still trembling, needing a fix—drugs or Ma's love, she wasn't sure. Ma finally stopped hugging the kids, crying and giggling. Her stomach had been making the kids' heads bounce by her belly jiggling from sighs of joy and laughter. She looked at Laura with a hard expression; a tear rolled down her cheek. Ma took a step toward her. Laura, trepidly, took a step too.

Didn't tell her I was coming home. Does she want me?

Ma let out a groan and hurried so fast to get to her that she worked herself into a jogging, hobbling mess, almost fell over, so Laura rushed to her too. When Ma got close enough, she threw her arms over Laura's shoulders with all of her weight and cried the loudest moan of want and love that Laura had ever experienced. Ma hugged her so tightly, for so long, it seemed she would never let her go.

"My baby's home," she cried out over and over. Laura knew then Ma had forgiven her for the way she'd left. Ma hugged her like she already knew all of Laura's pain and mistakes, and she was trying to draw them all out of her; she seemed to want to carry all of her worries, pull them onto her shoulders to bear them because she was stronger. Laura was still feeling a little insecure, still shaking. Ma probably thought she was cold from the wind because she took off her long multi-colored sweater and wrapped it tightly around Laura.

I'm home.

Then, like a queen, Ma turned to welcome them into her home, walking stately, proudly ahead of them, snapping off a few honeysuckle vines from the tired fence. Laura took her kids' hands and followed her, smiling, watching as Ma took the honeysuckle into the house. She knew that Ma would lay them on the table for air freshener.

I made it home to Ma.

2

The Mothers

PEOPLE WHISPERED AND JABBED AT EACH OTHER, GETTING everyone's attention—alerting everybody that the mothers board was approaching. More thumps and pushing as they parted themselves to make straight the mothers' path through the shrubs just left of Walking Town Road. It was midday, still hot. Some swatted themselves, ridding their bodies of mosquitoes, a plague that seemingly passed over the elders. The mothers walked as if floating; steps seemed to be coordinated. They dressed in colorful skirts, shawls, wraps, and turban-like headdresses. They looked like African royalty. Just as they reached the outskirts of the gathering, they peered to their right. A group of toddlers sat eating chicken legs, watermelon, and rolls. The young ones looked up at them as though they knew the mothers' importance too.

Mother Johns left the flock, taking a few steps in the children's direction and blessed them with her smile as was expected of a woman in her position. They were all mothers of the church, but she was the queen mother—the highest African royalty. The kids were cute to her. One boy ran near her feet and squatted, biting a chicken leg, with no shirt on and a droopy, full diaper. He bothered her.

Smells to high heaven.

She turned up her nose.

These kids out here naked, stewing in their own stuff while eating. Umh, umh, umh.

She took her smile back and stood in her place behind the mother flock.

Tsk. These young mothers ain't worth a quarter, don't deserve the respect that comes with the title, mother.

The other mothers were Mother Thompson, Mother Givens, and Mother Farrell, all walking in front of her like escorts in procession. Some people in the crowd moved back, weren't worthy for the mothers of the church to pass by them. The mass silenced themselves from whispering when they stood near them.

Musty like a slave ship. Ain't nobody washed today? She kept a straight face.

Mother Johns couldn't help but feel her strength as the crowd parted to let her pass by them from the outskirts of the commotion to the ugliness of its core. When the three old women in the front had fully reached the marsh where the boy had fallen dead from the white cop's bullet, they took out their handkerchiefs and shook their heads in sadness. The boy's mother wailed on top of the terrain's blood-wet vines, screaming, "They killed my son, took him and won't let me have his body." The crowd gasped and rumbled.

The mothers stepped aside, not too close to the bushes for fear of snakes, and mourned with the boy's mother.

Then Mother Johns moved closer. She heard someone whispering, "What a shame what's done happen to young Brother James, only fourteen years old. Ana seem to be close to death herself, losing her son at such a young age."

She heard another lady say, "She doing so bad. Don't seem like she gonna ever return to her right mind. Ain't fit to work at the market no more. *Tsk.* These white cops ought to be locked up with the key thrown away."

Mother Johns walked slowly, authoritatively. Her stacked square heels knocked on the large, flat rocks she used as a stage as she pushed forward with her cane. She made her way to stand directly above the bloodstained dirt and reverenced it like holy ground. Her pointy nose turned up, her gray loosely curled hair was combed back. She was an attractive elderly lady, statuesque and stately. She reached inside of her cape and took out her vial of anointed oil. She touched it with ceremonial seriousness and prepared for her libation. She twisted off the top and slung drops of oil onto the boy's blood as if the oil could make his blood stop crying out from the ground. She shook her head. They were all silent. The group's eyes followed her mourning rock from side to side.

"One for the Father, one for the Son and one for the Holy Ghost."

Some crossed their chest with two fingers, and most said, "Amen."

A tear rolled down her cheek. Some in the congregation let out groans they seemed to be trying to hold within.

Pastor Himley joined them upfront, trying to get Mother Johns' attention for a sidebar conversation. He coughed to get her to notice him. She turned and saw him as he touched her arm with the hand he had coughed in; she recoiled, feeling his germs crawling all over her.

"I done already notified Bishop. He was in the area, coming straight away," Pastor Himley said.

She nodded, couldn't speak, too busy staring at his hand still touching her.

Peoples ought to know when their touch is not a comfort but a thorn.

Everybody was watching her and wanting to be seen by her. She gave them smiles and nods. Some patted her shoulder as a show of respect. They wanted to acknowledge that her presence on such a day was appreciated.

More thorns. Got to grit down and bear it.

She smiled at a little girl, about five years old. She had turned completely around, gazing at Mother Johns, although her mother kept dragging her to the side.

So sweet at that age. She eyeballed her mother. *Too bad she can't stay that way.* Mother Johns looked at Mother Farrell and nodded. "Farrell, you can sing now."

"She's a mother, too, you know," Mother Givens corrected her.

Mother Johns was fit to be tied by Mother Givens' remark, but with Mother Givens being eldest, she held her tongue.

Better be her dementia talking, rebuking me and suchy, such.

Mother Farrell began to sing "Walk Around Heaven." Most joined in as though a planned choir selection, backing Mother Farrell up with soulful moans and high-pitched harmony to complement her deep alto voice. When they settled down from worship, Mother

Johns emerged to the front again. She paced across the span of the crowd. She walked with the help of a cane, but her stride was solid and sure. Pastor Himley followed her huffing; she shook her head. He was out of breath, but she knew he wouldn't admit it, not since the last time she preached about his gluttony and lack of self-control.

Ain't no model for the flock, can't control the desires of his flesh no better than that.

Mother Johns finally stood dead center and spoke. "I don't have to tell you, but I'm gonna say it anyhow." She leaned to her right side, supporting herself with her cane. "My father practically founded this part of town."

"*Ummm-hmmm,* sure you right," Mother Thompson chimed in as her support.

"Oh, Lord. Here we go again," Mother Givens mumbled to Mother Farrell.

Mother Johns heard the mothers mumbling, but more troubling was their facial expressions. Mother Johns bit her lip in pouting disapproval of Mother Givens and Mother Farrell. She cleared her throat again, rolled spit around in her mouth, swallowed, and resumed her speech. "My father built our faithful church, First Baptist of All Holiness Church of God. He built it practically by himself with his own bare hands."

Some in the audience seemed to hang on to her every word like spiritual food, Mother Thompson, sometimes called M.T., among them. Others looked to have grown weary, seemed to be pondering what her speech had to do with the tragedy at hand. She could discern them all. The latter group ruffled her feathers. She rolled spittle on the back of her tongue in disgust.

How dare they not exercise patience given all me and my family done done for these backward sheep? Makes me want to spit, but I'd rather shine them on for now, lessen I lose influence. So, she smiled.

"As I said, my family has a long history doing good for this community, and I ain't about to stop now. I vow to work with Bishop King and the authorities to get to the bottom of this great atrocity done here today."

The crowd roared with acceptance of her words. It was what they had anticipated and had rallied there to hear. They appeared to only want to know about what would be done about James' death. She prioritized reminding such a large gathering that she was the strength of the community before getting to the matter of the dead boy.

James had been unarmed, shot in the back by a white officer. It had been a couple of years since their community had experienced such a crime. Bovina's black population had all rallied together years before and protested police violence toward black boys. They had been successful with no more events of that kind until that day, and they weren't going to stand around and let those crimes resurface in their area.

"What you gonna do, Mother?" someone yelled.

She was indignant, felt she had already answered that question. But they seemed to want more, and she hadn't thought it out that far yet.

She widened her eyes, "What time is Bishop due to be here?" she whispered to Himley.

"Well, ah…" He looked up like he was trying to replay the phone conversation in his head.

This process of his always made Mother Johns rebuke herself for ever asking him a question.

"*Aw,* hush up, Himley, if you don't know." She shook her cane gently as she moved closer in the direction of where the question had come.

"W–What you say now?" she asked to give herself more time to come up with a response.

Bishop King's heavy steps broke twigs and branches on the ground and alerted the group to part again with mumblings and cheers at his arrival. He joined Mother Johns and stretched his arms wide toward the audience as they clapped at his simple gesture.

You swear somebody got healed the way they carry on about Bishop.

He smiled at her and touched her on the shoulder, as if letting her know he was there now and she could step aside. She didn't know how to take his arrival. His distraction had let her off the hook from providing a more detailed plan of action. But his commanding presence had stolen the spotlight from her. She always had this mixed reaction to Bishop. She admired him and even respected him, but she was threatened by him too. She moved to the side, joining the other mothers.

Mother Givens had a smile on her face. Mother Johns took it as mockery; she smacked her lips and ignored her rival's grin. Bishop King swayed from side to side and held his pregnant-looking belly as though he were in pain and sang "Amazing Grace." The assembly joined him with tears in their eyes.

Show-off.

When he finished, he stood resolutely in front of them and said, "This very night, the authorities are called to answer."

They all shouted in agreement, "This very night," and "Make 'em answer, Bishop."

"I am prepared to sleep in front of that police house for three days and three nights if need be until we get an answer. This crime against young Brother James and so many others within our community will not go without justice. No, sir. We won't stand for it."

Ain't that what I done already told them?

"We won't stand for it." They repeated after him.

"We gonna stand together in the face of our oppressors and fight the good fight until we see justice served…Are you ready to stand? Then say, 'I'm standing for Brother James.'"

The mass of onlookers repeatedly shouted, "I'm standing for Brother James, standing for Brother James." A car passed on Walking Town Road bringing them to silence. When they knew no other white folk were around, they started up again.

Bishop King raised his right fist in the air, still chanting. Mother Johns looked at the boy's blood then looked at her daughter Sal standing with her two grandsons, Noah and Joseph. More tears came to her eyes.

We got to save our black boys. Got to put a stop to this violence against them. But she had had enough of Bishop. She started her departure from the crowd, but they were less respectful. No parting of the Red Sea to let her through. Only a few stepped out of her way. She struggled to leave the way she came. The crowd was too thick. She stumbled. Pastor Himley ran to her aid, shaking his head, arms stretched wide, as though his gesture would stop the congregants from pushing. He was a short, balding, chubby man.

He grabbed her elbow and guided her through the crowd, creating a path, saying, "Move now. Mother is trying to get through. Get now. Get out of the way." His stubby arms barely fit around her long arms. They were too caught up in Bishop's chant to notice her passing by.

Bishop got y'all acting a fool, done lost your darn minds.

The other mothers had gotten caught up too. She walked all alone with Pastor Himley until she turned back and yelled, "Thooomp-son," in a high-pitched siren.

Mother Thompson, jerked out of her chanting frenzy at her sage's call, noticed she and the other mothers had missed their cue. She tapped Mother Farrell on the shoulder, Farrell nudged Mother Givens, and they all turned to follow Mother Johns, who fumed with each step.

Peoples ain't got no more respect for their elders these days.

She got hot, fanned herself with her Spanish-style fan, and stretched her arms wide. Like a rehearsed routine, M.T. took Mother Johns' cape from around her shoulders and carried it as though an armor bearer on assignment during church service.

Mother Givens, who they also called Old Mother, shook her head and mumbled, "Better her than me. I wouldn't be able to do it, treating human folk like they be gods and such. Got her thinking she's a queen and such."

Mother Johns grew weary of Mother Givens' mutterings all day. She moved to her, leaned into her face, wanted to speak obscenities, but that wouldn't have been appropriate for a woman of her stature. "Why don't you just shut your hole sometimes?" she said instead.

The other mothers standing guard didn't voice their opinions, but Mother Johns could tell they were not pleased with her treatment of Mother Givens. Even she knew that of them all, Mother Givens was the one who hadn't ever done anybody wrong. Mother Johns despised the discontent in their eyes. She hacked and spit it to the ground. She was perturbed, but she walked on without saying another word. The others followed her.

Mother Farrell touched Mother Givens gently in the middle of her back. The sound of Mother Johns' steps and stomps as she broke twigs in front of them now led their procession.

They gonna learn yet. I'm the pillar of this community. Ain't no Bishop or nothing else gonna change that, she seethed, stepping into mud.

3

***

Neighbors, I'm Back

MA'S BODY WAS MUCH WEAKER. SHE HADN'T BEEN TO THE STORE in a while, so there wasn't any meal already prepared like Laura imagined driving home. But that was okay. Laura was sad her mom had been alone while feeling so poorly. Ma said a local boy had been helping her with small tasks, picking up her medicine, grocery shopping, and such. But with her family home, Ma seemed determined to cook dinner after treating them to lunch in town.

She scuttled around, grabbing her purse, shawl and shopping list, weeping—overwhelmed, happy, shocked because her daughter and grandchildren were home. She maneuvered between the kids in the backseat for the drive to town. It took some doing, but she wouldn't have it any other way.

Laura drove, looking in the rearview mirror. She smiled. *I should've sent their pictures.*

Ma seemed to be making up for lost time, loving and hugging on them so. Laura held her breath, watching Ma shower her kids with big, wet kisses they secretly wiped away. *She can't get enough of 'em.*

"Mommy, I'm starving," Carl said.

Laura sucked her teeth. "I know you are. We all hungry. Going to get lunch now."

Ma rubbed Carl's belly; he froze and turned away. Ma chuckled and turned to Carmia, admiring her, not trying to kiss anymore, seeming to realize her affection was overwhelming. Ma looked at Laura in the mirror.

"I knows how you loves my yams."

"Sure do, Ma. I got all the time in the world to eat 'em now."

As Laura turned onto Orangewood Way, she felt itchy all over as if something was crawling on her. She scratched her arm, drawing blood. She sucked it, tasting her salty sweat mixed with another almost satisfying flavor—the cocaine she had sniffed hours before permeated her pores. Ma watched with familiar eyes.

There were hills all around for miles—shrubs, green trees, and dirt pathways. *Wild places where bad things happen, and no one ever finds out.* She caught herself and smiled for Ma and the kids' sake.

Fake smiles got Laura through uncomfortable situations. She hoped some fake things could become real, so she offered false words too. "It's good to be home," she said. Ma seemed to know she was lying.

Carmia broke her silence. "I hate this place. I dislike this place. I…" She pulled petals off of a yellow daisy with each phrase.

Laura could've fainted dead away; she quickly looked back squinting at the child, imagining how she might pinch the girl. She veered slightly into the wrong lane, and the scare caused her to hold her peace. *Ought to tear her heartstring out.* She sighed. *Gotta get a fix.* She looked at her mother from the corner of her eye.

Ma giggled. "Wonder where she got it from?"

Laura passed the impoverished rural land where Bovina blacks lived, driving into a suburban area. A wedding procession was taking place. Several white girls glided out of a medium-sized church nestled on a beautifully manicured lawn area, wearing dresses befitting the event. It didn't seem real that such a beautiful garden existed in those parts. A piece of paradise had sailed down to earth and anchored itself in front of the white people's church, as if the God they served favored them—gifting them with daisies, daffodils, roses, and all manner of beautiful green vines spread across fences and along the sides of the building, lurking around benches making the scene a place for angels to dwell.

Laura watched how intensely her daughter tried to see it all, as though memorizing the vision. The bride was smiling, carried by her new husband. Carmia's eyes seemed to lock with the bride's eyes, and her daughter smiled for the first time since they'd arrived in Bovina.

"Mommy, is this a place to find good husbands?" Carmia asked.

Laura looked at Ma, then their burst of laughter broke the girl's concentration on the wedding party. Their car entered another poor section of town. Carmia picked up another daisy from the seat as she glimpsed some black girls her age dressed in poverty. The girls were milking cows, their hands dirty from the task. Their feet were bare, covered with mud.

"*Tsk*" Laura's tongue tapped the back of her teeth as Carmia perched her chiseled nose in the air toward the dirty-faced black girls. Laura hated that her gorgeous child couldn't see the prettiness in darker skin. *She's only ten, and in her eyes, beauty is white.*

She gazed in the rearview as her daughter threw her wavy hair across her shoulder and away from the weary girls with matted hair. Carmia's actions reminded her of herself before she knew any better.

They finally arrived at the town's center. Laura parked in front of the grocery store on the shallow end of Brook Haven Road. Ma, escorted by Carl, went to buy flour, lard, and some other things she wanted. Laura and Carmia idled in the Supra. Just two stores down to their right, a group halted and stared at them.

Still nosy as heck.

Mrs. Mercer, who Laura's generation called Mrs. Mercy-Please because she was so stern and unforgiving, nearly broke her neck trying to look into the car as she walked by. Laura covered her face with her hair until she passed. She grinned, looking at the peeling, light-blue paint on her teenage, friend's family gas station.

He still just calls it Willie's Gas Station. Three generations of Willie's. Hmm, ain't never gonna change then. Same graffiti on the wall. Her nickname, Luscious, was next to her handprint in neon pink. *Frozen in place.*

Laura tried to brace herself for the unwelcome response she was sure to get from her religious neighbors. She heard a voice say, "Ain't you Ma Evans' daughter, Laura?" She ducked down in her seat, sorry his eyes had found her—not wanting him appraising her body.

It was Deacon Barnes standing on the passenger side observing her, then Carmia.

Get your nasty eyes off us.

He was a critter that lurked in Bovina bushes. His notice of beautiful flesh made him fail to see those who were watching him.

Yuck.

His lustful eyes were all the inspiration Laura needed to get out of the car and face the others.

"Yeah, it's me, Laura, but I've got to go. On my way to get Ma, my kids and me a table for lunch. Bye." She rolled her window up. *Hypocrites all around me.* Deacon Barnes stood there starring, wasn't done speaking to her. "Blah," she yelled.

He jerked back, collected himself and strolled down the road in his feeble, old–man-who-thinks-he's-still-a-catch sort of way.

Carmia giggled at her mother's impolite behavior then folded her arms, still unwilling to be where she was. Laura bent low, took a deep sniff from her purse. She shook her head. *Whew, now I'm ready to dance with demons.* She unskillfully powdered her face with CoverGirl makeup, a distraction for Carmia's sake. Now she was hyped. She looked into the mirror and wiped away any remaining white powder from her nose.

She wanted to appear refined and elegant. Laura lifted her legs and feet, turned her hips, got out of the car and wiggled to shake her skirt free from her butt. When she stretched her long model legs out of the driver's side, she knew she was causing every man watching to fall weak. Their mesmerized reaction made her feel powerful. She stumbled a little, less sophisticated than she'd hoped to be. She straightened her back and smiled, feeling sexy.

These women are still so insecure.

Laura was dressed in a cherry-red two-piece skirt suit with a pillbox hat to match, almost appropriate for church, but her red pumps were more cover than her skirt.

See, y'all. I'm wearing a church hat.

She looked toward the church at the opposite end of the street and shook herself free from the emotional willies running through her body at the sight of First Baptist of All Holiness Church of God.

Hmmm. Church seems smaller.

With cocaine-laced confidence, she walked to the passenger side and opened the back door for Carmia, but the girl refused to move. Laura desired to be longsuffering but lost patience with her daughter.

Carmia yelled, "You can't make me live here."

Laura snapped under the pressure of all the eyes on her. *This child gonna make me choke the devil out of her.* She moved close to Carmia, squinted her right eye and fake-smiled—quick flash of teeth, imagining what everyone was thinking. She spoke through clenched teeth. "This is where we're gonna live—here with my ma. Your grandma's lived through our kind of problems. Y'all gonna get money, land and other inheritances. Now get out the car."

It seemed the whole town was watching.

I'll beat you the Bovina way. Got me looking a fool.

Carmia rolled her eyes. Laura looked around, and it hit her that with all the distractions, she hadn't parked anywhere near Ester's Place—the restaurant that came closest to Ma's cooking. She spotted a nearer place, a newer restaurant called Carol's Diner, just five doors down from where she stood.

Don't know if the food is good, but it's gonna have to do.

"Come on here, child," she said. *Got to get all these eyes off us.*

She had just about gotten Carmia and a small bag out of the car when Ducky and Deacon George Pitts rushed over to help them. Ducky had a broad, long nose and wore his Jheri curl combed straight back, evidence that he was stuck in the eighties. Tall and thin, he wobbled from side to side as he walked with size sixteen feet flopping with each step to support his grand stature. Deacon Pitts was an average height white man—bold enough to marry a black woman and still live in Bovina. He possessed a book smart air, a little reserved. His patchy beard made him look slightly unkempt behind his thick glasses, and still, there was a kindness about him.

"Can I give you a hand, Laura?" Ducky said, picking up the small bag.

"Why, Ducky Johnson, when did you become such a help?" Laura said with a sniff. "Thanks, but never mind. We'll manage just fine."

She knew Ducky well enough to know her mild dismissal would reduce him from thirty-five years old back to eighteen. She was his high school crush and had rejected him then too. He seemed so awestruck he didn't realize she'd declined his help. He followed them anyway, still carrying their bag.

Deacon Pitts stood in the distance, but she felt his attention on them nonetheless. He always was an odd person. When they were in high school, George told her that his knowledge of African-American history rivaled that of Carter G. Woodson—well versed in African-American literature, religious studies, politics and history. Even as a teenager, he couldn't fool her.

Ma say he's always preaching about living a chaste life. Should've been a priest then.

She figured, he used his knowledge to judge people, elevating himself in his mind because of other people's lack of intelligence. Pitts made more noise about blackness than anybody, as though he were black. That got him weighed on the scales at a young age, wasn't fully accepted by either ethnicity.

Strange.

Remembering how he tried to commit suicide in high school, she graced him with grin anyhow.

"Mommy, that ugly man's following us," Carmia whispered.

"Forgive me, sweetie. This is Ducky, an old friend of mine." Carmia looked down. "Ducky, this here is my daughter, Carmia. She's ten." He reached for Carmia's hand. She ignored him. "My son, Carl, is a year older, but he's a big boy for his age. I just paged him about where we'll be." Ducky nodded, Carmia frowned, and Laura kept on yapping. "And you know me, I'm gonna make sure they don't have no problems around these parts." She looked straight ahead, walking and rubbing her nose. "I'll take my bag now." He didn't release it.

Carmia scowled at Ducky. Laura frowned at her girl. "I've got this handled." She expected her disapproving expression to persuade her daughter to fall in line and follow her. She walked on, too busy taking in the town through the corner of her eye, watching the response her presence aroused in her former neighbors, to notice that Carmia was no longer following her. The girl had stopped in front of the thrift store window. She stared at a mannequin modeling a wedding dress adorned with pearls. Laura searched until her eyes fell on her daughter with a sigh and a smile. Carmia's eyes had transfixed on the dress, and she was drooling.

"Come on here, girl," she said.

She watched Carmia brush her soft bangs to the side of her face for a better view of the gown. The girl's reflection appeared in the window. Carmia's eyes were as bright and as vast as the ocean, the color of seaweed, it was as if God had set them perfectly parallel to each other. The child was stunning, which made Laura proud.

Was it God or the devil who made her so beautiful?

Carmia's smile was the magic of her face—perfectly balanced, and pearl white teeth accented her brown complexion. Her smooth skin was a treasure other women couldn't resist admiring. Laura herself was gorgeous, but Carmia was more—she lived vicariously through her daughter, hoping for a better life. At ten years old, Carmia walked with a steady stride, a little sway-backed, already having the budding curves of an hourglass figure.

Look at what my genes made.

Carmia's hair was sunburned auburn with hints of crimson streaked in patterns befitting wild fields. Long hair with loose waves was not typical of people with her caramel tone.

She had what black people called baby hair—the soft edges around her forehead were slicked down in waves, outlining her face like a frame for da Vinci. She admired her daughter and worried for her too.

That child is a little too much like me…overly concerned with appearance and marriage.

She remembered watching the *Donahue* talk show with Carmia, seeing the beautiful story of a virgin bride dressed in the whitest white. They both had had tears of envy.

My baby's been stuck on marriage ever since.

Laura's smile faded. She shook herself from observing her daughter and returned to the reality of her scrutiny. Eyes everywhere darted away as she gazed in her viewers' direction. Weary with them, she focused on the buildings—run-down and depressing, except for Carol's nicely painted pink diner. It was the only new business on the whole street. Ducky was still standing with her when Ma and Carl caught up to Carmia, then they all caught up to Laura. Ducky had been talking; she hadn't heard a word. She mechanically nodded yes to whatever blather he was speaking. She could tell that Ducky was hungry too—for her, though.

"Well, Ducky, we're gonna eat now," she said, moving away from him.

"Yeah, okay, Laura. See you around," he said.

Ma looked at him but didn't speak. Ducky smiled at her, though she held a dismissive expression. Carl watched their silent exchange and frowned at him too.

"*Ugh.* Mommy, that man seems nasty," Carmia said.

Ducky looked sour toward the girl but seemed to hold his peace.

Carl glowered, more disturbed by the man's presence.

"Ducky isn't any harm, honey," she said, eyeballing him and smiling her way through her observers who had paused their lives to watch hers.

Deacon Pitts caught up to them. He patted Carmia on the head.

"Sure is a fine family you got here, Laura. Welcome home. Good afternoon, Ma Evans."

Ma finally spoke to someone other than her family. "Good

afternoon, Deacon Pitts," she said in her usual friendly way with all white people.

Laura liked the attention, but these men were making her, Ma, and the kids way too uneasy.

"Thank you, Deacon Pitts," she said.

He smiled with a gentle nod, gave Carl a handshake then his eyes lingered on Carmia, who leaned her head on her mother's arm. Laura kept watching all the people who were studying them.

If they want a show, it's a show I'll give them.

She caressed Ducky's ear, fixed his collar, and put her hand out to be kissed by him. Ma's mouth fell open; she shooed Laura's hand away from Ducky.

"I had forgotten about Bovina's southern charm. Thank you, Ducky, for reminding me of these disappearing treasures."

There she was, Sal, the girl Ducky had dated off and on in high school, hurtling like a locomotive toward them.

Step and snort, step and snort, huff and almost puff, interrupted by another *snort.* She must have gotten word Laura was back and Ducky was sniffing around her.

Not a good look since I stole her fiancé years ago.

Laura could see that Sal had rushed out of the hairdresser's chair with white cream perm turning yellow in her hair.

Girl, jealousy ain't worth going bald.

Ma seemed perturbed now. Laura took a good look at Sal's firm double chin; her eyes and nose looked like they had been squeezed into tight spaces by her bulging cheeks. Brown freckles covered her yellow skin.

She so proud of her light skin, but whew, them features.

Sal ran into the street and grabbed Ducky by the elbow, pulling him away from Laura—nose turned up, quivering lips, snarling at Laura's whole family. Sal never noticed that the overdone perm would soon cause her hair to fall out in clumps of salt-and-pepper cream turning yellowish-brown.

"Hello, Sal. How are you, girl?" she said, extending her hand.

If she don't get that perm out it'll be two years before she can grow a short Afro.

"Come on now." Ma urged Laura to go into the diner.

"Keep your dirty hands off my man," Sal snorted, out of breath, mucus caught in her throat.

"Just helping her with her bag," Ducky said.

"Sure you were, Ducky. You better keep away from that heifer." Although Sal was only about thirty-six, she was maturing nicely into a "Big Mama," a term of endearment given to elderly women in the Deep South. Laura looked at Sal's stomach and imagined how Ducky had to lift that thing to have sex.

Thunder-making thighs and arms in the developmental stages of old lunch-lady arms.

She shook her head in disgust and forced pleasant energy.

Pastor Himley strained his heart from a hurried jog-walk down the sidewalk. *Sal's missing caboose.* He had finally gotten word of Laura's return and tumbled into her path for a tight hug.

Too much touch from a pastor.

He hadn't noticed Ma standing in the group. Laura girded herself in the way her mother would expect for an equally awkward welcome speech.

"L–L–Laura, I–I c–couldn't believe my ears when everybody

said you done showed up. I was part of the important meeting today, you know. Got to save our black boys," Pastor Himley said then continued, "I was focused on the cause, then the news of your return reached me."

She was taken aback by the little chubby, balding man.

Breathe.

"Doggone it, I was c–c–compelled to come find you, welcome you back home." He smiled, curiously long, in silence. He finally became aware of the tension surrounding his behavior as a man of the cloth. His eyes met with Ma. He cleared his throat. "W–Well, my welcome is on behalf of the ch–church, of course. Yes, it's a happy day when one of our own comes home. Oh, happy day."

She graced Pastor Himley with a soft rub on his bald head and made him blush.

Such a sad old man.

Laura smacked her lips with sympathy. His wife, Clarice, had passed away several years ago, and from the way he was acting, she guessed he was unaccustomed to even a little affection. Himley appeared to be a teapot about to whistle and release stagnant aroma. He smiled, quickly turned his head, and grabbed her bag from Ducky. She chuckled at the brief tug-of-war between the two men. Sal grunted at Ducky, then, he finally gave in to the man of God.

"Mommy, we're hungry," Carl began to complain.

Carmia echoed her brother.

Laura winked at Pastor Himley, shook his hand and gestured for Carl to get their bag. Pastor Himley's face turned mauve then brown again. He looked around, soaking it up, then something broke his calm. He began to fidget. He stepped away from Laura.

His actions made her twitch, too, as she looked around to learn what the apprehension was all about.

Oh, God, help me.

Farther down the street stood Mother Johns peering in their direction. The commotion surrounding Laura's presence had interrupted Mother Johns' lunch down at Ester's Place. Laura moved out of view before the church mother could make her out. She followed Ma, who had already grabbed the children and taken them inside the diner.

Laura took an unusually long look around.

Carol's place is different, classy.

The door was made of fancy redwood. There were pink tables with matching chairs, and the space had air conditioning. Bovina didn't have pretty restaurants when she was a girl. Carol was a plump, white redhead. She was standing in the back behind the counter, but she rushed over to them, eager to serve.

"Hi, y'all. Now, we only got chicken today, but it's the best fried chicken this side of the Mississippi River, and we're plenty happy to have you," she said.

A big-bellied black man, Jake, came out from behind a half-wall where he had been cooking and smiled. "Have a seat. Saw y'all come in and brought you some of my famous tea." Laura helped Carmia remove her jacket as they took seats in the far-right corner of the empty diner. Jake stood almost in a military posture, one hand holding the tray and the other behind his back, as they sat. Jake eyed Carol as she spoke, explaining the meal of the day.

"We're only serving chicken until we get more customers that demand a variety," Carol said with regret. "Business been slow."

Her eyes looked down.

"But it's gonna pick up real soon," Jake said as though he needed to reassure her.

"A chicken meal be just fine," Ma Evans said.

"We so hungry, we not gonna be choosey," Laura added.

Carl looked toward the kitchen. "I could eat a horse, I'm so hungry."

Carol took that as a cue to hurry to the kitchen and make their plates.

"That's stupid. People don't eat horses," Carmia said.

"That tea looks just fine. Sure would look finer if I could drink it," Ma Evans said, smiling.

"Glad to serve you," Jake said, placing in front of them mason jars already sweating from sweet tea full of ice.

Carol and Jake seemed to be friendlier with each other than black men and white women in Bovina were supposed to be.

This place gets more different by the second.

Laura couldn't decide if they were a couple or not. She looked around, imagining the candy and ice cream store the building had been when she was a child—when she got two scoops for a dime. She located the booth she had often shared with her father. She could see her feet swinging, waiting for him to return to the table with their sweets. They used to sit in the opposite corner though. Laura returned to the present as other past thoughts distanced her from the fond memories of her father. Carol placed buttered cornbread on the table, which they devoured like cake, then she loaded their plates with fried chicken, yams and string beans. They ate in silence, too hungry, then too full, all of them about to burst, and still Jake kept the sweet tea coming.

Ma noticed Laura hadn't eaten her yams. "Why didn't you finish your food?" she asked.

Laura looked at Ma and smiled. *She wants to hear me say it.*

"These yams ain't my ma's yams," she whispered. "These white people healthy yams. Ain't enough sugar and butter."

Ma seemed proud. "I picked some yams up today. Gonna make my baby some tonight. Don't you worry," she said.

Laura learned later that although Carol's restaurant was cleaner, newer, and had lower prices, no Bovina blacks ever ate there. They had to pay more, and it took twice as long to get their food, but they all remained loyal to Ester and her rundown hole-in-the-wall. Her food tasted better to them anyway. Laura discovered that in full ignorance, trying to cure her children of their hunger, they became the only blacks besides Jake to ever eat at Carol's—the sole restaurant owner bold enough to open up on Brook Haven Road to compete with Ester. Laura hadn't done this on purpose, but she didn't mind that she had done it either. Ma seemed fine with it too. She felt it was about time Bovina got past all their lines of division anyway. Her rebellion against the religious boxes the townsfolk tried to pack her into as a teen was another line of division she was determined to erase now that she was back—even if someone got hurt in the process.

4

Generations

LATER THAT EVENING, LAURA TOOK THE KIDS FOR A WALK. SHE was still trying to ground herself back at home and help her kids start rooting too. She walked them down a trail that was blocked by an ocean of people when they first arrived but that she wanted them to know well. It could lead them to school, town or most anywhere locally.

Laura bent and picked up an unusually smooth rock. "Here. Look at this. It's the only trail around here like this because it used to be a small river," she said. "Remember this path; it'll always get you home."

She walked down a little farther to a large southern red oak tree. "See this here tree? I'm gonna tell you what my ma told me. This tree is a symbol of our family's strength."

"Why?" Carl asked.

"Well, that's what I'm about to tell you." She gestured for Carmia to sit on a large tree stump that poked high above the ground. "Not all trees are like this one," she continued. "Ma says this tree has the knowledge of our people in its branches and leaves. It was here where our first African ancestors, long ago family members, came to America as slaves and worked on the plantation that is Ma's house now."

"Do you really think that's true?" Carmia asked.

"Look at this tree. Don't you think it looks wise? I see thousands of our people. Every family member going back hundreds of years. It's true, all right. If you look deeply enough, you'll see them too. You'll see our ancestors' faces in the bark."

Carmia stood like she didn't want to sit on a tree like that. Carl stepped back, then moved close to the tree. He placed the palm of his hand on it and looked deeply, trying to see their faces. His eyes seemed to focus on the oblong patterns, some touching each other, until new visions formed in his mind. He stood with his chest out, back straight and head up—a young African prince—as though his body took on the form of his vision.

He nodded proudly and smiled. "I can see them," he shouted.

Laura smiled too. "That's right, son. You honor those who have journeyed this way before us."

"Liar," Carmia said, then she peered at the tree too. She must not have seen anything, turned away uninterested. Then the girl did a double-take. Laura saw in her eyes that she had seen a face, too, though her attitude tried to deny it.

"Let's go back now, all the way to Alabama," Carmia said somberly.

Laura wondered if faces in trees were too much for her daughter.

She left the tree alone. Carl looked down the length of the trail where other things seemed to call him. "Let's go that way, Mommy."

Laura was still gallivanting around in her high heels, stumbling and twisting her ankle. She was putting herself through more trouble to wear them in the rural South than made sense. She looked down at her shoes.

Feet hurt.

Laura took Carmia's hand and started them down the main road they had turned away from earlier because of the shooting. Just then, a young girl's scream startled them; they ducked low. Her kids pulled her in the direction of the crying child as though they thought Laura needed to help. They moved closer to the opposite side of the road, farther down, on the edge of Mrs. Annabelle's property. They listened and watched from behind trees and bushes.

Well, if that ain't Squeaky taking a switch to that child, carrying on the slave master's job—a generational steward of abuse.

Laura knew Squeaky was beating the little girl for dragging Mrs. Annabelle's clean white sheet on the dirty ground while trying to carry it to the washboard.

Looks like her. Must be her daughter.

When they were teens, Laura and Squeaky resented Mrs. Annabelle for insisting on washboard services when most other white locals had purchased washing machines for their help to use. Laura knew that Squeaky washed for Ma's laundry business now, and Mrs. Annabelle was still Ma's most important customer.

I've moved on, and Squeak's still scrubbing.

The area smelled of bleach, ammonia and lye. Needless to say, the crying girl wasn't the only one with tears in her eyes.

"Mom…Mom," Carl yelled as Squeaky again raised the switch to strike.

Laura pulled both her kids deeper into the tall grass.

This ain't none of our business.

Her retreat seemed to frustrate Carl. Laura managed a few more steps then pain made her stop again. Carmia smirked, thinking she was going to get her way, and they'd be going home now. Instead, Laura suddenly removed her shoes. Carmia frowned at the sight of her mother's feet in Bovina dirt, but Laura felt an odd childhood satisfaction—it was dirty, but it was home.

This cool soil between my toes is some kind of healing.

She smiled; her girl looked puzzled. In Mrs. Annabelle's yard, Squeaky started swatting the child's behind again. Carmia and Carl watched, horrified. The kids looked up to Laura, asking in silence if she was going to stop the abuse, but Laura still hung back, not wanting to be seen.

"Bearl, I've told you to lift those sheets higher when bringing them to the washboard. You gonna break yo' back this time to get them clean, then maybe you'll remember," Squeaky said, pausing between words to catch her breath as she beat her daughter.

Then Laura gestured for her kids to follow as she approached the washers.

Our presence might stop the beating.

Squeaky saw her, jabbed her co-worker Sadie in her side, and the two of them gawked at the family.

"Hey. Been a long time," Laura said. Laura could see Squeaky recognized her right away.

"Didn't expect to see you around here no more," Squeaky said in the same ugly tone she used on her own daughter.

Laura felt her lips twisting, but she calmed herself. *Don't start, Squeak. I ain't too proud to sling you across this field in front of your child and mine.* She looked at the crying girl, who was about Carmia's age. "And who is this cute thing? Your daughter, I bet. Looks just like you." *Hopefully, not a weasel, though.*

"Yeah, that's my daughter, Bearl."

Bearl was still crying but mustered a smile for her mother's eyes. Laura smiled back.

Poor thing. Ashy arms and knees. Lotion seem to be the least of their worries.

"Child abuse," Carl said to Carmia while looking from the road at Bearl. "I'd call 911 if somebody took a switch to me like that."

Laura looked back at him with an evil eye. Carl formed an "oops" with his mouth, realizing that he might get in trouble.

Squeaky used the switch on her daughter again, and Bearl screamed like a high-pitched firecracker. Laura saw Squeaky look at Carl who had wild, defiant eyes.

*He's stubborn but you bet not...*Laura cleared her throat. *I got beat years ago, in that very spot, for the same reason.-*

"I think your girl gets it," Laura said.

"Is you trying to school me on how to take care of my business?" Squeaky threatened.

Laura remembered their squabbles of the past and saw her kids' faces, already knowing too much about the negative vibes that can pass between adults and where they can lead.

"Seems I returned during a difficult time with somebody getting shot. Wonder who it was," Laura said, ignoring Squeaky's challenging tone for her kids' sake.

Sadie looked Laura over head to toe, then said, "They say it's Bertha's son, James. People gets what they deserve."

Laura's mouth fell open.

Squeaky looked at Sadie with scorn. "You wouldn't be saying that if it was one of yours. Doggone racist white cop."

Laura looked at Carl and put her head down. "Well, *ah,* it was good to see you all…"

"Don't act like we're friends. Why you back around these parts?" Squeaky asked.

"Well, Ma has always lived here…It's still home." *Can't believe I'm saying this.*

"She never left. You did, years ago. Ain't seen you visiting Ma Evans before," Squeaky insisted.

"Well, it's about time then, isn't it?" Laura turned her back on Squeaky, walked toward her kids, and Squeaky took another swipe at Bearl.

Sadie said, "I wouldn't bother if I was you, Squeak. That child touched. Heck, I'd let her carry them muddy sheets up the hill to Mrs. Annabelle's. After getting threatened by them white people, she'd be cured alright."

Laura looked back just in time to view Sadie sitting down to eat a hog head cheese sandwich. She rubbed lard from the sandwich onto the peeling skin between her fingers.

So glad I don't lotion with lard no more, but I do miss hog head cheese.

Flies attacked Sadie's sandwich, and she didn't bother shooing them.

Carmia gawked at Sadie. "Flies swarming around her like hungry kids on TV," she whispered to Carl.

When Laura was halfway between her old friends and her children, she gestured for her kids to be friendly and wave goodbye. They wouldn't budge.

Squeaky gave a sinister smile, like behind her eyes, she was thinking, *Um-huh. You got problems with yours too.* Laura wanted to pinch her kids until they died and were resurrected without three days to process it.

Sadie smacked her lips, preaching to Squeaky as she ate. "Shoot. If them white folks don't cure her, nothing will."

Squeaky lashed Bearl again across the tender flesh of her calves. The girl resumed screaming, "Sorry, Mommy."

Her voice faded as Laura and her kids walked on. She looked back, catching the women watching them with envy in their eyes.

Always judging, hating. It wasn't her fault they still wore the chains of Southern servitude. Laura stood between her children, took their hands, and purposely squeezed them too tightly. She led them down Walking Town Road, called that because it led to town, until they reached the scene of the shooting. Laura knew they had to witness it if they were going to survive in Bovina. The blood was still there, although the body was gone. She placed one hand on Carl's shoulder, the other across Carmia's eyes. She shook her head and said a prayer in her heart.

Another dead black boy. His flesh had oozed, making a puddled stain of red and purple blood. *Same old Bovina.* She shook herself. *Gotta keep my kids outta that number.*

She hadn't bothered to shield Carl's eyes—that scene was a reality about Bovina she wanted her son to digest, although he was only a year older than his sister. As her male child, he would have to be extra wise and submissive when dealing with the police.

Farther up the road, policemen stood barricaded to stop a mob of angry blacks and some angry whites who looked ready to defy the officers. A few of the cops were black. *Uncle Toms.* Confusion everywhere. Her heart sped up as some people pushed parked police cars onto their sides.

She heard someone ask, "Ain't that Laura?" She quickly ran away from the scene with her children.

I ain't ready to be seen by them. She put an arm around each of her kids' shoulders and looked down at Carl. "Got to grin and bear it, boy. Can't escape this disgusting reality in the country or the city these days." *Poor boy. Too young to die.*

It seemed that all the commotion was too much for Carmia; Laura wiped a tear off her daughter's cheek. Part of protecting her children from a world they had already seen too much of was showing them more. She turned and hit her vein, looking for a good one, thinking about where she'd go later that night.

She smiled down at her kids then started racing them. They ran until they couldn't run anymore, then walked the rest of the way back to Ma's house. Laura lagged, trying to see if her children had paid attention to all the signs she had pointed out to them to know their way home. They navigated with ease, looking for the red oak tree. They each touched the tree with the palms of their hands like a prayer. She hoped that seeing the dead boy's blood would somehow cause them to see the faces in the bark of their ancestors who had hung there. But the ways of the South were still too foreign to them for their souls to summon these visions. They walked on the dried-up river and trails that reached Ma's fence.

"You see, Ma. I did it." Carl stuck his chest out, taking full credit for finding their way home.

Carmia glared at him. "I did it too," she said.

Although Carl had led the way, she smiled at them both and said, "Good job."

Carmia strutted in front of them like she had won a battle—getting her mother to agree that she was an equal compass to her brother in guiding them home. Laura didn't know if she should be proud or worried by her daughter's burgeoning sassiness, a carbon personality to that of her own. She wondered if she could keep the girl from going down her own destructive path.

Carmia's facial expression changed when entering Ma's house.
Little snob.

She behaved like it was an afflicted house of infestation and didn't want to touch a thing. Laura was agitated but understood too. Everything was ancient, the walls papered with newspaper. Then as if singled out for a plague of biblical proportions, Carmia was surrounded by mosquitoes who bit her legs and arms, covering them with welt-like bumps. She sighed in irritation, slapping herself all over, trying to kill the mosquitoes.

"Mommy, I want to go back to the city in Alabama," she whined.

"This is home now, baby," Laura answered, rubbing her nose and swatting the mosquitoes away from her daughter. *Gotta get a fix* tonight. *Gotta get to The Shack, no matter how rundown that club is.*

At times like these, she was thankful for a son with limited emotions; Carl had an adaptability they all needed.

Sometimes it's easier to be male. She thought men could be unkempt, unruly and downright unattractive and still have plenty of women broken enough to want them.

Carl had run from corner to corner and scoped the whole place out. He ran back inside. "Carmia, guess what? We got a real-live outhouse."

Ma entered with him, a bit out of breath.

"That's so disgusting," Carmia said.

He slapped his knees and held his stomach in laughter.

"We got an outhouse outside and bathrooms inside, missy," Ma said, laughing too. "Carl, go gather the trash in the back. I got to make smoke to drive these mosquitoes away from your sister's sweet flesh before she faints."

Ma chuckled from the gut, her belly jumping with each giggle. Carl ran out the door.

Carmia stomped her foot in a tantrum. "I'm not living here."

Laura soothed her, wrapping her arms around the child. Carmia was taken to fits like she had as a girl. Under normal circumstances, she would have punished her, but she had already been through too much. *You got to help me, God. Are you listening? Are you there?*

Laura's eyes glossed over. A single tear fell as she rocked Carmia. Ma prayed under her breath, then walked away to give them a moment.

"Baby, I thought you didn't want to live in our house anymore after everything that happened there."

"I want to live back in the city," Carmia said.

"I know, but you're gonna have to get used to living here."

"You should've picked a better daddy for us."

"Baby, Mommy didn't know he was hurting you," she said.

"Didn't want to know." The girl trembled in tears.

"That's not true. You gotta put all that behind us now, baby girl. I need my ma now…We need her. Ma's gonna help us heal, baby, but you got to try our new life," Laura said in a whisper, crying with her daughter.

Ma overheard them. She came back into the living room and looked deeply into Carmia's eyes with tears behind her own. "You listen to me, child, and listen good. We got us here multiple generations. We stand here in three generations of strength, and many more forerunners went before us too. They witnesses in heaven, helping us to get through this life's journey. Their lives and our lives witnessed by our family tree out yonder—a great red oak. We are a people who gets through what we have to get through, no matter how hard it is."

Grandmother and granddaughter stared at each other, like ancestral knowledge and strength were passing between them— an inheritance from one to the other. Ma looked fiercely strong. Carmia seemed stunned. No more fits, everything calm like Ma had tamed a wild bull.

"Everything you need," Laura mouthed the rest as Ma spoke, "Is already inside, so look inside for strength." Ma looked at Carmia with matriarchal authority. "Now you say it." Carmia mumbled Ma's words. "Don't you dare whisper," Ma threatened with a mock sternness.

"Everything I need is already inside," Carmia said with a mustered-up obedience.

Me at her age.

"You remember that, you hear?" Ma asked. Carmia nodded.

Ma is stronger now than when I had my fits, but it's probably easier to tame a bull you didn't piss off yourself.

Laura was the bull that Ma's mistakes had created.

Ma, the bull tamer, touched Carmia's sulking face, which had smoothed out. "Do you understand me, grandbaby?" she asked again.

"Yes," Carmia said, then ran out the door just as rain began to fall.

Laura reached for her daughter. "Come back here, girl."

Ma looked steadfastly at Laura. "Same way you used to be. Let her go. She'll be back after while."

Laura had a flash of herself running underneath the house when inside of it was too much for her. Her face hinted at a smile, not ready to let Ma know how right she was.

Ma meandered to a chair. "When you gonna stop punishing yourself and me behind the past?" she asked.

Laura felt a childhood fit rising. "I ain't been home a minute, and here it is, can't even fake it for a day after twelve years apart."

Ma moved closer, trying to put her taming hand on Laura, but she wasn't having it. She moved away. Ma continued, "That man hurt you enough. Stop hurting yourself. I done took care of it so you'd be free. I done paid for it before God and conscience and aloneness all these years. Done missed out on knowing my grandbabies." Her face turned stern with grief. "I done paid for my sins. Forgive me, baby. I don't know what happened between you and that child, but forgive me like you wanting her to forgive you."

Laura swung her arms around her head like she was shooing gnats. She held her ears. "I got to get out of here." The whole day—all its events and conversations—were too much. On top of it, her body needed cocaine. She needed anything besides the unpleasant high of that moment. She also ran out into the rain, leaving Ma in an internal storm of pain all her own. A generational pain Laura didn't fully realize until then, how it spanned across many centuries in her bloodline. It was passed down to her and now extending from her like a bad omen. Wrongs done to her family in the past by African traders desiring gifts for the price of others hurt, slave owners' willing disbelief in her ancestors' humanity due to greed, and the men in her family's own natural inclination to iniquity had all been mixed together as the toxic ingredients for her pain. Now the past was reaching for her future—her daughter. Bad things were repeating, like her own twisted childhood of rape and self-hatred. It seemed as if the lack of love and flat-out rejection from the men in her life wasn't content to affect only her. This pain and abuse had reached for the fruit of her womb, Carmia. Now, the faces in the bark of the oak tree looked like Ma's, hers, and Carmia's too.

5

That Jezebel!

SHE WASN'T TOLD ABOUT LAURA'S RETURN, BUT SHE FELT IT— worries paraded through her mind and disturbed her. The Bovina community's matriarchal elders had their daily lunch at Ester's Place, seated at the sidewalk tables. Mother Johns could hardly enjoy her meal.

Something is wrong.

The other mothers' chatter about nothingness irked her all the more. Her spirit stirred. She stood and leaned her sixty-four-year-old self on her cane, moving close to the sidewalk rail, peering in every direction, then she caught a glimpse of herself in one of Ester's decorative mirrors hanging in the doorway. When she saw her nose twitching and her mouth in a stern pout, she was upset with her face and straightened it out.

She looked back at Mother Thompson, her right-hand man, who was the youngest of the mothers. She preferred to call her

M.T. because Mother Thompson was barely a senior citizen at fifty-two years old. Mother Johns despised her more youthful face and demeanor, but she disliked her manner of dress more than that. She felt M.T.'s eyes on her—gazing at her as intently as she watched their surroundings.

Ester set pork ribs, collard greens with ham hocks and hot water cornbread in front of Mother Thompson, so her eyes left Mother Johns to herself—Mother Johns felt that too. She looked again at M.T. and the others and shook her head.

Would miss God standing before them, all for setting a plate down in front of them.

Ester placed another plate with hog maws and chitterlings in front of Mother Farrell. Shortly, Mother Johns returned to her table. She and Mother Givens had already started eating pot roast, southern fried potatoes, cabbage and bread pudding.

Mother Farrell said to Ester, "Child, you sure are holding down Mississippi cooking traditions. These here hog maws is bursting with flavor." Ester noticed Mother Farrell rocking in a chair with a missing knob on the end of the leg. She proudly brought the church mother a sturdier chair. The seat was decorated with the same fabric as the wallpaper—pink flowers and green leaves.

Mother Johns grunted, shaking her head at the pattern. *Need to pay some attention behind the counter, remodel thangs where she prepares food.*

She managed to eat at Ester's Place by forgiving the impoverished setting, forced herself not to think of the mess going on in the kitchen. Her gut feeling wouldn't let her eat that day anyway. She wiped her mouth, stood back up, her eagle eyes peering again, landing on Pastor Himley standing in front of Henry's barbershop.

"Them can't be Christian folk what's down yonder with Pastor. Ain't fitting for peoples to be so gaudy, driving flashy cars, when it be folk starving in this world," she said.

"I wonder who they are," said a man walking by.

"That woman looks awful familiar," Mother Farrell added, peering, too, as she gobbled.

Mother Johns watched Mother Farrell's chin move like rippling waves of skin. Mother Farrell shook her plastic cup of iced tea, lifting her arm so high her short blouse rose above her navel. It revealed evidence of her nine children—jagged lines stretched in multiple directions.

She frowned at her. *Intimidated so easy, no backbone. Now go pee.*

Mother Johns figured out a long time ago that stress made Mother Farrell need to pee—a thing she suffered over four years since she had turned fifty-eight. Sure enough, Mother Farrell rose to relieve herself. She was wobbling like a fat jellyfish, leaning on her cane with every step.

"Some people don't have any elasticity in their skin. Need always to girdle their bodies. Shame befo'God." She grunted, watching Mother Farrell walk away.

Mother Givens rolled her eyes at Mother Johns, then spoke in a small voice with high authority. "First, take the plank out your own eye, then you'll see clear to take the speck from yo' sister's eye," she said. "Ain't you one to talk," Mother Johns half-mumbled.

"Now Mother...*ummm*, what your name is...you too mean. Too mean," Mother Givens repeated.

"My name is Janice Johns. Mother Johns. You hush up." *Don't need to give nobody a piece of your mind. Need all the parts you got left, dementia having old goat.* "Can't never remember people's names and such."

"You ain't gone worry me." Old Mother shook her head and rocked herself.

Mother Thompson mustered courage. "Be gentle, Mother Johns. You know that's…well, the dementia is talking," she said.

Mother Givens shook her head. "I still gots most of my mind, praise the Lord. Whispering about me. I have trouble remembering thangs, but I still got the Word of God in me. His Spirit is a present help in times of trouble. I ain't worryin' about y'all."

Mother Johns gazed them over without patience and zeroed in on Mother Thompson. "You feel the need to speak, so today, prepare words for women's bible study this evening, using scripture."

M.T. retreated into what Mother Johns knew was a deceptive silence, paying attention to everything and everybody with photographic memorization. She pulled out a mirror and fixed the curls of her hair as Mother Johns refocused her judgment on the scene down the street.

I know that ain't Pastor flirting with that woman…and in public. Ain't got the wisdom God gave a gnat.

She walked a little closer to the disturbance to see what was going on in front of Henry's barbershop.

"Mothers, some strange whore done crept into our midst. Got to pray. Her and two children done entered the barbershop."

Mother Farrell returned to the table, asking, "Well, are we going down yonder to see what the ruckus is or not?"

Mother Thompson tensed, watching Mother Johns. "Wait.

Shush up…I gots to tell you what's done happened." She leaned to whisper into Mother Farrell's ear and told her all she had missed while using the bathroom.

"I don't understand," Mother Farrell said too loudly, frustrating Mother Thompson into squinted eyes. Mother Johns watched Pastor Himley and contemplated that scene without missing a beat from the mothers' conversation.

Mother Farrell don't seem to have her full mind either.

All of M.T.'s attempts at secrecy, and Mother Farrell couldn't understand her. Mother Johns sighed, gazing at them through the corner of her eye. Mother Thompson watched for her return to the table but continued her gossip, trying not to let Mother Givens hear. Old Mother shook her sixty-seven-year-old head and hummed, "Kumbaya."

I ain't old as them. Never needed glasses. They depend on me to know what's going on. "Here come my Sal—crying." *With her Ducky.* "Arguing like Chihuahuas," she mumbled. "Sal, you come here," Mother Johns demanded as she moved away from the sidewalk table.

Sal crossed to her mother's side of the street.

"Yes, Mama," Sal said in reluctant submission.

"Who them people down yonder got everybody in a stir?"

"That be Laura. That tramp done come back here, Mama, and already flirting with my Ducky."

"Laura. You sure? What in hell?"

"Mother, watch your language. Now…moving right along," Old Mother said. No one quite understood all of her words.

"*Hell* is in the Bible," Mother Johns retorted, then looked at Sal.

"Sal, you sure?"

"I'm sure. She already got Ducky acting a fool."

The devil done come to torment me.

Ducky put his head down. She squinted at him then glared at Sal.

"How long she been back?" They both looked away. "How long?"

"As far as we know, two days," Sal said.

"The devil done descended on us two days, and you ain't told me?"

"I was gonna…" Sal slurred.

"Shush." Mother Johns bit her lip, paced, then stopped in front of her daughter. "Get some backbone in ya. We ain't about to have thangs the way they was."

She sniffed Sal, scowling as her eyes climbed up to her scalp, which was covered with red, swollen balding patches. "What the hell is wrong with your hair?"

Sal hiccup-cried like a child. "I ran out of Mary's beauty salon when I heard Ducky was flirting with Laura, and…"

"No, never mind. Go put a scarf on, walking around looking like a leper," Mother Johns said. Her head got hot, felt dizzy.

Sal and Ducky crossed the street, but she called Ducky back.

"Now, I ain't forgot your cut from the drug sales money, Mother." His hands shook, passing her an envelope. "This all the money Earleen sent."

She looked it over and grew hotter. "Tell my sister it better be more next time, and I don't want my nephew, Mosley, hanging around here doing business in my town no more."

"It won't go right for me to tell Earleen that. You know how she gets." Mother Johns was unmoved by his concerns. "Yes, Mother," Ducky said, running to catch up with Sal. They kept bickering down Brook Haven Road.

Mother Johns spun around, her mind moving faster than her body. She balanced herself with her cane and yelled back to the flock, "It's that whoring jezebel Laura done come back into our midst." She plopped into a chair weak-like.

Mother Givens pursed her lips to correct; Mother Johns stopped her with a cold, prolonged glower. She had no more tolerance for Givens'desire to reprimand her for using the word *whore, jezebel,* or any other so-called profanity. Mother Johns had shushed her with her eyes.

All this done made me hot.

"I ain't surprised she still looking trashy. Never was a nice girl," Mother Thompson said with her cleavage peeping into all the mothers'views.

"Ain't you one to talk? Now moving right along." Old Mother spoke in a stern confusion.

Finally a fitting reprimand, nothing worse than elderly peoples dressing trashy.

Mother Johns pondered what she saw in Pastor Himley's behavior. She rose from the table. "Mothers, I'll be back directly."

Mother Johns walked toward Himley, where he stood outside the barbershop with some of the locals. Mother Thompson walked behind her in a step-for-step fashion until she turned and stretched her arm to stop her. M.T. shrieked back—an abandoned pet. Pastor Himley yammering away with the crowd, had begun to sing "Oh Happy Day" as Mother Johns walked up from behind.

She spoke slowly. "Disgraceful for a pastor to behave so."

Pastor Himley jumped two feet in spirit, although his feet never left the ground. "Now, Mother, I ain't did nothing unseemly for a pastor."

"Why you hanging in these streets then? Can't get you out to feed the homeless no time, never."

"Our former neighbor done returned home. Be my business to invite her to church this Sunday. Right thing to do." His lips perched into a perfect baby "O."

Mother Johns looked him over keenly. "Not when they be kin to Evans. You know what that woman and her seed did to me and my fruit."

Pastor Himley looked her eye to eye, but his low hum of "Oh Happy Day" revealed he hadn't heard her.

Darn fool.

They sat on the bus stop bench and waited in ghostly silence for Laura and her kids to exit the barbershop. Mother Johns still raged inside.

The stupidity around me is draining.

Laura's family exited Henry's shop and started toward their car when Mother Johns grabbed Laura's arm. Mother Johns'face twitched, seeing Carmia roll her eyes.

"You better respect your elders around here, child," she said.

Laura spoke with clenched teeth. "My children respect them that deserve respect."

Mother Johns was vexed. The blood pumping through her veins sounded like balls rolling on a pool table. Carl snickered in the background. She lost balance.

I'd love to slap the heck outta them wayward kids.

Carl looked up, seeing dark clouds fill the sky and said, "Mommy, it's gonna start raining again. We need to go home."

"We just wanted to welcome you home and to come to church," Pastor Himley said.

Mother Johns heard pool table balls again, listening to him try to keep the peace.

A few people were watching. She remembered her position, so she softened her expression and smiled and waved at a few passersby. It seemed that a buildup of offenses stretching across their bloodlines for generations had come to settle accounts and she was ready. She turned back to Laura and let her sternness permeate the space.

"What brings you back here, gal, and how long you be staying?" She hoped to be just rude enough to make Laura speak obscenities to her in front of their neighbors. *Show them the devil you are.*

Her thoughts were interrupted by the shuffling steps and commanding voice of Ma Evans. "These here are my grandbabies. Come here, children, and stand at Grandma's side."

The devil comes in doubles.

Ma Evans had a deep, strong voice that made Mother Johns levitate. She had just left seeing about her laundry service in time to join the supposed sidewalk welcome meeting for her family. She wore a cotton calf-length maxi dress patterned after all the flowers of the fields in all the colors of the rainbow. Mother Johns relished that Ma Evans lost her leg five years before to diabetes and walked with a prosthetic the color of white folks' flesh. Yet, even with a missing leg, Ma Evans was a more mature version of voluptuous, beautiful flesh. She had the curves that Johns had hoped for during puberty, but her butt remained flat and had become even flatter.

Don't make no sense; people carry so much weight. Butt too big to be seen attractive.

After loving on her grandchildren, Ma Evans hobbled over to Laura. Her good foot stepping solid, her prosthetic one dragging softly on the cement, she put her arm around her daughter. Mother Johns snickered at the sight of her bad leg. She watched Carl stare from Ma Evans to Laura, probably wondering how Ma Evans, black cherry in complexion, had given birth to Laura, who was bright yellow. She figured he was already digging up skeletons in his mind that no one wanted him to excavate.

Mother Johns hated that Ma Evans, at sixty-two, was the wealthiest black person in town. However, her appearance and personal surroundings didn't show it. She didn't attend First Baptist of All Holiness Church of God but was faithful to tithe. Mother Johns, who was also church treasurer, made no qualms about that.

Ma Evans turned to Mother Johns and Pastor Himley, smiling proudly. "These here are my family. Laura was born and raised here, and the good Lord done blessed me to meet my grandbabies before I die. They be welcomed to stay here long as they wants to, ain't that right, Pastor?"

Mother Johns applied a nonverbal pressure as she observed Pastor Himley contemplate his response, trying not to offend either of the ladies. Mother Johns, an informal church power, could sway Pastor Himley in or out of favor with the congregation by the wave of her cane, yet he needed Ma Evans' faithful giving.

Pastor Himley smiled like he had gained a revelation from heaven on high. "*Arrr.* I rely on the scripture," he said like a hacking Baptist preacher. "Suffer these here little children to come unto me, and do not turn them away."

He cleared his throat and opened his arms in acceptance to Carmia and Carl, which appeased Ma Evans, while his neglect of Laura pleased Mother Johns. He had his arms extended to no avail with the children until Ma Evans grunted at them in disapproval. Only then did they ease slowly toward Pastor Himley for a cold touch.

Mother Johns felt some victory as Laura, still ruffled, guided her family in the direction of their car. She sniffled with each step, Ma Evans studying her behavior.

Mother Johns couldn't help but gaze at Carmia further. *A beautiful-looking child, ugly inside though.* She'd never compliment Ma Evans' lineage aloud. She always wrestled with the disappointing features of her daughter, Sal. She observed Carmia's stroll behind her grandmother and how she stared into the storefront at the wedding dress display.

"I'm gonna marry a nice boy one day," Carmia said, looking at the old woman.

Curious for a child to think on marriage so.

Mother Johns shuddered when Carmia smiled deviously into her eyes.

Little hussy.

Carmia nudged Carl's side, winked and stuck her tongue out. He mimicked her gesture then they turned to show Mother Johns what they thought of her.

Carl yelled, "Mean old witch."

Mother Johns started in their direction to tear pieces out of their behinds. Her arthritis slowed her down, agitating her, so she focused on Ma Evans wobbling down the street.

At least I ain't like that.

She sped up, trying to reach the kids. Her knee locked, and she doubled over. She would've fallen if not for her bejeweled cane—mostly an accessory—and Pastor Himley restraining her by linking his arm into hers. "H–H–H–Hold your peace now, Mother. They just children."

Laura looked around. When her eyes found her kids, she said, "Come on here." They ran to their mother. "Do you want the whole town to hate us?"

"Yes. Then we can leave here," that snotty girl said.

"It ain't so bad being from around here. You just wait and see," Ma Evans said as she pulled Carmia into the car.

Mother Johns watched Pastor Himley lick the corners of his mouth where saliva frequently formed like a frothy foam. He wiped it with his thumb.

Nasty. Don't touch me, fat roly-poly.

He gently pulled Mother Johns down the opposite path as she tried to avoid his hand.

"I ain't never seen such sassy children in all my life. Them young ones make me want to cuss. Hope that woman and her rebellious seed don't stay around here long." She shook her cane in midair. "That's just what this town needs—more sinners." *Gonna make it my business to bring them to their knees.* "Laura coming back ain't nothing but trouble. She come from a family of loose, trashy women. That bloodline is cursed."

6

What Does Purity Look Like?

CARMIA AIMLESSLY RAN PAST THE RED OAK TREE THROUGH A small forest, letting her pain guide her direction. She was at odds with her mother again, and like Laura, getting away from home was how she cleared her head. She was afraid of getting lost, but that didn't stop her from running. She was angry at the world, wanted to be strong, but didn't know how.

She finally stopped. "Mommy, Mommy." She knew no one heard her—just needed to say the word out loud.

I'm lost. She ran faster, hurting inside and out. She fell into the mud crying, her clothes as dirty as she felt inside. She looked up and realized she was near one of the white houses on the hill.

After crawling to the steps, she sat, drenched from the rain, muddy and shivering. She breathed off rhythm with a high-pitched wheeze. She wiped her tears and watched her bosom rapidly push the buttons on her shirt up and down. Her body was still sore from the bad time she'd had in the city.

I'm so dirty; nobody will ever love me.

Her sorrow was interrupted by the sound of little girls playing. She limped toward the large picture windows. Her inner thighs burned with cold, sharp soreness. She leaned in carefully, secretly, and peeped into a world unlike her own. Two little white girls she recognized from the wedding procession days ago were playing with dolls. They were slightly younger than her, but she wanted to join their pretend world anyway. Carmia's eyes lingered on one of them— the most beautiful girl she had ever seen. She touched her hair while staring at the curly blond with crystal-blue eyes. The other girl, a naturally tanned brunette with brown freckles, was also beautiful.

Nevertheless, her standard of beauty was simple—anyone with a lighter complexion than her own. They were dressed in their wedding clothes again—white gowns of purity. She hoped for an invitation into their world, but her reflection in the window brought her back to reality. Her right hand rubbed her left palm so hard it turned red. She stood shaking, listening, watching for what purity looks like.

"Now you be a good girl, eat all your vegetables, then you can eat a whole pie," the blond girl said to a doll that looked like her.

"Don't be silly, MacKenzie. No mommy would let her baby eat a *whole* pie," the brunette said.

"My mommy said I could imagine anything I want, Kelly."

The tanned-looking girl smacked her lips. "I suppose, but all that pie will give her a tummy ache."

"Let her get one then. What do I care? Just pretending anyways," MacKenzie said.

"I'm going to be a vegetarian and stay skinny for my husband."
Kelly made Ken kiss Barbie.

Carmia smiled.

White girls are funny.

Her hands muzzled her laugh.

"Hey." Carmia heard a boy's voice. "Hey, girl."

She looked around and saw a black boy's head peeping out of a
bush. She looked at him like he was daft. With foliage hanging over
his head, he looked like a black and green-colored sheep.

He came out a little more, trying to show her he was a nice
person. "You better come away from there," he whispered.

She didn't like his bossiness. "You can't tell me what to do."

"*Shhh.* Shush up around here, girl. You're being foolish," he said.

"You hush up," Carmia said.

The boy hit his forehead, looked around, then walked over to her
on the porch. Carmia calmed, seeing him up close.

He ain't no harm.

His clothes were nicer than hers.

"You that new girl, huh? What's your problem? Trying to get
yourself hurt sneaking up on them rich white folks' houses?"

Carmia rolled her eyes. "What you doing here if it's so dangerous?"

He smirked. "Nothing. Just followed you here. You looked pretty
upset, so I followed you."

She stared at him.

He's not like city boys. He's kinda goofy.

"You stupid or something?"

"Or something." He laughed.

Hmmm. Goofy jokes too.

"Why you following me?"

The boy smiled. "You looked like you needed somebody to be here for you," he said.

"Well, I don't need you," Carmia said more sharply than she felt.

"Doesn't look that way to me. I saw you crying and acting weird a little while ago."

"I'm not stupid."

"Well, then you're *something* too." He laughed again.

Not funny, country boy.

"I'm not crazy *or* something."

"You are if you stay by them white folks'windows."

Ma Evans and Mommy's voices surfaced with the stories of her ancestors born in Africa, then slaves in America. Family members who once lived near Mount Kilimanjaro in Tanzania, Africa. Ma Evans' great-grandma told about where they came from, and the story kept passing down until now. She had no idea where that was; it sounded like a scary place to her.

Carmia watched the girls playing again, looked down at herself then moved away from the house. The porch creaked as they both crept away. The boy shrieked, following her noisy steps.

"Aye, what's your name?" he asked, smiling.

She liked his smile. "Carmia. I'm ten. What's your name?"

Kinda cute Superman dimple in the middle of his chin.

"My name is Joseph—Joseph Johns. I'm eleven years old. Been living here my whole life. Know everything about these parts."

He rubbed his hand over his curly hair; seemed to be trying to make himself look more presentable. His actions made Carmia self-conscious too. She turned and cleaned her face with saliva, then looked him over again. She was color-struck when it came to the female ideal of beauty, but she liked Joseph's dark, silky skin and his very white teeth. He was unusually tall for his age and carried himself with a confidence that made her seem safe.

She felt a warmth she hadn't felt since her family had arrived in Bovina, so she stopped pushing him away. She exhaled and smiled. *Wait a minute.* "Your last name is Johns. Are you related to that mean old mother of the church?"

He chuckled. "Yep. My grandma is Mother Johns, but she's not so mean," he said. "You just have to get to know her."

"She doesn't like me, and I just got here."

"My grandma just worries about strangers changing the way we do things around here. She's trying to keep our area godly," Joseph announced like a proud preacher in training.

"You believe in God and all that stuff?"

"Sure, I do," Joseph said. He paused. "You sure are a pretty girl."

"Can't say the same for you."

"Well, I ain't a girl." They laughed.

"You alright yourself." Carmia blushed. If stuck in Bovina, she needed a friend, and Joseph was far better than anyone else she had met. He seemed to accept her, so she accepted his friendship back. "I'm from Montgomery, Alabama."

They began walking down the hill. She nearly slipped on a rock. He grabbed her hand and steadied her. The sky was clearing, and she could see the red oak that led to Ma Evans' house.

"Your family is from here, right?" Joseph asked.

"Right," she said.

"So, in a way, you're from here."

"*Ummm,* I guess so. But I'm not claiming this place. You can just say I'm an Alabama city girl."

"Where's your daddy? I saw your mommy and brother, but no daddy."

She tensed up. Joseph seemed to know he had asked the wrong question. She stopped smiling and looked very sad.

"I'm sorry. Didn't mean anything. I ain't got my daddy neither."

"Haven't you been told to mind your own business?" she asked.

"I was just trying to get to know you."

"Don't ever ask me about that no more."

"Okay." They stood silently until her soul seemed lighter again. "Stick with me, Carmia. I'll show you how to make it around here. I'm eleven; I can help protect you."

"I got a brother named Carl. He can protect me if I need it. But I usually take care of myself."

He thinks I need him?

"I ain't weak."

He smiled. "No, you ain't no weak girl."

She smiled on the inside.

Never met a boy like him.

She liked his ways. He made her smile on the outside too. She heard Carl calling her in the distance.

"I got to go now," she said, turning in the direction of Carl's voice.

"Yep. I guess that's your brother. See ya around," Joseph said.

She turned back toward him and extended her hand. "Want to be friends?"

Joseph grinned, revealing his large, white teeth. "I ain't never been friends with a girl before. Guess you can be the first." He ignored her hand and gave her a quick hug. "I'll see you around, Carmia."

She frowned and pushed him back, then she ran toward Carl, smiling.

Ma's house made Laura claustrophobic; she never could understand how Ma's spacious house maintained the feeling of a much smaller place.

Ma's clutter drives me mad.

The furniture was homely—hand-me-downs from wealthy white families—fabrics of velvet and lace, patterns of flowers and leaves, colors of beige and pink and green sofas.

Same crap from my childhood. Ma way too frugal.

The seats drooped a little but were still in fair condition. Doilies lay on the armrests. Ma's amateur crochet throws draped the backs of chairs.

This stuff has got to go.

Laura longed for the simple, spacious environment that she had created in her own house. Hardwood floors and leather sofas. No wallpaper, just beige walls with a pale-lavender accent wall here and there, and a few items of furniture for everyday use.

Carmia ran into the house, still covered in mud. Carl chased her because of it.

"Mud monster," he yelled.

"At least I'm not ugly like you." Carmia said as they ran past Laura and up the stairs.

Glad to see them happy.

Laura flounced around Ma's place, trying to read her peeling newspapered walls. They were brown where the glue had aged and yellow where the paper had done the same. She remembered when they had pasted them up there to hide some confederate carvings but they had been poor. Ma still living like that made no sense. She could still make out a few headlines: community bake sales and the grand opening of Goody's Department Store. Then her eyes fell on the obituary of Ma's dead boyfriend, Bo, who had died a mysterious death—some kind of foul play.

Hmmm. Never figured Ma for hiding things in plain view.

She moved into the hallway and viewed black-and-white photos of mean-looking great-grandparents with no smiles, but Ma resembled them. She walked into the dining room and picked up little figurines of white ladies dressed up for one occasion or another from the worn China cabinet.

Gotto draw the line somewhere.

She shoved them into her pocket to toss out later. She turned to leave the dining room and ran into Black Jesus hanging on the wall. She held her chest and laughed.

No doubt, Ma's full joy.

"Well, Black Jesus, I hate to tell you, but this painting of you is tacky." She held her stomach in laughter.

Some poor little boy on the corner must've painted you.

She folded her hands and prayed. "Let him into heaven despite this sin."

She did like the deep, warm colors of her mother's house. It was calming. The house itself wasn't so relaxing, but Ma made it feel like a place of healing. Her personality made everyone and everything around her still. Laura knew plants grew in Ma's presence and humans, too, when they recognized the fertility of her ground—she was late in this discovery. Ma had lived a full, eventful life; both sorrows and joys had wrought her much wisdom, pearls Laura couldn't see during her youth but wanted to inherit now.

She ended her tour of Ma's home and joined her in the kitchen. "You've done a lot with the place since I left," she said.

Her fake smile and false politeness provoked Ma to roll her eyes. Laura felt uncomfortable, knowing her mother knew her too well to fall for flattery; they stood in awkward silence. She felt like a girl again.

Shouldn't have tried it.

Laura watched Ma tilt her head to the left. It meant she was about to get a speech. Ma straightened her head back up; she seemed to oblige Laura's manipulative behavior to keep the peace.

"Well, I tries baby."

Ma looked like the Pillsbury Doughboy, covered in flour.

She smiled.

Do what you must. Nobody cooks as good as you.

She watched Ma knead dough to make her famous buttermilk biscuits. It smelled sweet and sour, like the way she was feeling about being home. She stood near her ma and followed her from corner to corner of the kitchen.

She was her little girl again, and that made Ma spoil her. Ma was patient, although they bumped into each other once or twice. She touched Laura's cheeks, leaving a bit of flour on her face.

Ma smiled. "I'm so happy to have my baby home."

Ma's big smile revealed her terrible dentures, and just like that, Laura felt grown-up again.

Ugh. Gotta do something about that.

"Laura, baby, reach above the stove and get the pickle jar. Take the money in it. Why don't you go to one of those fancy stores in Vicksburg or Jackson and get you some new clothes? I know how you likes to shop."

You got teeth like that, but you're worried about my clothes?

"Ma, it's my body and my life. I ain't concerned about those old crows down at the church."

Laura softened as Ma walked over to her and held out a spoon dripping with homemade syrup. She licked it clean.

Ma smiled gently, rubbed the edges of Laura's hair, and said, "That's my baby. Do you remember how I used to cook for you all the time?"

Laura was okay with getting flour on her face, but in her hair broke the mood.

Ma, you don't touch black women's hair.

The little girl in her gave in. "Yeah, Ma. I remember."

Ma nearly bumped into Laura as she moved to the other side of the kitchen.

"Baby, how did you leave the business concerning yo'dead husband?"

Laura moved to the other side of the kitchen; tears welled up in her eyes. "Cremated. Then flushed him down the toilet just like you did Bo. Only I killed him by accident."

Ma turned to look her eye to eye. "Ain't nobody judging you, so don't you go judging nobody." She turned and kneaded the dough.

Laura wiped her eyes. "My marriage was a living hell for the kids and me. I've screwed the whole mother thing up. Carmia hates me."

"That girl loves you. Why you say such fool things?" Ma said, slapping the dough.

"I made some terrible mistakes—Carmia…God must be punishing me for the way I treated you."

I was so strong-willed, so disrespectful. She threw herself on her mother's shoulder.

Ma rubbed Laura's left temple as if she were an infant again. "God heals everything in time. All y'all need is time for you and these kids to mourn. Y'all trying to be too strong. It ain't normal not to grieve. Ain't nothing so bad family can't get through it by sticking together. Ma is here. It's gonna be alright."

"I hope so, Ma." She hugged her desperately. "We gonna be alright, baby. I been sick, but I'm trusting the Lord like you got to do."

"Okay."

Ma took some biscuits out of the oven and put others in, and as she lifted herself, she lost balance and couldn't find the counter. Laura guided her hands. "Ma, how come you didn't tell me about your health problems?"

Ma's face dimmed for the first time since she had arrived. "Let's not take the conversation there today."

Laura could hear in Ma's voice a hint of accusation; now she couldn't let it go. "What, Ma? What do you mean?"

"Leave it be, child. Know when to leave things alone," Ma snapped.

"Why are you angry with me? Everyone's angry with me."

Ma hesitated, then blew it all out. "You kept my grandbabies from me until now. Until I don't know if I'm gonna live or die." She slammed down a pan.

Laura held her stomach.

I can't be the daughter or mother they want no matter how hard I try.

She didn't know anymore if it was safe to tell Ma all of her weaknesses and failures.

"I couldn't be around these people, Ma," she said, clenching her teeth.

"And here you are."

They stood face-to-face in pain, speaking through their eyes the hurt they each harbored. Ma's face was drenched with tears. Laura ran out of the kitchen, wanting to forget the pain in her mother's lonely eyes. Instead, she saw herself in those eyes.

7

Family Ties

FALL LEFT LAURA DYING WITH WANT AND NO ONE TO LOVE HER loneliness away. She hugged herself, dancing around her room, sniffing cocaine.

If Ma knew what I was doing in her house, she'd go to her grave.

Aretha Franklin's "Baby, I Love You" played as she spun around like she had that kind of love near her. Laura caressed her waist. Carmia stood in her doorway. She jerked, then leaned into the girl's face. "How long you been there?"

Carmia's eyes filled with worry. "What's that stuff you sniffed?"

She squinted at her daughter. "I asked you a question: How long you been there? Y–Y–You ain't got no business spying on me." She put her hand on her daughter's shoulder.

Carmia moved back. "Mommy, you're scaring me. Why you taking drugs and dancing like that?"

"Get out of my room and go to bed." Carmia didn't budge. She rolled her eyes and kept staring. "I said get out." Laura took a step in her direction. Carmia moved to the doorway. "Looking at me like I ain't nothing," she mumbled.

Carmia ran away in a panic.

Laura sat on the side of her bed and sniffed more coke, waiting to feel lighter. She listened to the music again. Her room seemed filled with swirls of color. She smiled, then her head fell to her knees. She swung her head around, shaking her hair. She stood, bopped back down, and giggled. She pushed herself up and staggered to her vanity table. She touched her neck then picked up her bottle of Poison perfume. She sprayed it into the air and stepped into it. She was proud that she knew to spray and step into the scent. She didn't want to have any backward behavior like the rest of backward Bovina. She frowned, laughed and glowered.

She remembered the smell of the cheap perfume that the mothers of her childhood friends used to wear.

Glad I've done better.

Laura looked proud.

My feet pedicured, my hands manicured. Everything cured, but my heart.

Sniff, wipe, twirl, laugh. Laura focused on Aretha and let the Queen of Soul's voice take her to another place.

"Ooo wee. Sing it."

She hummed with the record that played on her childhood record player.

Can't believe Ma held on to it. I sang up a storm back when I wanted to be a famous singer.

The mustard yellow handheld travel-type record player still sat on the same corner table in her room.

Ma's a packrat; everything has value to her.

Having her authentic record player made her happy. Laura hummed along and blended well, but there was a flaw somewhere. She stood silently and listened. Nothing, not a sound.

Need another hit. Make all the pain go away.

She lifted a small mirror tray and sniffed a line of cocaine from it. "I tell you, I love you," she sang.

More noises interrupted her. She lifted the needle off the record. This groan wasn't the kind of utterances her mother used to make in prayer; these sounds rang of pain. She followed the moans to her mother's room.

"Ma. What's the matter? Let me help you," she said.

"Go back to bed, child. I'll be alright."

Her mother's urine reeked as she approached the bed.

"Ma, what is it?" Laura sat on the edge of her bed but soon realized she was getting wet. Her mother's urine seeped into her gown.

"Go away. Leave me be," Ma cried.

"Peeing in the bed ain't no reason for shame, Ma. Just call me to help you."

"I feel like I'm turning right back into a little baby. Can't feel my left side sometimes. I–I–I can't hardly see how to get down the stairs at night," Ma said.

Laura held her arm out to her mother, and Ma took hold of it to raise herself from the bed. As they headed down the hallway, Ma peed on herself again, crying and moaning.

I came home for healing only to find Ma dying. Got to find a way to be a better daughter and mother.

Ma stood still, trying to balance.

Mother Givens can help.

Ma groaned with each step toward the bathroom.

"Ma, don't worry. I'm here." Laura's body trembled.

Ma smells sick, something inside rotting, making me nauseous.

She wondered if the meds sitting on Ma's dresser could get her high. As they reached the bathroom, some stray animal howled outside. She helped her mother sit on the toilet. Ma seemed embarrassed, crying as her pee hit the water. Laura stood on tiptoe looking out the small window, trying to give Ma some privacy and needing fresh air to hit her face. She had sobered up faster than usual. The sky was dark, but a single ray shone in the distance, struggling to transition into a new day. She half-smiled.

Three hours later, the sun shined brightly in the pale blue sky, bringing Laura hope—renewed strength sufficient for the day. Ma managed to rise early, cooking like the previous night was a bad dream. Laura entered the kitchen, wondering if she really had it in her to take care of Ma.

I can't take care of nobody being addicted to drugs.

She wanted to be that kind of daughter, but she had never been that better version of herself before.

Aww crap, who am I fooling? I ain't no good daughter.

"Good morning," Ma said with thankful eyes.

Laura wanted her eyes to say, "You're welcome," but she grinned and turned away. She was still hungover and groggy as she came down from the previous night's high.

Carmia woke to the smells of Grandma cooking bacon, sausage, eggs, biscuits, and the anticipation of fresh milk.

I promised to help cook breakfast.

It was time to get ready for school, but she lay there just thinking about her grandma and mother cooking together—the only times they got along. She admired the way they laughed and the important-sounding words Grandma expressed during those moments. Pastor Himley always said that old folks were wise. She tried to gather Grandma's wisdom remembering her sayings like: "Love each other so one can't fall for the other one holding them up." Also, "Be quick to forgive today; it'll be you needing forgiveness tomorrow."

She listened carefully because she didn't hear Grandma's chuckle that morning. But she told herself that things were fine. She yawned widely, trying to let the butterflies out of her belly. She knew that the silence wasn't a good sign.

Mommy had a drug problem, and Grandma was sick, but they were hanging on. At least she tried to convince herself that they were hanging on, although she often saw on their faces that they were drifting apart. She shook her shoulders as if problems were dust that could be brushed off. They had made it through their first month in Bovina; things weren't as bad as she thought they would be.

I got Joseph.

Within those few weeks, though, Mommy had changed in ways that made her mad, using and staying out late. Carmia didn't feel comfortable enough with her mom to share her secrets. Instead, she and Joseph spent weekends swimming, picking berries, and catching fireflies at night. They were boyfriend and girlfriend, although they hadn't really said so.

Carmia smiled brightly and stretched her arms. Breakfast was calling, and she wanted to get it while it was still hot. Grandma was cooking less and less. Carmia and Carl usually woke to the sound of their mother singing, but her voice wasn't so sweet anymore.

Them drugs more important than us.

It was an important week for Carl. He had a big game the next day after school, starting on the community boys' basketball team for the first time. Carl had told his sister he wasn't sure he wanted Laura there. Carmia seemed to worry about him more than herself. The girl finally got out of bed and tensed up hearing her mother's sad imitation of Tina Turner singing, "Rolling, rolling...."

God, don't let her go to Carl's game.

She heard her mom stumble with sloppy dance moves—bumps against the wall and eerie laughing.

I bet her breath stinks.

She used to think her mother was perfect. Now she didn't want to be anything like her.

She heard Carl jump out of bed, and out of habit, she raced him to Mommy's arms for a morning hug.

Don't want a hug, but if I'm first, won't be a long one.

She almost always beat Carl into their mother's arms, but he didn't seem to mind it much. Whenever Mommy scooted Carmia over to the face bowl to brush her teeth, she showered Carl with long hugs and scratched his back. Mama's boy. He didn't seem to mind her stench.

She watched him melt into her embrace.

"I love you, Mommy," he said.

"I love you too, my strong man." Mommy rubbed her nose,

squeezed him tightly, then squeezed herself. Carl hugged her tightly too. She knew he liked feeling her soft, smooth skin. She also knew he was trying to comfort her. Mommy smiled at him.

"I love you, Mommy," Carmia said, teasing Carl. She walked by them wrapped in a big white robe. It looked like fresh-picked cotton. "I look like a sheep." She giggled.

"Baaaaa," Carl said.

"At least I ain't no mama's boy," she said.

"Ain't nothing wrong with loving your mama," Mommy said, leaving the bathroom. "Y'all hurry and get cleaned up. Don't want you late to school."

There was a knock at the door. Ma Evans shuffled over to open it. She wasn't surprised to see Joseph.

"I don't reckon I'll be needing you to help me with small jobs no more," she said, handing him an envelope.

"Figured…I mean with your grandkids around now," Joseph said.

"You're early anyways," she said.

"Yes, ma'am. I thought I'd walk to school with your grandkids."

"Boy, I done told you it'll be the death of you if your grandma ever figures out you been helping me and hanging around my family. You best go on to school."

Joseph looked hopeful. "But I—"

She closed the door.

Ain't got the sense God gave a rock.

Ma Evans shook her head and looked out the window to make sure he was gone, then she gave in to the smell of her own cooking, sat in the kitchen nook, and started eating. She had nearly finished before her family came downstairs. She cherished the sight of Laura with her children each morning, though her vision was often blurred. The more her eyes failed, the more she tried to hide it. Having her family with her brought her joy, but she despised the nightlife-laced kisses Laura gave the kids. She wanted more from her daughter but was coming to accept Laura for who she was rather than who she hoped her to be—a better version of herself.

Laura's appearance in a robe and house shoes was to act as though she had spent the night at home. It conjured up ghosts too similar to Ma Evans' own past and deepest regrets for her to play the judge. Her mind idled a moment on her days down at The Shack. The pain she harbored from breaking up families and hurting other women's kids during her youthful days broke her heart. Her selfish younger self hadn't counted the cost that her current wisdom could weigh in years of loneliness and tears.

She shook her head.

Can't worry now. Got to accept what is and do my best with it.

She shifted her stiff body in the chair and smiled, hearing her grandbabies running in the hall.

They my hope now.

A loud thump and crash, and she knew Carl had jumped four stairs down again.

"Carl, haven't I told you not to run and jump in the house?" she reminded him with a sternly sweet voice—couldn't make up her mind which way to be with her grandbabies.

"Yes, ma'am. Sorry," Carl said as he, Carmia and Laura joined her in the nook.

"Grandma, how come you never wait for us before you start eating?" Carmia asked.

"Oh, no. Y'all takes too long in the mornings for me. My food be cold waiting on you," she said.

Ma Evans' stained dentures with a white plastic fingernail glued on them peeped into view as she talked with her mouth full. She washed jam-packed scrambled eggs down her throat with a gulp of hot, black coffee. Her teeth looked like they'd fall out when she chewed, and she knew Laura couldn't stand it.

"Grandma, it's Mommy's fault we come down so late," Carmia said, pouting.

Ma Evans watched her granddaughter rubbing her hand on the sleeve of her dress. It was brownish pink with ruffles dangling on the hem and three-quarter sleeves.

Don't blame her for liking beautiful things. Raised Laura spoiled, and now her children more spoiled. Guess I'm the only humble one.

She snickered and kept her eyes on Carmia.

And this one likes to smell like lilac 'cause it makes her feel wealthy.

She giggled, belly jumping. "My, you done got fancy. Decorating yourself with pretty ribbons makes you late to breakfast," she said.

"No. Mommy's got to make us look perfect, wiping spit on our eyebrows to make them lay down and spit on the edges of my hair. And if we get our mouths dirty at breakfast, it's more spit on the corners of our mouths. Spit, spit, spit." Carmia shook herself in disgust.

"That sure is a nasty habit she got, ain't it?" Ma Evans laughed.

"I wonder where I got it from," Laura said, smiling. "Hurry up and eat, girl. It's time for y'all to go to school."

"She eats too slow because she talks too much," Carl said, smirking at Carmia.

"Hush up, boy. Don't make no sense; nobody swallow food without chewing way you do," Ma Evans said. Her granddaughter smiled.

"Carmia likes a boy."

His words wiped the smile off her face. Carmia gave him the evil eye and headed for the door. Laura squinted at Carmia and then at Carl. She couldn't tell if he was making it up or not.

Her daughter moved to the back door just as she had done years ago, seeing Laura off to school. Laura peered at her watch, then at Carmia, and took a sip of coffee.

Ma Evans smiled, reenacting the scene herself.

Carmia eased over to her mother and tilted her head sweetly. She put her arm around her mother's waist and rubbed her forearm gently. It tickled Ma Evans so much that her tummy started jumping again.

If this child ain't Laura all over again.

"I got to pray extra for you, Laura. She's a tricky one to raise," Ma Evans said.

"Mommy," she almost sang, "You remember that mean old lady with Pastor on the day we came here?"

"Mother Johns? Don't worry about her," Laura said.

"You think she'll like us eventually?" Carmia asked.

"I wouldn't bet on it. It'll be her loss." Laura covered her cleavage.

"Maybe if we give money to the church, she'll like us."

Carl huffed at Carmia from the back porch. Laura's mouth hung open. Ma Evans watched Laura bite her lower lip. She knew the thought of giving money to people who loathed her daughter and hadn't forgiven her for leaving town the way she did would stir up Laura's defenses. It was mildly fun watching her daughter stew in it.

That's what it's like trying to defend what's wrong, way I did when you left home.

They were silent, but Ma Evans wanted Laura to support her daughter's idea.

Want to see you be there for yo' child in spite of your pain.

Ma Evans cleared her throat. The vibrations straightened Laura's spine.

Go on, spew that liquor out your mouth and use your tongue to bless that baby. Help your baby survive our sins.

Laura's shoulders drooped.

Why won't you be the mother I know you can be—the woman I know you are?

She looked at Laura and shook her head. "Daughter, listen to your ancestors."

My only hope.

Laura tried to laugh it off. "Grandma, don't pay me enough to manage the laundry service." No one else laughed. "That won't be nothing but a waste of money," she said.

Carmia lowered her head.

Ma Evans swung her prosthetic leg around the side of her chair and pulled herself up with her cane to stand. She walked over to Carmia and hugged her. "I'm going into my savings to put together the best offering I can, then we'll go to church and give the biggest offering yet."

"Ma, we can't buy friendship," Laura said, huffing.

"No, but kindness can turn away wrath," Ma Evans said.

Carmia looked from her mother to her grandma, not knowing if she'd get her request.

"We gon'do it, grandbaby," Ma Evans answered before her daughter said another word.

"Now get out of here, child." Laura scooted the girl out the door. "Carl, you wait on Carmia."

"If we don't run, we gonna be late," Carl said.

"You two stick together the way I told you. Family is all we got," Laura yelled as she watched them run. Ma Evans remembered the many times she had said those words about family to Laura.

She never forgot, passing them to the next generation. Don't seem like they ever penetrated her heart.

Ma Evans froze.

Oh, Lord, help me get to the toilet fast.

Ma Evans shuffled toward the bathroom, trying not to be seen. Ma was proud. Laura walked over to help her and then took a step back before sighing and sitting at the table. She didn't want to bruise Ma's ego, so she pretended not to notice.

Carmia might be sweet on Joseph.

Laura had had crushes on boys at that age, but she hoped curiosity in boys would bud more slowly for her granddaughter. She made her way to the bathroom and listened as her daughter cleared the table. Silverware jingled, plates clinked, Laura danced, her voice muffled as she sang. Ma Evans knew the muffled sounds in her voice were from her daughter taking the leftover biscuits off Carmia's plate, sopping them in syrup, and stuffing them into her mouth. Feeding her family made Ma Evans happy, so she listened well, smiled instead of crying, her body racked with pain from nerve damage.

Ma Evans returned from the toilet and stood in the archway that joined the kitchen and dining room. Laura had pulled the hem of her gown up to her thighs as she danced.

Food always made her dance and sing.

"What you gon'do with them children of yours? They strong-willed like somebody else I know." Startled by the insinuation, Laura twirled in her direction. Her eyes locked directly on a plastic fingernail her mother used to cover a missing tooth, and she frowned.

Ain't gonna change the subject.

Ma Evans smacked her lips. "I said what you gonna do with them kids?"

"I don't know," she answered, then she prepared fresh dishwater. "What's gotten into that girl, trying to please Mother Johns?"

Ma Evans grew solemn and limped a little more. It felt like a jellyfish sting had started in her foot and moved up her calves. She wiped a tear before her daughter noticed. Her body hurt, but that was nothing compared to the aching concern she had for Laura. The burden she carried for her family filled the room. She looked at Laura, holding her breath in a changing-the-subject kind of way, squinted her left eye, and raised her right brow. Laura held her breath, too, and her words.

"What was that you said, baby?" Ma Evans asked.

"Ah, I'm just wondering what got into Carmia. When has she ever cared about giving money to church?"

"I don't know for sure, but I suspect it's that Johns boy."

"Ma, you spoiling that girl past what anybody else gonna be able to tolerate, giving her all that money to put in church." Laura put her hands on her hip and said, "Give it to me if you don't know what to do with your money."

"My grandbaby wants to give to the church, and give is what we gonna do. Carmia is new around these parts, gots to make friends, and it ain't easy around here," she said. *Got my family back with one foot in the grave.* "I've lived here alone, abandoned by husband and child. Don't want her to be lonely that way."

The mood changed; small talk had ended. Ma Evans looked her daughter in the eyes.

Laura's aura seemed to scream, Don't question me about last night.

You know you getting a speech.

The old woman groaned, playfully preaching. "Laura, I say, Laauraaa, wheeeere you been allllll night?"

Laura hated the sound of whining sing-talk the old deacons on the church mourning bench performed.

"Ma, don't start. Nightlife is how I have some kind of happiness for myself."

Laura's reaction jerked her out of her playful religious spirit and into an emotional one. Her daughter began to cry more than their current conversation could've stirred. Ma Evans' eyes filled too. She felt cold. Spirits of the past were entering the room, refusing them peace.

She stared at Laura, wanting to hug her, but she was paralyzed by her thoughts. Then she reached out. Her daughter moved away and said, "You left me alone."

Ma Evans hung her head low. "How long do I got to pay for not knowing what my boyfriend, that man, was doing to you? I was wrong to trust him; I didn't know he was evil." She faced her daughter again. "You done ripped this town up, feeling that everybody around here needed to pay for what he did. You done lived like the trifling floozy he wanted you to be." Tears fell from Ma Evans' eyes. "Everything I ever did for you since then was to say, ' I'm sorry. Forgive me.'" She wiped her face. "I'm dying now. When you gonna move past it? Stop hurting yourself and your kids. Get up outta that pit, child."

Ma Evans had tasted the bitter flavor of tears for too many years to allow herself to remain wrapped in shame. She had shaken that kind of guilt and pain off. She had learned to forgive herself for when she hadn't known any better. She had done the best she knew how at the time.

Everybody wants to rewind the clock for a do-over. Can't though. What is anybody supposed to do? Forgive themselves just so they can keep on breathing?

She knew Laura needed to forgive herself too. Trying to hide her mistakes in drugs was killing her.

"Got to let it go, baby. Just do better now that you know better." She wasn't gonna hug Laura while wrapped in pity—her daughter had kids now too. She wanted Laura to gird herself with that same strength she had found.

Laura got to be stronger now than she ever knew she could be.

Ma Evans looked at her with a beautifully stern, loving face. "That man hurt you one time when you was little, but you keep hurting yourself over and over, so who done committed the greatest sin against you?"

"Ma, can we just for one day not talk healed or hurt, saved or sinner, God or the devil?"

Ma Evans wanted to end her speech with a short prayer and a smear of anointing oil on her daughter's forehead. She burned inside as Laura walked away before she prayed her last word.

"I knooow you don't like it, but it's whaaat yooou neeeed."

She wasn't teasing in the way of the deacons' sing-talk anymore. It was real for her. She felt it in her gut. Her body trembled, leg wobbled as she lay face down on the floor, crying.

"Don't know what I'm gonna do. Ain't got much longer with them to help them, and Laura ain't got no mind to listen. So stubborn, so hurt, too long laying in that hurt. Help me, Jesus."

Got these grandbabies depending on us.

"We done lived too full of self, not always walking with you, Lord, but I got to stop this hurt from passing to my grandbabies."

Ma Evans shook her head, trying to drive away, once again, the demons she had cast out of her mind years ago. She could hear Sal as a toddler crying and Janice—young Mother Johns—yelling, beating on Ma Evans' front door, begging her husband to come out.

Sal kept yelling, "Daddy, come home." She held her ears.

Sal keeps yelling for her daddy.

She slammed her hand onto the floor. "Make her stop. I done paid for not honoring marriage."

Letting my pleasure be above the pain of other people's families, men's wives, their children.

"Done sinned against my own family."

She thought about how the Lord had blessed her with money and how she would give it all up for peace, to have not been alone in the world all those years. She breathed heavily, wheezing with tears, then stopped. She got on her knees, humbled herself, pushed aside her pain, and said, "Don't let my wrongs continue to visit my child, and please, Lord, don't let them visit my grandbabies."

8

To Heck with Them!

CARMIA SAT ALONE ON THE PLAYGROUND BENCH, PICKING DAISY petals. For most students, it was six weeks into the school year, but only three weeks enrolled for her and Carl. She still didn't have any friends except Joseph. She removed the handkerchief from inside her book to dust her shoes like her mother taught her to do. They were alike in looks and behavior; she wasn't sure if that was good or bad. She watched the other kids play.

Oooo wee. That boy is fast. Nobody will ever tag him.

She took chewing gum from her Wonder Woman lunch box, blew bubbles, and popped the gum between her teeth. It sounded like little firecrackers. She learned that trick from city life. She watched the girls from Bovina run around, not caring if they were clean or dirty.

They been friends from birth, ain't got room for me. I don't care about them stupid country girls no way.

Carmia remembered Bearl screaming from Squeaky's switch during the first week of their arrival and guessed that's why she was so unfriendly.

Some seem to like me, but they're scared of Bearl—mean old bully.

She figured Bearl was jealous. Some city girls had been jealous of her too—only the other pretty girls ever liked her.

Mommy says girls like Bearl feel bad about themselves, that's why they so mean.

She figured if she had a mother like Squeaky, she'd be mean too.

I feel sorry for her, but I ain't gonna bend down and kiss her shoes for no friendship.

Bearl sashayed over to the bench, smiling, and sat down with her. "Pretty ribbons in your hair," she said.

Carmia stayed on guard. Bearl's face reminded her of her mother's fake smiling ways. "Thanks," she said.

"I wish I had pretty things," Bearl continued.

She had compassion because Bearl wasn't wearing anything pretty—a dirty white T-shirt and overalls like the boys, holes in them and all. She reached up to remove her ribbon, wanting to give it to Bearl, but it was tangled in her hair.

"Show off," Bearl said angrily, watching Carmia twirl her fingers around the ribbon. "You think you're better than the rest of us; well, you're not."

The bully walked behind Carmia and yanked the ribbon, plucking several strands of hair out with it. Carmia screamed. Her entire head was woozy, face red, hot all over. The part of her mother she wasn't sure she wanted to be like was taking over. She balled her fist and looked at Bearl with twitching eyes. The other girls ran over laughing.

"Give it back."

"Come and get it," Bearl said as she passed the ribbon to another girl.

The girls giggled and passed the ribbon from person to person. As Carmia approached one, the fabric passed hands. She was so angry. Bearl teased her, holding the ribbon up high to show her that she had it again.

I'll show you.

She reached down, grabbed a handful of dirt, threw it into Bearl's eyes, and snatched her ribbon back.

The boys ran over too.

"Fight, fight!" one boy yelled as the circle of children formed a miniature-sized mob. Bearl tackled Carmia, and the two girls wrestled on the ground—scratching, biting, kicking. Dust whirled above them like volcano smoke. Carmia felt sharp rocks scraping her knees and arms; tiny beads of blood appeared on her dress. She felt like one of them—a dirty country girl—which was worse than the pain of her burning knees.

I hate these dumb girls—didn't do anything to them.

Carmia hit, slapped and socked Bearl with all of her might. There was a scream that wound down into a deep moan. Bearl lifted herself. Her eyes were blood red. She spat dirt out of her mouth and ran away, holding the rest of her screams inside.

I beat her good. Where's her pride now?

The boys laughed, pointing at Bearl as she ran away. Carmia got up and dusted herself off. The girls had a new respect for her but still didn't make friends.

Mrs. Davine rushed over after nobody needed her. She jog-walked toward the playground just in time to catch Bearl running away. She grabbed Bearl's arm to help her, but Bearl snatched away. "Don't leave the school yard," the teacher said. Bearl ran toward home anyway. Mrs. Davine threw her hands above her head in confusion and ran to the crowd of kids who were still laughing.

Carmia was upset at how dirty her ribbon was and walked over to the water nozzle on the side of the building to wash it. She pulled locks of curls from it as Mrs. Davine approached her.

"Are you alright? What happened?"

"I'm okay. Bearl took my ribbon and wouldn't give it back, but I managed."

Carmia wasn't crying, but her heart was still pounding. Mrs. Davine picked a couple of leaves out of her hair. Carmia sighed when she smelled her teacher's perfume; it put her in the mind of lilac.

She smells wealthy, like I'm gonna be when I get married.

Carmia looked Mrs. Davine over more carefully. She was the same kind of high-yellow pretty as her mother.

I wonder if people dislike her because she's pretty.

She figured any woman from that area who cared about the way she smelled might be okay.

I like her.

Mrs. Davine shook her head. "Don't seem like that girl is ever going to learn to keep her hands to herself. Disobedient, I told her not to leave. You must've got her good the way she went running home."

Carmia wasn't sure if the teacher's words were a trap or not. She sat quietly until the teacher's smile inspired trust. On the other hand, she didn't care about getting in trouble because Bearl had it coming.

"I did get her good," she said. There was an uncomfortable silence, then they laughed.

She's laughing; I'm not gonna get in trouble...I do like her.

"Most times, I'd say keep your hands off people, but with Bearl, I already know you probably couldn't help it. But, if anybody asks, I haven't said a thing." They smiled.

"She's a mean cow," Carmia added as she washed the ribbon.

She dripped a little water from her cupped hand onto her scraped knee. It burned like stick pins poking her, then slowly numbed. Tiny spots of skin had raised on her knee—thin pieces of skin that put her in the mind of grated cheese.

"Did you get all of the dirt out?" Mrs. Davine asked, ready to pour more water on her knee.

She shied away, "I think so."

"You remind me of myself years ago," the teacher said.

Can she tell something bad happened to me?

"How do I remind you of you?" she asked.

"Well, you're lonely for no fault of your own."

"I'm not lonely." Carmia sighed, then looked up to her teacher. "What did you do about it?"

"Glad you asked. I have a funny story. My aunt, a beautiful white woman named Lily, saw me crying my heart out one day because I didn't have any friends. She walked up to me and said, 'Whatever are you crying for?' I said, 'Because I'm mixed race. Blacks don't like me and whites don't either.' Then my Aunt Lily said, 'They're just jealous because mixed girls are the prettiest of all,'" Mrs. Davine said, laughing herself into a mild cough. When she calmed down, she said, "Can you believe a white woman said that mixed girls are prettier than blacks *and* whites?"

"I ain't mixed race like you, though," Carmia clarified.

"No, but you're lovely."

"Do you have friends now?" Carmia asked.

"Yes, I do. Honey, it gets better. They hate you now because you're beautiful. But one day, your beauty will open doors for you. Mine sure did," the teacher said.

"Then why do you still live around here?" she asked.

"Well, Miss Fancy-pants, some people enjoy living around here, and you will, too, when you stop your pity party."

"Mommy always says people don't like me because I'm pretty, but I don't care anymore if they hate me. Besides, I'm not pretty like them white girls."

"No, prettier. And you do care, but one day you might not." Mrs. Davine wiped dirt off Carmia's cheeks. "My aunt got downright angry with me and said that she wouldn't stand for me being sad and lonely when I got confederate general's blood running through my veins."

"You do?" Carmia said, although she had no idea what confederate was.

"Yes, but I learned that's not what's essential. What's important is Auntie taught me to stop crying and said I was stronger than bullies. She said that when I feel lonely, I need to yell out loud, 'To hell with them.' Oops, I'm not supposed to say *hell* to a child, so say *heck*."

Carmia laughed uncomfortably at her teacher using that word. "Did that work?" she asked.

"It sure did. I never cried again because of loneliness."

She felt proud as Mrs. Davine looked over her hair. Her mommy had perfectly parted it into six ponytails, but one had unraveled during the fight. Mrs. Davine started twisting it back like the others.

"Ouch."

"I'm sorry. Your scalp is red in this area. Bet it's sore." Mrs. Davine continued more gently as Carmia struggled to put her ribbon back on. The teacher tied it back into her hair.

"There you are. Just beautiful. The sun will dry it quicker than two shakes of a tail feather."

"Thank you."

"You're welcome. I'd better get ready for Bearl's mom. I know she'll be here soon, and she is some kind of mean."

Carmia turned to walk away, but she felt her teacher's eyes on her, staring at her just long enough to seem odd. Mrs. Davine snapped out of it. Carmia watched the light-skinned woman as she turned toward the classroom. She took out her pocket mirror and observed her reflection. Mrs. Davine was beautiful, but she was getting older. Her light skin was almost white.

She's one of the blacks Mommy said passes for white.

She was getting deep lines around her eyes and mouth. Mrs. Davine's white family and black family had left her many blended birthrights. The inheritances showed which side they came from—wealth was probably the white side, and youthfulness the black side. Carmia watched the teacher pinch her cheeks and blush filled her wrinkles. She smiled, put her mirror away, and went back into the classroom.

Her mother had told her that white people have many advantages in this world, but Mother Nature evens the playing field in time through wrinkles on their faces.

When Carmia returned to the bench, she found Joseph there. That same comforting warmth as the day she met him trickled through her. He showed his beautiful smile and said, "You alright?"

Carmia grinned back, ignoring his question. Then Carl ran toward her, looking ready to fight boys and girls alike. He found her sitting quietly instead. She was embarrassed by how Joseph kept his eyes on her—she didn't want Carl teasing her anymore.

Carl looked at her, still trying to catch his breath. He grabbed her arms, stood her up and turned her around, looking for any severe bruises. "What happened?" he asked.

She shoved him away, not wanting to be babied. "Nothing I couldn't handle."

He exhaled after he saw she was okay and she sat back down. She had been in more fights than him because girls always disliked her.

He never has to fight; everybody likes him or scared of him.

She already knew it was different for handsome boys and ugly ones; she thought her mom was right about males having it easier. Carl sat on a nearby stump, looking at her, disappointed he wasn't there to help. Carmia stood; her movement knocked her brother out of his gaze.

Mommy was walking in their direction, wearing a hip-hugging jean mini-skirt with a black leather belt and a large silver buckle.

She had cut her white cropped T-shirt off her shoulder, and her black low-heel boots glistened. She was the rebel they loved, with her hair combed back and a loose curl hanging on her forehead as she sang "Bad" by Michael Jackson. They laughed because that was her way to let them know she knew all about the fight, and everything was okay.

Mrs. Davine must've told her it was Bearl's fault.

Mommy looked at Carmia with a serious face, then smiled. "Did you beat her butt good?"

"She looked worse than me," Carmia said.

"Alright then." She looked at Carl. "Did you protect your sister?"

Carl shrugged. "When I found out, the fight was over. My sister is tough," he said.

Pride covered Mommy's face. She stretched her arms out to them for a hug, and this time Carmia wanted to be last. Carl ran toward Mommy, stumbling over his untied shoes. When he reached her, he bumped into her; his dimples popped into view as he snorted. Mommy raised a suspicious brow toward Joseph, making him put more distance between himself and them.

"Dang, Carl. You always tackle Mommy," Carmia said.

"I ain't trying to tackle Mommy."

She scratched his back, then Carmia eased up and received a long, warm hug.

Mommy looked at Carl as he stumbled again. "My baby is a little clumsy, but he's big and strong and sure does love his mother."

Carmia smiled, watching the two of them hug tightly.

Yuck. There she goes again, spoiling her mama's boy.

Mommy scratched his back, and he purred. Carmia loved her

mother, too, but she didn't need all that affection in words or actions. The proud hug Mommy gave her was enough.

"Now tell me the details of the fight." Mommy raised her eyebrow. "Did you touch her first?"

"No, Mommy," Carmia said with a grin.

"Good. Don't ever hit first, but after somebody hits you…"

Carmia and Carl laughed and said in unison, "Take them out."

"There's mean, jealous girl troubles here, too, Mommy. They hate me because I'm caramel, not dark-skinned like them." Carmia lowered her head, but Laura lifted it back up.

"We are descendants of strong people," Mommy said.

Carmia walked proudly alongside her Mommy and felt their strength together.

Laura wanted to stop by Mrs. Ernestine's roadside market on the walk home from school. It was along the dried-up river near Ma's place, and everybody in the area either traveled it or worked it. She grinned inside when she laid eyes on Buckeye Belinda and her buckeyed sisters, who sold lemonade to the field workers. They were lined up just like in the old days for a cold drink.

Boy, I remember them. That whole family got buckeyes—big, round, slightly protruding eyes.

But no one's eyes were as buck as Belinda's. She knew people shouldn't tease others for how they were born; they couldn't help it. Bovina folks were void of compassion. Everybody had made it part of Belinda's name.

She must put her baby's pee in that lemonade, though—best lemonade I've ever tasted.

Laura was glad Carl was too busy knocking rocks with a stick to notice Reggie looking at her like she was the sugar intended for his lemonade. She wanted to cut another man—a stranger her age winking at Carmia. She shoved him away as they passed by.

Reggie got in her way and said, "You sure is looking mighty fine today, Laura."

She walked faster. Her children didn't know the man, but they kept their eyes on her, following his comment.

She tried to hide their association, but he would not have it. He rubbed himself against her.

"Stop trying to look big in front of the crowd, Reggie," she warned. She smirked and walked on, shooing him like a pest.

Everyone laughed, and that must've bothered him. His face turned cold—veins bulged in his neck and forehead. "Eh, baby, why don't you give me some of that good stuff for free tonight?" he said.

Low down...talking to me like that while I'm with my kids and in front of everybody.

Laura looked at her children.

Now I don't have a choice.

Laura clenched her teeth, walked close to him as if she would kiss him, and whispered, "You will never get this again." She slapped him so hard that her handprint tattooed his face purple.

He fell to his knees, laughing, then turned his other cheek toward her. He wrapped his arms around her legs. The crowd roared in laughter with *oohs* and *aaahs*.

She was embarrassed.

I guess now you got the attention you wanted, idiot.

Buckeye Belinda ran toward her, yelling, "What you slap him for? You is a slut anyways."

She couldn't believe her ears—she was every bit ready to street fight. But she came undone when Carl ran and tried to jump all over Buckeye Belinda. He was all revved up, swinging in the air, being held by Big John at the back of his pants. He lifted Carl off the ground just in time using only one hand. Carl's legs kicked like a puppet; his arms swung like a boxer. All that energy was getting him nowhere, so he eventually fell limp, causing Big John to turn him loose.

Carl wasn't free for long before Laura had to yank the back of his collar and pull him away from Belinda again. He kicked and screamed down the road as she whacked his arm.

"Stop. Let me go. I ain't gonna keep letting them people say stuff about you," Carl yelled.

Laura looked assuringly into Carl's eyes and lied. "It ain't true, honey. It doesn't mean a thing."

All I neeed is for Ma to hear about this.

They continued toward the market. Laura stopped a few steps from the store to calm her children. She hugged Carl and rubbed his head. He moved away from her, but she pulled him close again. Carmia laughed as he pulled his bunched-up underwear out of his butt. Laura laughed too.

Carl wiped his face. "Mommy?"

"Yeah, baby."

"Why don't you stop dressing like that? Maybe they'll stop talking…"

"I ain't letting no so-called Christians who do more devilment than I ever have tell me how to dress. That's why." She spoke before thinking and regretted not considering Carl's pain.

I guess I'd better bend a little for my kids' sake.

"We love you, Mommy. Who cares what these dumb country people think?" Carmia said.

They reached the market door just as Mother Thompson was pushing the door open with her rear end.

Really?

Mother Thompson's hands were full of groceries, but that didn't stop her from trying to eat Ruffles, all while trying to balance her bags. She looked at Laura and her kids.

"Oh, Mrs. Ernestine, look who done come to your store now."

Mother Thompson smiled as the family entered, seemed momentarily bewitched by Carmia's face. She studied the child's features beyond comfort. Laura moved close to her daughter as the church mother touched the girl's smooth cheeks, which glowed with rosy radiance.

"Hello, pretty. How are you?" she asked.

"Fine." Carmia forced respect.

The elderly woman put one of her bags down, dug in the bottom of it, then pulled out a lollipop.

"If you give Mother a kiss on the cheek, you can have it, pretty girl," the old woman said.

Carmia looked at her mother, then back at Mother Thompson, but not even candy could convince her to kiss the bad-breath mother.

Before Laura could stop her, and before Carmia could realize her actions, she yelled, "You ain't my mother."

Carl laughed so hard that he forgot all about his mother's previous encounter with Reggie. "Fat old hag," he said.

"I was going to offer the lollipop to you next, chubby boy, but never you mind. Ungrateful, snotty kids."

Laura knew Mother Thompson would never forgive them. She watched the church mother scratch her scalp in frustration. She wiped sweat from her forehead and rubbery, mildly-wrinkled face. Unlike all their other encounters, Mother Thompson hadn't offended them, so Laura was sincerely embarrassed by their actions. She repeatedly apologized to the mother.

Ought to kill them myself when we get home.

She was exhausted, trying to be Bovina accepted. She knew Mother Thompson left the market angry in her version of a speed-walk.

Hurrying to gossip. Mother Johns at the top of her list.

9

Salon Talk

THERE WAS AN ODD SILENCE IN MARY'S BEAUTY SHOP. SAL stood massaging her nearly smooth scalp with *Don't Be Bald-Headed* hair cream while looking down on the table at a few *Sophisticate's Black Hair* magazines highlighting the 90s Black royalty like Mary J. Blige on the covers. Mother Johns flinched, remembering how Sal had lost her hair during Laura's disturbing return. She shook the thought away and sat like a peacock on a pink plush stool. She fanned herself with her Spanish-style fan, waiting for the rest of the mothers to arrive. They were late, and she wasn't happy.

Leave me alone with these showy young people.

She looked at Sal, the brightest jewel on her cane—her only child. Her pleasant thoughts were interrupted when Patti Labelle's hit, "Somebody Loves You Baby" came on. She shooed for them to change it, but no one seemed to notice her gesture because the rest of the ladies were singing along with the radio. Mary had the nerve to rock like she was slow dancing while she worked. Mother Johns looked on her prized possession again. She was proud of her daughter's constant effort to be like her, the next generation running their town.

It's her birthright.

Sal commanded respect from the community, too, just by being her daughter.

She'll keep growing, learning the Bible—letting the bitterness of life turn into fuel for influence in the community the way I did.

She watched Sal stir a bit of strife against Laura. Mildly amused, she grinned.

Sal paced, seemed to have gossip rolling around in her mind. The church mother watched. The others stopped what they were doing to watch her too.

Young peacocks…scandalous, messy, deceptive, but trying to gain my good graces.

Mother Johns shifted in her chair; her butt hurt to the bone with hemorrhoids. The mothers had regular biweekly appointments, a time when all the young women wanted to shine brightly in their elders' eyes.

Where are those senile hens?

They wanted to be a shiny jewel on her cane next to Sal, but she never paid them any attention. There was no space in her mind for anyone to upstage her Sal.

They sat quietly. Buckeye Belinda was sitting on the fancy new purple chair eating a box of chicken. Mother Johns grinned at Mary, snarling every time she touched the chair with greasy hands. Next to

Buckeye Belinda was Mrs. Davine humming "My Girl" and other Motown songs as Mary curled her hair. She sat in the Hollywood chair, called so because bright lights surrounded the mirror.

Mother Johns rolled spittle around in her mouth like she was about to spew.

Marilyn Monroe wannabe. Ain't never seen a black person so proud to have the slave master's blood running through her veins.

Squeaky nodded to sleep from time to time while pretending to listen to Sister Pitts, who fingered through a *Jet* magazine.

Ain't got the sense God gave a rock. Ought to go home if she that dang sleepy. Head bouncing like a basketball. No room to shake her brain any more than already been done.

Six other women and girls lounged on off-white fake-leather chairs in the back center of the salon, which also housed a coffee table covered with decades of *Essence*, *Ebony*, *Jet*, and more *Sophisticate's Black Hair* magazines. The women seated there were eating boxes of chicken and drinking cans of cream soda. Mary eyed them repetitively.

Sal picked up a chicken breast; Mother Johns sent her corrective energy, so she put it back into the box.

Several young women began to congregate at Mary's, whether they were getting their hair done or not, since Laura had returned home. Sal was pacing again, looking like she couldn't contain herself. Finally, she cleared her throat in a theatrical way that caused them all to lean in. This moment was the anticipated time they were waiting for, and Mother Johns' presence made Sal bold.

She roared, "I heard Laura already been messing around with Old Blind Barney, taking that disabled man for all he's got."

Mother Johns watched proudly. Sal paused, making them want more.

That's right. Feel the room, baby.

The women seemed eager to hear the gossip that Sal's soul conjured up. Her voice rattled with mucus, but this irritated her mother. The women scrutinized Sal's every move.

Now you got them.

Mary turned the dryer on to warm up for Mrs. Davine—the finishing touch to add body to her curls. The ladies moved closer to Sal, causing Mary to have to step over them.

"Congregating in my salon, not wanting any services," Mary grumbled. The Styrofoam boxes of chicken they brought from Ester's Place were left everywhere. Mary usually didn't gossip, but her frustrations were aimed at Laura too. "We ought to be happy Laura zeroed in on Barney, only way he'd ever have somebody," Mary said.

A few of the ladies nodded in agreement.

Mother Johns saw Mary's comment didn't go over well as Sal's words—heartless choice to criticize the disabled, like her grandson. Mary seemed upset the ladies left her hanging. She shrugged and massaged more Don't Be Bald-Headed onto Sal's patchy scalp with heavy hands as she passed. Sal frowned.

"Be careful you don't take nothing out on me," she said.

Mary looked at Mother Johns and lightened up.

Sal continued, "She goes after married men too. Mrs. Davine, you better watch your husband around this whore."

Mother Johns knew her daughter intended to inflict fear into their hearts. "I'm sure gonna be watching after my Ducky," Sal continued.

Mrs. Davine turned her nose up like she was smelling something sour. "People say she already been hanging down at The Shack trying to get business," she said.

The schoolteacher was beautiful and knew it, but she feared the sagging cheeks that began to reveal her age. Mother Johns watched her gaze into the broken mirror that added more lines to the ones already forming on her face.

Shameful vanity. My skin looks younger than hers.

Mother Johns hated how she passed herself as white at times and then claimed to be black, too, when it benefited her.

Worse than an Uncle Tom.

But for the most part, the black community took pity on her. The local white folks despised her kind, didn't want any blacks around them that could deceive them.

Buckeye Belinda bit a chicken leg and said, "I saw her down at The Shack myself, half-dressed as usual."

The women mumbled to each other slanderous words about the types of women who hung at The Shack. Time moved in slow motion as it hit them that if Buckeye Belinda saw Laura there, she had to have been there herself. Sal gawked at Belinda—they all stared her down.

Buckeye Belinda covered her mouth.

Done told on yourself.

"*Tsk.* Just a club for men to find prostitutes," the church mother said.

The other women rolled their eyes at Belinda, then continued their gossip.

Mrs. Davine eyeballed Belinda like she was a wrinkle she wanted to remove from the corner of her eye and said, "I'll be six feet under before my husband, Willie, gonna be hanging down there."

Mother Johns looked at her watch as the rest of the mothers board entered the salon in a slow, decisive manner. They searched the place over, finding Mother Johns in her seat. Canes clunked, heels clacked, and their demeanor clucked like the majestic hens they were. The young ladies instinctively gave up their seats and scattered to beanbags and wood crates as their elders perched upon their rightful nests—the best places to sit. They joined Mother Johns, and the flock was finally together. Mother Thompson groveled at Mother Johns' side with apologies.

Mother Johns smirked as Mary twisted her lips watching the young ladies finally throw away their trash. Sal refocused attention on herself and said to Buckeye Belinda, "Some of us ain't no better than Laura hanging down at that shack."

Belinda seemed unable to bear the hate stares. She pretended to need something from the back of the shop; her A-line miniskirt rode her butt like a bird flapping its wings.

Mother Johns tapped her tongue on the back of her teeth.

So trashy.

She shook her head.

Entire community going to hell.

Mother Thompson couldn't wait to gossip. "These single women nowadays act like dogs in heat. Don't care who or what they sleep with, even go after older men using them to buy their drugs and such. They tell me Laura's been winking at Deacon Barnes too."

She looked for confirmation, but the ladies stayed silent.

Mother Johns turned her nose up.

M.T., please, don't nobody want that old bag of bones but you.

Sal mourned her hair loss in the mirror.

Every time something terrible happens, Laura's somehow tied to it.

Sal looked at her mother for assurance. Mother Johns nodded, and Sal geared up to preach—a Baptist pastor in the making. She moved through the salon swinging her arms wide, clapping her hands and yelling. "Them Shack women, like Laura and some others around us, is just as bad as these nasty men—no, worse. I'm telling y'all, you better watch your man, or you'll be without one around here. We got to protect our men, children, and town," she said.

"I hate that Laura. I hated her years ago for being a tramp, and I hate her still for the same reason," Squeaky said. She had never married and didn't know who Bearl's father was.

They seemed to believe people like Laura made it hard for other women to get married. *Why buy the cow if the milk is free?*

Women giving sex without marriage give men no reason to settle down. Mother Johns looked at Mary.

Ain't never gonna marry or have kids, thin as a train track.

Sal circled the room one last time with a speechless warning upon her face. The intensity in her eyes said, "You better watch your man."

"Amen," they said one by one as Sal looked on each one individually.

Mother Johns smiled and nodded, giving Sal the approval she seemed to desire. Sal nodded back and slumped into a chair, drained by her successful preaching debut, acting as though the spirit had left her.

"Ma Evans is to blame. She should have raised her in church, same as the rest of us did with our daughters," Mother Johns said as though the spirit had left Sal and passed to her.

She smiled at Sal to affirm her daughter further. Her eyes turned evil as Mrs. Davine rose from the hairdresser's chair and squinted her green eyes into the cracked mirror to check her hairdo. No one said a word.

Mrs. Davine felt their gazes. "What? I got to go now." Mrs. Davine swung her long, honey-blond hair, pinched her white cheeks to produce blush, gave Mary a two-dollar tip and left the shop, switching her behind like a bunny's tail. Mother Johns spoke obscenities in her mind as she watched her exit.

Sal fanned herself with a paper church fan advertising a funeral home. The younger ladies flocked to her. They gave her a glass of ice and a can of cream soda, then relieved her from fanning herself. Sal sat propped up like a Buddha statue.

Mother Johns smiled and continued, "Now we got to do something about that floozy. Drive her and her seed back where they come from." She looked at Sal. "It's time Laura pay for stealing your man, luring away my grandchildren's father." Mother Johns looked around at the other women. "Evans did the same to me, and when I saw her seed do the same to my Sal, I knew it was the devil working in them women, generation to generation. It's a curse, and I declare war on the devil and Ma Evans' whole bloodline. I woulda held my peace but Laura had the nerve to come back here. The devil be bold."

Some of the ladies murmured, "Amen."

I'm gonna make them think they in hell.

She wanted to make them want for love, protection and a father the way she and Sal wanted it.

Ain't nowhere Ma Evans and her seed can run from me where I won't hunt them down.

Her eyes were fixed on the ladies fanning her daughter. Her heart hurt, remembering how she carried Sal away from Ma Evans' door so many years ago as her husband peeped out through the curtains. Ma Evans pulled him away from the window, and he never returned home.

Mother Johns' mind flashed to the day she had exited the church doors just in time to watch Sal, pregnant with Joseph at the time, beg her fiancé not to leave her.

"Stay with me, William. Don't leave our children," Sal cried, then she carried two-year-old Noah, who was blind from birth, and set him at his father's feet.

He wrapped his little arms around William's ankles, but his father shook him loose. Sal worked herself into a snot-filled cry. Laura watched from a charcoal gray Ford pickup truck.

"You ain't nothing but a piece of trash."

Sal ran toward the truck to fight her, but William stopped her. She socked him until she lost strength. Then Noah and Sal were crying; lookers-on cried too. William jumped in his car with Laura looking back through the passenger window. Her face wore excited desperation that seemed to already fill up with regret.

Mother Johns made her way through the crowd that day and saw how Sal had thrown herself down on the sidewalk in tears. She was humiliated. She lifted her daughter—the whole town watching—and mourned the times she'd ever let Sal spend time with Laura. She believed her religion had numbed her common sense—not wanting to blame Laura for her mother's wickedness. Mother Johns thought of how they had trusted Laura to babysit Noah and how many times she had seen William and Laura alone together, supposedly choosing a ring for Sal.

"Them women are cursed to act out lewd behaviors," she proclaimed that day.

Then she recounted past hurts in her mind: Ma Evans had walked out of the market unaware, saw everyone in tears, didn't know what her daughter had done. She moved toward them, wanting to help, but they refused her. She offered her handkerchief only to have Mother Johns spit in it and throw it back.

"I managed to forgive you, but I ain't gonna never forgive this what Laura done to my Sal and her children. You and your seed are cursed."

The crowd got between the two women; their eyes demanded that Ma Evans leave their presence.

"Laura done left town with William," someone yelled from the crowd.

Ma Evans got weak, and stepped back as if a boulder had been thrown at her by Janice. They were once thick as thieves, loved each other. Until pain and fighting came between them. Ma Evans grew further away from the church and Janice became Mother Johns. Evans seemed to think the title "mother" had changed Janice into someone she didn't know anymore. Mother Johns took it that she was jealous because Evans was no longer the only highly respected black woman around.

Mother Johns moved toward Ma Evans. "The sins of the mother

126

done visited the daughter. Wipe yo' tears. You ain't got nobody but yourself to blame."

The community didn't seem to care that Laura had deserted Ma Evans. Her heart had seemed to be breaking too; only Mother Givens tried to comfort her for her loss.

Mother Johns came to herself as Sal called "Mama." Sal was now fanning her mother, who was sweating profusely.

She looked firmly into her daughter's eyes and said, "We gonna drive that wench back from whence she come, so help me God."

Sal smiled and said, "Amen."

Laura drove down Brook Haven Road, a little floaty from last night's high. The church seemed bigger and brighter like Jesus' aura surrounded it.

I think I see Ma's Black Jesus.

She smiled as she left the black part of town. Ma had sent her to see about getting her will drawn up, which meant entering the white folks' section of the town—territory she rarely went to as a girl. All morning, she drove in circles, looking for a small rundown law office that Ma told her to find. She finally laid eyes on a raggedy red sign next to the alley that read: *Something, Something Law Firm.* She couldn't make out the first words.

Laura didn't know if she had found the right place, but she was done looking, so she parked and got out of her car. A thin white woman, seemingly in her mid-forties, slammed the door as she left the firm. She held two preteen twin boys' hands tightly.

A frail much older white man followed her, saying, "You have my boys home by the time I get there for dinner."

Her stomach got sick, just imagining that pretty white lady laying with the likes of him.

Looks seventy, probably mid-fifties.

He didn't have the good manners to hide his lustful eyes, which had locked on her. "Can I help you?" he asked.

She hated every moment she nodded. "I'm here to get a will drawn up for my Ma."

"You must be Evans' girl." He extended his hand. "I'm Mr. Fibbs," he said.

"Woman." She cleared her throat. "I'm her daughter but a grown woman." She nodded rather than take his hand.

He looked her over. "That you are…Come on inside."

The door squeaked, then slammed shut on its own.

Hmmm. I guess Fibbs' wife didn't slam the door.

The office was dusty and smelled musty with mildew. One big desk nearly filled the whole space. A bookshelf full of legal reference books and a coffee maker percolating stale-smelling coffee seemed to be all he had.

"Have a seat," he said.

Laura took a piece of newspaper off a small table, spread it on the only chair on her side of the desk and sat on it.

"How much does it cost to draw up a will?" she asked.

He chuckled. "Too much if you have to ask." He struggled to realign his backbone as he reached out to touch her hand. "It could cost a lot or not so much, depending on how much I like you."

Laura stood and squinted her right eye at him.

"No need to act so uppity. I can draw up a will for two hundred dollars," he said, recoiling.

"I'll need two, one for Ma and one for me." He was staring at her cleavage. "We gonna need you to come by the house to do it, though. Ma too sick to come to town much."

He licked his lips. "That'll cost ya extra."

"We can pay." Laura exited the office.

The door appeared to slam just before he got a good look at her butt. He hurried to open the door, calling out to her, "What day?"

"How about you come to the house any morning over the next week?" she said.

"Tell Evans I'll be over tomorrow morning."

Laura nodded, then drove out of the white folks' part of town like the air itched her. She crossed Walking Town Road and passed the future prison site. She was about to turn toward the red oak near home when she remembered that locals used to get high in the bushes near there.

Maybe I'll get lucky.

Laura pulled the car over and followed the sound of men's voices into a cove. She spotted Ducky and Reggie getting high.

"Hey, baby," Ducky said as he slapped her butt.

She wasn't bothered by it; she had her eyes fixed on the powder. Reggie put some on the tip of his tongue and French kissed her. Ducky rolled a dollar, poured some coke on the back of his hand and let her sniff it clean. She laughed as they whacked her behind. When she turned to leave, they pulled her back.

"Where you going, baby?" Ducky asked.

"Ma waiting on me to tell her what he said about the will."

"I forgot, y'all rich like the white folks, writing wills and such," Reggie said.

"What will? For who?" Ducky asked.

"Mr. Fibbs is gonna write us wills so my kids will have an inheritance…They gonna have Ma's house, her laundry business and her money after I die." She swayed as if the wind had pushed her. "I'm gonna have a will too." She smiled.

"Ain't that nice?" Ducky asked, smiling back.

Reggie grabbed her butt, still focused on trying to get him some.

Ducky pushed him off her. "Leave her alone." Reggie balled his fist, shaking it at Ducky.

"Think, fool. That old white man owes Mother Johns his right arm. Wait until I tell her about all this," Ducky whispered, trying not to be heard.

Reggie smiled. "Points for us with the old lady." He put his hand back down.

Laura managed to get in the car and revved it toward home, realizing too late that Ducky couldn't be trusted now that he was son-in-law to Mother Johns.

10

The Offering

DEACON BARNES, THE WALKING DEAD, CLEARED HIS THROAT and went to the front of the church to take up the offering. Every December, Pastor encouraged everyone to give a special end-of-the-year gift.

Been waiting on this moment.

Ma Evans looked at Mother Thompson, smiling ear to ear at Deacon Barnes.

And she thinks no one knows they're dating.

She held her stomach.

Nasty man. A shiver ran through her body.

Whatever do she see in him?

"Everyone bow your heads. We gonna pray before the offering," Deacon Barnes said. "Good Lord, touch the hearts of your peoples to give to your house. Malachi 3: 10 say, everybody needs to bring all your tithes into the church house so that it be meat in my house.

And prove me about it, I will drive away from you the devourer for your sake. Amen."

"Amen," the congregation said.

Ma Evans pulled herself up with the help of the pew in front of her. She stood still, giving her blood time to flow so she could walk. It felt like a porcupine was rolling its back across her good leg.

They looking at me, wondering why I stood. Wait until they see.

Carmia assisted her until she gained her bearing. She walked in a shuffling way, leaning on Carmia's shoulder until they stood below the pulpit. The ushers' board had started marching in almost military fashion—rhythmically endowed by the organ's tune, "We Are Soldiers in the Army of the Lord."

No one ever moved when the ushers' board marched, or they might get ushered right out of the building. Ma Evans and Carmia were in their way. They had to march around them. Sadie, the head usher, grimaced at them. Pastor Himley shooed the ushers and seemed to hurry them as if he knew Ma Evans had a huge offering. Even Deacon Barnes' lifeless face perked up.

Now they gonna show my family some respect.

She looked at Mother Johns. *Acting so holy, hating all the while.*

Pastor Himley interrupted the ushers' performance—a ritual offering march displaying the importance of giving and serving. They ended with irritated sharp soldier turns back to their post.

Mother Johns, as church treasurer, assumed her duty and stood side by side with Ma Evans—something only money could ordain.

"Carmia, come closer to Grandma."

The girl hugged Ma Evans, smiling uncomfortably.

Pastor Himley stood for the announcement as Ma Evans lifted a thick envelope.

"Today, I'm making the biggest offering I've ever given because my grandbaby here urged me to."

"Out of the mouth of childrens...." Pastor Himley said. He fidgeted with his program, not remembering the rest of the scripture.

Ma Evans continued, "Yes, and she's only ten." She handed the envelope to Mother Johns. "Here's three thousand dollars in cash. We sowing this to help the homeless ministry."

Pastor Himley fell back into his seat. Mother Johns received the money and gave a small nod of approval and a flash of a smile—no teeth. "The good Lord provide a return on your giving equal to the gift," she said with a cold, rehearsed obligation.

Ma Evans wanted to cuss her out.

Not in the Lord's house.

She thought of the days when they liked each other—childhood. They played patty cake and made crochet dolls. She missed Janice, who she was before she became Mother Johns. Although she knew much of their division was her own fault. They used to love each other before things had gone wrong between them and the men in their lives.

Ma Evans was morose, standing so close to Janice, remembering their better days. She seemed to notice a tinge of regret from Mother Johns, too, as their eyes locked just long enough to see the girl in each other, but there was still no bridge over the troubled waters between them.

Mother Johns took the envelope back to her office, and Ma Evans tottered back to her seat with Carmia's assistance. The congregation provided a soft clap for the offering. Hot flashes ran through Ma Evans' insides, but she was well past menopause. She sat down calmly, out of respect for being in God's house, and didn't show her family her disappointment with the congregation's response.

The choir sang and the sermon was given, but Ma Evans could tell her family hadn't heard a thing since the offering. They wore expressions of anger, especially Laura, whose nostrils enlarged with each inhale. At the end of service, Pastor Himley, Deacon Barnes and Mother Johns stood at the door of the church shaking hands with church members and visitors as they exited the building.

Ma Evans watched as Laura extended her hand toward Mother Johns, but the old woman coughed and turned away. Carmia's smile turned to stone, observing the same.

They ain't gonna never accept my family and me. My grandbabies ain't did nobody wrong.

She resolved that day she had to teach them how to survive it, how to be better than what people expected from them, how she had endured all those years on her own.

Joseph reached out to help Carmia down the steps, but Mother Johns pulled his hand back. Carl was close enough to stabilize his sister after missing Joseph's hand. Ma Evans had learned Carmia well—there was no way her grandson could steady Carmia's soul after experiencing Mother Johns' rude behavior.

Carmia's anger caused her stomach to turn, and Mother Johns was her throw-up target. She moved toward the church mother, but Grandma Evans, the old bull tamer, had been watching. She stopped the child with a touch on her shoulder.

Pride rose in Carmia.

Don't care about none of these people.

She remembered her conversation with Mrs. Davine.

To hell with them all.

She was numbed to the warmth of Joseph's presence too. She didn't want anymore to do with Bovina.

We ain't no dumb farm people who say we nice but hurt other people. They like Bearl, just grown-up bullies.

Pastor Himley and Mommy were still standing on the church steps. Carmia saw Mother Johns gesture for Ducky to approach them with her. When they reached them, Mother Johns said, "Pastor, I sent Ducky to check out the gossip about Laura's behavior down at The Shack."

Mommy looked hurt as she turned to Ducky.

Mother Johns puffed out her chest like a boxer and said, "It's all true, Pastor. Ducky, tell him what you found out."

Ducky put his head down, reluctant to share these things in front of the kids. "I seen it with my own eyes. Laura is a regular down at The Shack, and she don't hide being intimate with different men," he said.

Mommy looked as if she wanted to kill him, but he avoided her eyes. Carmia kicked Mother Johns on her ankle, then Carl charged Ducky like a linebacker, pushing him to the ground.

"Liar," Carl yelled.

Carmia's eyes filled with tears. She looked to her grandmother. Although Ma Evans' face was angry, she didn't say a word.

Why don't she say something?

Grandma Evans tried to pull her family away from the church steps. Carmia stared at her mother. Disappointment gleamed in her eyes. Her lips were tight.

Defend yourself the way you taught me.

"They hit you first with their words. Hit them back, Mommy. Hit them back," Carmia said. She could see that something was wrong. Her pride vanished as a single, salty tear rolled down her cheek with her first step toward home. There was no confederate general's blood in her veins. No family pride could help her the way Mrs. Davine had won the war with her bullies. Carmia's war was greater than Mrs. Davine's battle—her teacher didn't have to fight the truth; she only had to fight mean lies.

As she walked away, Carmia overheard Pastor Himley say, "Mother Johns, I must offer my deepest apologies. You discerned Laura right, and I was wrong. Surely, that woman is filled with the spirit of harlotry."

Carmia's soul recoiled at the words, but outwardly she smiled with a hardness behind it. Mother Johns smiled back but she knew that they were both lying. Carl joined Carmia and grabbed her by the arm, leading her away from those church people.

"They ain't good, always talking about other people," he mumbled. But Carmia could tell he was a bit worried. Knowing her brother, he was going to get to the bottom of it, and when he did, she was gonna be right there too.

It was 1993. Although it was still winter, the day was humid. Carmia, who was two months from eleven years old, sat alone in the back of the dimly lit church. She hid in a cove where the ushers stored paper fans and a few service agendas on a wire rack. She chose this corner, not wanting to be noticed by anybody but God.

Don't care if my family worries where I am…better leave before it gets dark though and before mean Mother Johns comes.

Joseph was playing his Gameboy under the piano and watching her.

God, I want to be pure, not like my mommy. She hunched over and cried. She looked up. "I want to be a good wife one day."

Joseph heard her crying, left his Gameboy, and stood close to her. "I'll marry you," he said.

She stood and wiped her tears, angry he was eavesdropping again. She was fickle; she smiled, then spoke with firmness. "Your family hates my family for no reason."

Mother Johns approached the two children, shaking her head. "Hate is a powerful word," she said.

Carmia froze as Mother Johns headed their way. She made slow, solid steps—scarily strong and confident. The old woman kept her head raised and looked down on the girl. Carmia flinched as Mother Johns stretched her arm toward her face and gently wiped her tears. She turned Carmia's head from cheek to cheek, observing her beauty.

"Pretty, ain't she?" Mother Johns asked Joseph.

"Yes, ma'am," he said.

She released Carmia's face, then wiped her hand on her long, pleated skirt. "I got all the reason in the world to dislike your matriarchs, but I ain't gonna bust hell wide open by hating them. You might be told your bloodline is better than others—ancestor talk and such. But it ain't. You come from a long line of adulterating females, worse than most. You remember that."

Mother Johns walked down the center aisle with dramatic footsteps looking from side to side, slightly switching her bottom. Carmia noticed Mother Johns' steps grow less confident. She had a swollen ankle.

Ma Evans call that elephant leg water on her ankles. Wonder if my kick did that.

The church mother held her Spanish-style, white-laced fan with both hands as if it were a bouquet. Joseph swooped in and handed her her cane, following her as though she expected him to, as if it were his duty to guide the imaginary train of her dress to the door.

Mother Johns faced Carmia. "Your grandma pretends she done cleaned up her life, wants people to forget thangs, but it's too late. That sickness is your matriarch's payback for sowing bad seeds in the past. Money can't wash no sins away." Carmia's mind lingered on the word: *payback.* She squirmed, had trouble breathing.

Sowing bad seeds.

She didn't want to be who she was, didn't want the parents she had, or to be a part of the family she was in, not even the ancestors in the tree bark. *Some great cloud of witnesses they are.* She was doubting all the Bible stories too.

Carmia's heart beat fast. She took a step, exhaled and stammered, "Mother Johns, can you help me? I don't want to be like my ma-matri…"

"Matriarchs, *hmmm.*" She smiled. "Well, I sure can." She tilted her head, giving the idea more consideration. "But you have to do as I tell you." Mother Johns looked downward at Carmia.

"I will, Mother Johns. I will."

Joseph put his arm across Carmia's shoulder and tickled her neck. She smiled at first—felt butterflies, then nauseous. Mother Johns shrieked disapprovingly and removed his arm.

I hope she don't change her mind about helping me.

She stepped away from Joseph.

She don't want us to be friends.

"Just trying to comfort you," Joseph said.

Mother Johns looked resolutely into Carmia's eyes. "Little girl, your family is cursed, and there's only one way to break a curse—the power of the spirit. You gotta be willing and obedient."

"I will," Carmia begged. Joseph stood with her.

Mother Johns walked in her confident way. "Well, then. I'll put you in my prayer journal and seek the Lord about your request."

Thank you, God.

"But, in the meanwhile," she added, "You need to keep your distance from the women in your family."

But I live with them.

Mother Johns passed through the church doorway, Carmia hanging on to her every word.

"Okay, I will. I promise."

"Very well then. I'll show you the way." Mother Johns nodded.

Now my family is gonna be pure.

"You see, Carmia, my grandma ain't so mean. She's gonna help you," Joseph said.

"Of course, Mother isn't mean. I tries my best to live by the Bible. It's other peoples that draws out the worst."

Carmia ambled out the church, walking side by side with Joseph, who was still following in Mother Johns' footsteps.

She looked at Joseph.

Maybe one day she'll like us being friends.

She jumped when a gust of wind kicked up onto the porch and closed the church door behind them. Carmia walked slow, proper and confident too. Mother Johns slowed down, put her hand on Carmia's shoulder and bowed her head in silent prayer. Although Carmia didn't know what she prayed for, the gesture was a gift that entered her heart.

"You keep coming by the church, and Mother Johns will teach you how to intercede for your family. You watch your mother. Write everything down, then come tell me what to pray for. We gonna snatch her soul right outta hell, okay?"

Carmia stood and nodded to her every word.

Laura lay in bed, feeling too heavy to move. Months of nightlife at The Shack were taking its toll on her kids. Carl spent most of his time away from home, and Carmia had grown distant.

She yawned.

My breath smells like rotten tilapia. I'm so tired.

She finally got out of bed and went to look in on Ma.

It's a sad day when my sorry self is the caregiver.

She shook her dragging feet, trying to wake herself up. She sat in the rocking chair near her mother's bed.

Her mother's health had grown worse. Diabetes, which had already claimed her leg, was working on her mind and had been closing in on her very life. Ma stayed in bed, trying to stifle her groans.

She tries to be so strong—strength that's really a weakness.

Ma cried again. Laura stroked her forehead. Her yellow fingers lingered on Ma's dark skin. Watching her physical struggle caused Laura's mind to drift into the memory of her mother's emotional hurts.

She was ten when her father walked out. He never bothered to say goodbye or even get a divorce. He walked out of their lives twenty-one years ago and never looked back. He had married Ma contrary to the advice of his parents about only mixing with blacks of his fair shade. In the end, the seed his parents planted took root, and he gave his heart to a Creole woman named Lizzette.

Should know not to trust somebody with a name like that. Lizzette, lizard, what's the difference? Either way, it slithers in weeds and gardens. She destroyed our garden.

Laura and her mother had entered the house like any other day, laying their coats on the couch. Ma put her purse on the kitchen counter, then noticed the disheveled appearance of the hall closet. It had been left open with things that had fallen out all over the place. Their routine was interrupted by panic.

"We been robbed," Ma said. "Or your daddy done something wrong and got the attention of the Klan."

They stood afraid in the hallway, then signs of their new reality began to stand out in plain sight. Only *his* things were missing. His side of the closet was empty, his drawers vacant, his items gone from the bathroom counter.

My heart settled from a racing horse to a slow, skipping beat.

Ma pretended to be okay, but Laura witnessed her heartache from that day right up to the present.

I thought her heartache was too dramatic—too sorrowful—until now.

Laura was so young when this happened; Ma lied to her to ease the hurt of her father's disappearance. She told her Daddy loved them so much he wanted to take better care of them, Ma said, so he went to work on the railroad in California. Ma said that taking better care of them meant he wouldn't live with them anymore.

I believed it, cried because I was so loved. Daddy made such a sacrifice.

Four years later, Ma had to tell her the truth because Laura had seen him eating in Ester's Place with the other woman—the Lizzette "lizard" woman. She cried then because she was old enough to figure out she had been abandoned too. That's when Laura's soul stopped breathing. Her heart locked up, making it hard for her to love and believe that she was loveable. When Ma realized Laura had such low self-esteem, she told her that her fair skin was a type of inheritance from him, a blessing that would cause her luck with men to be better than her own.

Ma was a fool in her relationships, trying to teach me what she didn't know herself.

She always aimed low when it came to men, trying to make up for having dark skin.

Ma's words got Laura through the pain of that day and gave her false ideas about how far her looks could get her in life and love. She was too young then to know that luck with men isn't wrapped up in complexion or appearance. As an adult, she realized that female attraction is a balance of softness and strength, intelligence and stupidity, innocence and worldliness, beauty, and a little ugly, too, that's all bottled up into a kind of confidence.

That's the stuff that keeps a man. Not many women have it. Me and Ma don't have it.

Laura looked at her mother and remembered the ten-dollar bill her father had left them on the bedroom dresser and his picture on the bed. When she was older, Ma said, "He had a lot of nerve leaving his image." She thought to take it to a voodoo priestess. She told Laura she'd never use the money or picture for any reason other than to remind her never to marry again. She placed them both in her Bible and prayed, "God, you be my husband now, a father to the fatherless and our provider. Now I'm trusting in you. Sweet Jesus, don't let me fall."

Ma wrapped herself in God's strength from that day forward— worked herself like a mule—washing white folks' clothes, saving her pennies, until one day she had enough to start her own laundry business. She took her first one hundred dollars from her business and gave it to the church. Since then, she'd never stopped giving to God because of how He had given to her.

Ma found favor in the eyes of local white folk. They liked her, trusted her with their clothes and their children. White folks used to let their kids hug Ma's belly to feel it jiggle when she laughed.

I wanted to know why they got to hug her jiggling belly all day, then when she came home, she was too tired to laugh for me.

Ma was a comfort to them. Wearing her rag-tied hair, apron and sundresses must have been a fond memory to them, a vision of the way things were. *Gone with the Wind kinda crap.* Stupid country whites wanting slaves again. All the while, Ma was focused on changing the way things were. She took their money and trinkets and saved up, moved up into a better life.

I hated watching Ma serve them white people, but in time, I respected her. She made it so I didn't have to serve them on that level.

That was her goal all along. The white folks who were Ma's playmates when they were young were the same ones who lavished her with their unwanted items for her services. Her house had evidence of these exchanges everywhere. Ma had learned a long time ago about how to find favor with whites. She let them think she understood her place with them.

A thing that she tried to teach me, but I was too ornery. I learned what really guided Ma's actions with whites was her understanding of their place with her and her position with God.

One time, a white woman tried to cheat Ma—thought she couldn't count money. The white lady wanted to give her $1. 75 less than what she was owed, but Ma stood her ground until other whites came into the store, the ones who loved her. They made the woman settle things right. Laura had watched Ma that day, and Ma became her hero for standing up to the white woman. Laura had watched Ma take so much from white people. She needed to see that she didn't have to kiss their butts, and she saw it that day through Ma's actions.

I wanted to be just like her until she let that man stay with us. How could any responsible woman trust her new boyfriend alone with her daughter?

Laura desperately wanted to get the hero feeling back, especially with Ma dying.

I want Ma to see in my eyes again that I know she's a hero.

When Laura thought long about her relationship with Ma and all the trouble they had been through with men, she wondered about her daughter.

Don't want Carmia to be without the kind of confidence that makes men stay.

She didn't want her to live her life fighting men off her either. Laura wiped tears from her eyes.

I don't know if I'm the kind of woman who can teach her, though.

She didn't know how to give someone what she didn't have.

Got to try. I want to see in my kids' eyes that I'm their hero.

They were in the midst of their second unusually hot summer. It was 1994. The sun melted the sap on the trees, so the kids scraped it off and mixed it with sugar, trying to make chewing gum.

Carmia was suffering from puberty at twelve years old. She felt betrayed by her own body, sweating out impurities in the form of small pimples.

Blackheads on my forehead, making me look like a chocolate-chip cookie.

She combed her bang down over her forehead and sat on the church pew next to Joseph, trying to be a good Christian. She had been attending vacation bible school, led by Sal and Mother Johns. Even though her mother told her she was changing for the worse, she was faithful to the church—an unholy offspring of the double-minded Bovina church. Carmia didn't care what her mother thought, no matter how much Laura complained about her false humility. The kind of meekness her mother said was personal judgment hiding behind the Bible.

Carl was in the corner of the church, blowing paper spitballs through a straw at her and Joseph. Although her brother was thirteen now, he was still childish in many ways.

"Sorry, Joseph. My brother acting a fool in God's house just because he was forced to come with me," she said.

Joseph frowned at Carl and brushed the spitball off his T-shirt. Joseph was thirteen, too, but he acted more mature than a lot of boys his age. Carl was tickled by Joseph's discomfort, but he stifled his laughter, trying not to be discovered by Mother Johns.

At the end of the summer services, Carmia always sat at the piano, having private discussions with Mother Johns. Their relationship bothered Carl more than anything else; he showed it by punching the back pews.

Mother Johns handed Carmia a homemade toffee chip as though a diamond. She licked it slowly, trying to stretch the treat beyond what was reasonable.

"What news you done brought Mother today?"

Carmia leaned toward her and whispered, "My mommy dates a lot of men."

"Gonna slip-n-slide right into hell," Mother Johns said as she balled a piece of her calf-length skirt into her fist.

"Huh?" Carmia looked at the mother's balled fists. "Ain't you gonna get her saved?"

"*Ummm-huh.* Laura be saved all right. Did you find your grandma's deed to the house I told you to look for?"

"No."

Mother Johns slapped her hand on her knee. "What's taking you so long?"

Carmia was sad. "I don't know how to find stuff like that in Ma Evans' house. I'll keep looking, though."

Carl walked over to them. "What's wrong?" They both frowned at him. "I'm leaving now, and if you don't come, I'm gonna tell Mommy not to let you come here no more. She don't like it no way."

Mother Johns touched him on the head. He moved her hand away and left them. "You see, gal. Darkness don't mix with light. See how he moved away from me?"

"Yes, Mother."

Mother Johns looked at her with corrective eyes, direct and demanding. "God's people relies on His word: Obey your mother and father that your life can be a long one. Well, I don't know nothing about your father, and your mother ain't fit, so that leaves me. You do as I tell you. You keep our talks a secret, you hear? And find that deed, bank statements or anything else."

"Yes, Mother." She ran to catch up with Carl, and they started home.

11

Courage

LAURA SAT ON THE PORCH IN MA'S ROCKING CHAIR. ALTHOUGH she was only thirty-three, she felt weary like a much older woman. She dozed, looking like her mother on the day of their return. She had been back home for two years, and she regretted it.

Should've listened to Carmia.

Instead of things getting more relaxed, things kept getting worse, Ma getting worse. Mother Givens was her only friend; she came by as often as she could to check on them.

Ma was too sick to see after her washing business. Laura tried to keep it up, but with all that was facing her, things weren't going smoothly. Squeaky, Sadie and Bearl frequently came, demanding back pay.

She hated that Carmia had withdrawn from her and was still getting into fights at school.

My baby girl hanging around nothing but boys—Joseph and her brother.

She was thankful for summer. Carmia wouldn't be in any more fights for a while. Laura wanted her kids to have fun and rest, but she balanced their lives with chores too.

They always started their season off in what she called summertime shock—spinning for a couple of weeks trying to find a new routine. Their first summer together, they developed the filthy habit of mud fights.

Carmia was now twelve, less interested in dolls except for sentimental reasons. Carl and Joseph, a year older, weren't enticed by mud anymore. Instead, they spent hours sitting around the yard making fun of Drunk Man Barney as he walked to and fro talking to himself. Barney lived in a cabin just beyond the small pond and stream that was thought to have its roots in the Mississippi River. The kids kept threatening to follow the flow to the river, and Laura kept threatening to beat their behinds if they did.

Carl watched Barney fight off a June bug until he gained scientific inspiration that healed them from boredom. He ran into the house and back with Grandma's yarn, tied a string onto three different June bugs, gave one to Carmia, another to Joseph, and kept one for himself. And just like that, he invented June bug kites. Laura watched them play day after day. It made her feel close to her kids. She nearly cussed them the day they sprayed her perfume, trying to make the bugs race toward the scent. At times, Carmia seemed to think the game was cruel, but their fun outweighed her sentiment. She always had the fastest June bug and won every race. The boys watched her pick her bugs, wanting to learn her secret, but it never worked. "Is it the fattest ones, the more bluish-black ones, or the more greenish-black ones?" Carl and Joseph asked her daily.

Laura didn't like Carmia spending time with Joseph when Carl wasn't around. Their friendship seemed to be growing in subtle, intimate ways. Whenever their hands came near each other, Joseph would touch the tip of her fingers and walk his index and middle fingers up her arm and neck to tickle her. Carmia would shake herself as if chills were running through her body. Other times, she'd push him away like his touch was unwanted. Laura preferred the latter.

Carmia's pushing never seemed to deter him. He appeared to be under her spell from the day they met. Laura had fickle feelings about their friendship, but what was she gonna do? So many issues going on: her drug problems and Ma being sick. Her plate was full.

She had secretly tried to kick her addiction many times, wanting to be a better mother and daughter. Still, her attempts ended with irritations that led her to sniff her way to her desired calm. Unfortunately, she didn't have Ma's broad shoulders, couldn't carry all their problems and the burden of Carl hanging out with teenage hoodlums. She had slowed down but still found herself hanging at The Shack from time to time.

The summer of 1994 was filled with lazy days and capturing June bugs. That season of discovery soon gave way to fall. Winter was around the corner, and more demanding routines were required. A new school year had begun for the kids. Carmia had joined Carl in junior high. He had started the year before. Laura worried about how Carmia and Carl seemed to want space away from each other.

Carl was thirteen and he had his own friends. Carmia troubled her the most, but as much as she tried to focus on her daughter, she had to give Ma her full attention—a greater separation was on the horizon.

The kids ate cereal, then ran out the door for school without so much as a goodbye to her. Laura threw the plastic bowls into the sink and started upstairs to get ready to see Ma.

I hate her being in that nursing home, but what am I supposed to do?

Her mother's eyesight and mental state had given way to dementia; diabetes was causing her to slip away. She went to the nursing home and prayed all day, but Ma wasn't herself. When Ma was first diagnosed, the doctor told Ma that a better diet could cure her, but even Laura knew a change in Ma's eating habits wasn't going to happen.

We all have our addictions. Hers was sugar. And sugar was gonna be the death of her.

Laura wasn't herself a few days later when she picked up the kids after school. She tried overly hard to prepare them to be unfamiliar, foggy figures to their grandma now. They stood in the hallway outside Ma's room.

"Now, when you go into her room, go gently, stand by her and see what she says," Laura said to Carmia while fidgeting with her fingers.

Carmia looked sorrowful; her mother never bit her nails.

"I don't know if I can stand to see Grandma this way," she said.

"Carl, don't do none of that running around and being loud—might scare her." Laura was trying to think of any scenario that might throw Ma into a fit.

"Okay. I'll try not to bother her," Carl said.

They eased into her room. "Ma, it's us. Laura, Carl and Carmia," she said.

Ma turned her head the other way. Her heart broke, seeing how Ma's skin had birthed sores all over her body that refused to heal. She beat herself up for not being strong enough to roll Ma's massive body on her side to wash her thoroughly and help her blood flow. A new depression filled Ma's eyes when she had been moved there. Laura had tried but couldn't care for Ma at home anymore; she needed help.

They were juggling between school, the washing business and tending to Ma during the week, but on the weekends, they spent all day at her bedside. They brought pieces of home to her—crocheted blankets and homemade biscuits—but she still didn't seem to have the will to live. Before her health had fallen so low, Ma agreed to have Carmia set up visits from the congregation. However, Laura didn't trust them. She resented Carmia for arranging visits without her knowledge, so she made sure to be there for Sunday visits after church.

Carmia's twelve-year-old mind had been manipulated by Mother Johns for several months now, and things came to a head. One late afternoon on the third Sunday in January 1995, the mothers board was in the nursing home chapel waiting their turn to visit Ma, who was drifting in and out of consciousness. Laura walked by and snarled at them. Mother Johns was riled up but held her peace under the circumstances.

Then Carl ran to his mother's side and grabbed her arm. "Mom, hurry. Grandma mumbled something."

The mothers stood as quickly as they could. Laura gestured for Mother Givens to join her and gave the rest a don't-even-think-about-it look.

Mother Givens shook her head in sorrow at her friend's fate. Ma Evans spent her last days in a tiny room with hard, colorful furniture. The window had happy face curtains on them that someone thought would cheer up the dying. Ma's skin was darker than usual—an old dying dark. Her full face and jiggling belly had disappeared, and her skin drooped in all directions. By the time Mother Givens reached her, she had settled down and drifted back to sleep.

They sat with her for almost half an hour before Ma mumbled again. "Whether in the body or not, I do not know," she said. Ma looked around, seemed to be more in her right mind than she had been in months. "Where's my Laura? I got to tell you, baby…"

Ma hadn't spoken for days. When Laura heard Ma say her name, she rushed out of the wooden rocking chair and knelt by her mother's side. The kids followed her.

"Yes, Ma?"

"I can see Him now," Ma whispered.

"Who? Who can you see?" Ma looked around as though she had sensed another presence in the room.

I'm sorry for the way I been—left you alone all those years. Sorry I wasn't the daughter you deserved.

Ma smiled at Laura, seeming like she saw her more clearly than ever before. Laura could tell Ma recognized her. She and all her flaws had been seen by Ma again, looked at with the eyes of unconditional love—pure, forgiving love. In times past, she hadn't liked Ma's discerning eyes, but now she just wanted to be seen by her; however, she could be.

"You gonna be okay, baby," Ma said.

Laura and the kids' eyes filled with tears. Carmia threw herself across Ma's belly.

Laura cried. She hoped her mother could feel what was in her heart and her soul, then she said the words, "You're my hero, Ma."

Ma smiled at her as though Laura were a toddler again. She raised herself slightly and touched her daughter on the shoulder.

"You see there? I can see my husband. He's coming to get me now to take me home."

Laura looked in the direction where she pointed. "Who do you see, Ma?"

Ma, don't leave me.

Ma smiled and said, "I can rest now. Don't have to worry no more. You find Him before you leave here, child." Then she breathed her last breath.

Laura wanted to be strong, to wear her mother's heavy mantle, but she wailed so loudly that she fell to the floor and threw up. Her heart ached, and her teeth rattled as she curled into a fetal position. Mother Givens laid a hand in the middle of her back. Carmia blocked the old mother from getting soiled by Laura's vomit. A nurse came, helped the kids lift their mother back into the rocking chair, and cleaned up the mess.

"Why did you take her now, God?"

I don't have her kind of strength.

Then she remembered the red oak tree, took a deep breath, thought of her ancestors' guidance, of Ma with them now. And she got up.

Laura reached for her kids. Carl hugged her tightly while Carmia stood aside with her head down, crying. The rest of the mothers board entered the room with Mother Farrell singing, "Walk Around Heaven."

Mother Johns approached Ma's bed, shaking her head with tears in her eyes, and fell over her body, moaning a long, sorrowful wail. Laura regained her strength, lost all control by Mother Johns' showy act of grief.

I'll go to my grave, too, before I let her walk in here wearing fake sackcloth and ashes. Not on my watch.

She pushed Mother Johns away from her mother's body, nearly knocking her down. When the church mother regained her composure, they looked eye to eye, deciphering each other's fury.

Then Mother Johns cried out with a seemingly sincere grief that confused Laura.

"Why are you here? She's gone now. Leave her be," she said.

Mother Johns took her handkerchief and wiped her eyes. "Girl, it's so much you don't know nothing about between your mother and me. Now let me say my goodbyes."

Laura's nostrils flared in her face. "It might be things that I don't know, but what I do know is you should've loved her in life."

Mother Johns stood in her pride, looked at Ma Evans' body, then her eyes moved across the room. She seemed taken aback by the many flowers that were sent to her rival. She discreetly read a few cards, but Laura saw her shock in noticing white folks' names signed on them.

Jealous of Ma in sickness and death.

"What the heck is wrong with you?" Laura hurled her body back then forward as if she were ready to charge Mother Johns. The entire mothers board stood in her way, so she turned her fury on them.

"You wicked witches hiding behind the cloth, pretending to be mothers for the community. Ain't nothing nurturing about you. You torture people's souls, driving wounds deep so they won't never heal. Ma tolerated your evil ways longer than she should've, but I won't. Get out, all of you."

Mother Johns' jaw dropped, then she spewed her venom. "You ain't seen me wicked yet. At least your mother knew when to get outta my way. You done come back here stirring ghosts you best leave in the grave." Mother Johns clapped once and then left the room, followed by all the other mothers, except Mother Givens.

Carmia gazed at her mother with a hardened face that troubled Laura, then she ran to catch up with Mother Johns. She consoled the church mother with a hug as they walked down the hallway. Tears rolled down Laura's cheeks. Carl took his mother's hand as Mother Givens wrapped her arms around them and prayed.

Mother Johns loved that Carmia wrapped her delicate arms around her in rejection of her mother. It nearly made up for Laura's insults.

I'll limp a little, gain her sympathy. She dramatized the need for her cane.

Carmia provided more support. "Are you okay, Mother Johns?"

She could hardly answer; her thoughts were all over the place. "Yes, my little darling." They sat on a bench in the hallway; the others returned to the chapel.

I'll run that whore and this baby whore clear out these parts.

She smiled at Carmia. "How you feeling about your grandma passing?" She rubbed her back softly.

Carmia laid her head on her lap. "Don't really want to talk about it."

Mother Johns was uncomfortable about the girl's head on her lap. She hesitated, then rubbed her back again. "And how you doing with finding the things we discussed?" She rubbed Carmia's palm too. "It's normal for you to miss your grandma. She must've helped you tolerate that mother of yours."

Carmia exhaled three breaths rapidly. "Sometimes I feel bad about staying away from Mommy all the time like you told me to, especially now."

"You mustn't feel bad about breaking the curse off your family."

"I guess so."

Girls are too much work. Much prefer boys. But she the best way to get at her mother.

Carmia reached into her dress pocket and pulled out an envelope. "I think this is what you want."

Mother Johns brightened up and opened the envelope.

Bank statements, will, deed to the house and other important papers.

"You sweet girl."

Makes all that bereavement worth it.

She patted the top of Carmia's head and looked over the documents. "You know, your grandma promised her house to the church before your mom came back here."

Indian giver done changed it—have to see Fibbs about changing it back.

In her mind, the house and everything else now belonged to her or the church. She cleared her throat.

"Even though I don't have to, I'm gonna allow y'all to keep living in Evans' house."

Or as long as I can tolerate you.

She finished reading the documents, folded them back into the envelope, and tucked them into her bosom. "Good girl." She winked at Carmia. "Still our secret, though." She gave her a piece of licorice and patted her knee. "Now, what's on your mind for my prayer list about your mother?"

She could see that Carmia was conflicted about telling her mother's business, so she rubbed Carmia's palm again, and the girl relaxed. "Mommy still comes home late."

This is too easy.

Mother Johns wrote notes on a paper, which she folded into her Bible. "So, she still hanging down at that Shack?"

I'm gonna have to send Ducky down there to get me more details.

Carmia looked as if she had said the wrong thing. "I guess so. I begged her to stop going, but she won't listen."

"Anything else I can pray about?"

Carmia took a deep breath. "She smells like alcohol, and she still on some kind of drugs. I think she's trying to stop it, though." She fretfully rubbed her palms. "Will you pray harder?"

Mother Johns sat up straight and smiled.

The path to her ruin.

"Obscene, riotous living."

Carmia looked up at her. "What's obscene, r–ri-o-tous mean?"

Mother Johns slouched and wrote in her Bible. She noticed Carmia staring at her, waiting to know what the words meant. "Oh, filthy and unruly."

Carmia rubbed her hands. "I stay away from her, just like you told me."

She smiled then looked intently at her. "You need to get your mother to join the church if you want to see her free from liquor and drugs. That's the only way to save her soul."

Carmia took a deep breath, nodded okay and sat quietly for a while. Mother Johns could see her contemplating. She gave her another piece of candy.

"Well, out with it. Aren't we friends?"

Carmia wiped her tears. "Yes, we're friends. Well, *ah,* I was w–wondering if I–I'm a good girl now. Am I pure now?"

Mother Johns had been on the edge of her seat, thinking she might hear something else juicy about Laura. She slouched again.

Ain't nothing pure in your DNA.

"That's a good thing to wonder…You're going in the right direction. Mother is praying for you, but these things ain't easy. It's spiritual warfare. Mother Johns will let you know when you're pure." *Never.* "Don't you worry."

Mother Johns had what she wanted and lacked the patience for any more of that talk, so she stood to let the child know she was leaving.

Carmia looked up to Mother Johns, but the old woman walked away, leaving her with no more clarity about her standing with God than she had before. Mother Johns paused when she heard the child earnestly pray, "God, please help me not to be like my mother." She looked at the child and almost pitied her.

"Good prayer." The church mother smiled and walked on, contemplating how she'd get revenge on their entire bloodline.

12

The Shack

A FLORAL AREA RUG LAY BENEATH CARMIA'S BED. THE EDGES
stored her house shoes and ripped out pages of the bridal section
of a JCPenney catalog. Her childhood doll and teddy bear lay in
privileged places around her pillows. A single light hung from the
corner of the ceiling, putting a spotlight on her twin-size bed. She
sat, twisting her hair into several locks, ignoring her mother's call
to dinner. She was too old for dolls and too young to be a birth
mother, a thing she already wanted to be. She picked up her white,
blonde toy that was missing an arm.

"You're strong and pretty even without all of your parts, like
Grandma."

She lay her head on the frilly pink pillow and sobbed. Carl
entered her room, catching her off guard. She jerked. He handed
her a plate of fried chicken, string beans, potato salad, and a dinner
roll. He told her every day that he wouldn't keep bringing food to

her room. Carl seemed tired of the women in his family not getting along.

"I'm trying to help Mommy," she said.

He frowned at her, seeming to have no sympathy for her tears of loneliness, and looked at her like she was bringing it on herself.

Carl shoved the plate at her. "You got to stop being so mean to Mom. She needs us now."

She set the food down and folded her arms. "She ain't my mom no more if she don't stop them drugs and come to church. It's what Grandma wanted too." Her stomach rumbled. She looked back at the plate.

"You're still living here and eating her food, so show respect."

"Mother Johns told me the women in our family did bad things. That's why nobody likes us."

Carl threw her pillow to the floor. "Mom ain't no nasty woman. They just don't like the way she dress. Why you trust that old hag anyway? Go live with her then."

"Why so much bad stuff keeps happening to us then?" She whimpered.

He sat next to her, put his arm across her shoulder, and looked into her eyes. "The men in our family ain't doing no better. Dad is gone. Mom is all we got now. Mom always told us that we got to stick together."

"I don't trust Mommy no more."

Got to break the curse, or I'll always be lonely.

Carl stood. "So, you gonna just drop your family for them mean church people?"

She missed her mother but wanted things to be different. "I

got to stay away from Mommy if I don't want to be like her." She lowered her head.

"All y'all crazy. Grandma dead. Mom always depressed, and you always talking stupid." He yawned and scratched his head. "I'm going to bed."

"Thanks for the food." She took a bite of the chicken leg. It was full of flavor, although it was cold.

Mommy does make the best chicken.

The string beans she typically avoided tasted good too. She finished eating, yawned and rolled onto her side.

Don't want to lose Carl. She closed her eyes.

Gotta break the curse, then me and Mommy will be like other women.

She fell asleep.

At almost midnight, Carmia threw her cover to the side—hot, sweating, unable to sleep.

"Carl." She heard a voice repeatedly yell with a persistence that made her follow it next door to his room. She peeped in as he lifted himself and wiped the sleep out of his eyes. He grabbed his crotch.

Yuck.

He scratched and moved toward the voice in the dark.

"Carl," the voice continued as he finally reached his window. He was thoroughly awake now and irritated.

Sounds like Sammy.

Her brother's friend was a dirt-brown color, always ashy.

What he want with Carl this late at night?

Sammy might have been a cute boy if he had paid more attention to his appearance.

Mom calls him a young hoodlum.

She pictured his large, yellow front teeth.

Yuck.

His lousy breath stole all beauty from the big, black curls which bounced around his head.

Carmia stood in her brother's doorway.

It'll be the death of me if Carl catches me spying on him.

She watched him lean too far out of the window, trying to hush Sammy.

Be careful.

Carl's quick movements made the situation worse.

Sammy fell from the window ledge, yelling the whole way down. *"Aaaaahhh. Oooouch."* Sammy hit the ground.

Probably woke Mommy.

She laughed, covering her mouth; Carl didn't hear her. *That was close.* She smiled. Carl poked his head out the window again.

Boys are stupid.

Carl was groggy and frustrated. "Man, shut up before my mom hears you…What you want?"

Sammy spat. "Ricky sent me to get ya. He said you should come hang out with the fellas tonight…so are you coming or not?"

Carl sighed and grabbed his crotch again. "Man, you gonna get my butt beat. Stop talking so loud."

Sammy yelled, "Well?"

Carl left the window. "I'll be down in a minute. Just shut up," he said.

Carl dressed as quietly as possible. "Ouch." He grabbed his foot—seemed to hit his toes on the leg of his bed when looking for his shoes.

Carmia was now on her knees watching him. Carl managed to climb out of his window undetected—toe hurting and all. Carmia ran to her room and got dressed. *I ain't gonna miss this.* She snuck out the back door. It was dark. She watched them from a short distance and wondered if she were really up to a nighttime adventure following boys.

Sammy was still brushing dirt off and picking the sharp, round burr stickers from dried-up burweed out of his hair. The earth in the corner of his mouth turned into specks of mud. "We got to hurry," he said, then Sammy took off running like a cheetah, so Carl took off behind him, limping from his hurt toe.

Carmia raced after them both.

Glad his toe hurt, or I couldn't keep up.

They ran down winding roads that she didn't know existed.

"It's spooky out here," she whispered to herself.

What am I doing following these dumb boys?

Her heart was beating fast, and a knot formed in her chest, but Sammy and Carl kept running like wild animals.

She heard Carl ask Sammy, "Where we going, man? How far?"

"You'll see," the cheetah boy replied.

She was scared, tired, and her heart seemed to hurt, but she had to keep going because she was sure she was lost.

I'm so dumb following these boys. She ran with all her might.

I want to go home… We better get back home before the cock crows.
They had school the next morning.

Carmia knew she'd better keep up, even running through the tall, itchy grass. Her shoes were covered with mud.

Gonna have to do an especially good cleaning on them.

The running seemed endless; she felt like passing out. The boys seemed out of breath too.

Thank God.

Sammy stopped; Carl bumped into him and flopped to the ground into a puddle of water. He seemed angry.

Is it still worth it to him to be one of the fellas? She giggled.

Carl looked like a mangy animal. "Sammy, this is enough. Where are we going? I ain't going one step farther until you tell me," he said.

"Hush your whining, man. You sound like a girl," Sammy teased.

"I didn't come out here for this. I was sleeping good too."

"You act like I woke you up from a wet dream or something," Sammy said.

She frowned. *Eewww.*

They were standing at the end of the field. Sammy separated the tall grass standing in front of them. Carmia struggled to see what Sammy was showing him. It was a small house-like building just a few feet away. The porch was lit with specks of light here and there, but darkness dominated the area. The small club rocked as if it were the sole place from an earthquake. However, the people within The Shack and the booming music created the rumble.

She watched Carl and Sammy creep in closer. They tried not to be seen by any adults lurking about in the dark. She could hear soulful music bursting from inside—Tina Turner's "Rolling on the River" had just ended. The Shack's roar lulled to the mellow roll of Lou Rawls singing, "I Wish You Belonged to Me."

Male and female voices threw curse words around like everyday language. It made Carmia uncomfortable, more afraid. She had to stay a good distance away from the boys, but she wanted nothing more than to hold Carl's hand while going back home. The boys moved closer, so she did too. A liquor-laced vapor filled the air with the stench of all manner of spirits hovering over them. The two boys approached the place from the back. Ricky and the others stood on whiskey barrels while peeping in the window. Then, the volume of the music crept down while the slow song played.

"Oh, baby, turn this way again," Ricky said with a wicked smile.

"Let me see, let me see," J.J. said. Then, hastily, he pushed Ricky out of the way just as Carl and Sammy moved toward them.

"What's up?" Ricky said. He eyeballed Carl and laughed at his appearance.

"You look like a bum," he said. Ricky extended a sideways fist for their special handshake.

"I'm Ricky."

"Yeah, I know." Carl hit his fist on top of Ricky's hand.

"You got any money?" Ricky asked as a stipulation for further conversation.

"Yeah, a little bit," Carl answered.

"Cool then. You wanna be part of my gang?"

"*Ummm,* yeah, I guess so." Carl exhaled a sigh of relief.

Oooo, you gonna get in trouble.

Carmia watched and listened, shivering from the cold and hiding behind a car. Her teeth rattled.

I hate that I left my bed.

"Come with us." Ricky marched like a general. They obediently followed. One by one, they ran from The Shack, still seeking cover from adult eyes, and so did Carmia. She watched Carl turn back as if something he had overheard caught his attention. He struggled to look inside The Shack, then jumped on top of the wobbling barrels, and his eyes filled with pleasure.

What's he looking at?

She got on a barrel, too, just around the corner from her brother. She could see inside, and she could see her brother looking at Henry, Carl's barber, was dancing with a woman, pushing his body against her. She frowned at the club stench that wafted through the open window.

"*You'll never find...*" Lou Rawls sang on the record player. Henry swung the woman around on the dance floor, drooling.

"Baby, you sure smell good," she heard Henry say.

Even though the place wasn't packed, she could barely see Carl. He seemed to be struggling to get a good look at the woman. Carmia tried, too, but still couldn't see her. He climbed higher onto the barrels and began to sweat. She climbed higher also. Then their eyes locked on the face of their mother. Mommy was on the dance floor, allowing herself to be handled that way by Henry.

Carl fell off the barrel, and someone yelled, "Big John, it's a kid out here."

Then Big John, the bouncer, ran toward him. He grabbed for Carl, but Carl was too quick for the heavy man.

"Come here, boy." Big John yelled.

Carl ran with all his might as Big John chased him to the edge of the grass. Carmia panicked and ran to the grass too. It seemed like Henry's hands were touching her also; she was filled with anxiety. She got dizzy.

Mother Johns was right.

She held her stomach.

I'll kill myself if I'm like her.

She covered her eyes and wished she had stayed in bed. She ran, wiping tears from her face, and caught up to the boys, following close enough not to get lost.

Big John yelled, "I done told y'all, young hoodlums, to stay away from 'round here."

The boys disappeared into the tall grass, and so did she.

Carl looked back. His eyes seemed to glow red, but no tears flowed. He seemed so angry. His shoulders looked bigger, more muscular, as if his pain had made him a man. He probably lagged behind the others on purpose—running just close enough to them to see his way home, and she ran close enough to him for the same reason. Finally, he reached the oak tree and socked it.

"What you do that for?" Sammy asked. "Don't you know this is an important tree?"

"Everything around here is stupid," Carl said.

"You ought to respect the dead, man. These here parts is like a graveyard. Some of your ancestors and mine, too, got hung on this tree." Carl moved away from it and seemed to see bloodcurdling faces all over it. He jerked away and slumped over like he saw creepy African ghosts with missing limbs and lashes across their backs.

Go home, Carl. I'm scared.

He moved on as though he heard his sister's thoughts.

That Sammy boy done stole all the pride Carl felt from that tree.

When Carmia saw Carl reach Grandma's yard, she exhaled. The earlier drama at The Shack had caused her joints to tighten.

I hate her now. I hate that I'm her daughter.

"See you tomorrow, Carl. We'll be at the alley about eight o'clock," Ricky yelled.

The gang vanished out of sight. Carl paused for a moment at the gate to catch his breath. She wanted him to hurry so she could go home too. Her feet and hands were almost frozen. It didn't look like he cared about his appearance anymore. But, heck, she didn't either. Carl chewed on a stick while he walked up the porch steps. He kept wiping his face; he didn't look like a man anymore. He cried like a boy.

"My mom is a low life, for real, not just talk," he mumbled. "She ain't worth nothing." Then he cried so loud his voice got hoarse. He socked the front door over and over until his knuckles bled.

Stop, Carl. Stop. You're hurting yourself.

"Aaaaaahhhh!" Heavy breathing between his teeth. "Aaaaaahhhhh," He yelled over and over.

She couldn't remember the last time she'd seen her brother cry.

"She ain't my mom no more," he said.

Carl stayed outside for hours; his heart had hardened. Eventually, Carmia went inside the back door and cleaned herself up. It looked like his stomach was turning just like hers. Two hours later, Carmia sat in front of the living room window watching Carl. The front window was still open, and even though the night air chilled her, she didn't close it for fear of drawing attention to herself. He was dirty and cold, sitting in the rocking chair. He sat like a mad dog; his mind didn't seem right, like he was peeling inside, just like the white paint shedding off the wooden rails on the porch.

Carl scrambled to get inside before his mom saw him. His eyes met with Carmia's in the dark, and he seemed to gather that she knew the awful secret about Mom too. He pulled his sister close to him and put his arm around her. They both watched and listened from inside the house at what the darkness began to reveal.

In the distance, two people came out of the night.

"You got the best body this side of the Mississippi River, baby," a male voice said.

This man had a different sound than Henry the barber. Carl balled his fists.

They heard their mother say, "I'm yours any time."

"You ain't got no mercy, Laura. You'll drive a man to the poor house, but it's worth it. I'll be back all right," the man said.

Carl looked with shame as he watched his mother kiss a man who was a stranger to them. She headed for the door. Carl moved to the kitchen and squeezed into the dark space between the fridge and the counter. It was where the eggs hung from the ceiling in a basket. Carmia moved to hide in the bend of the hallway where she could still see her brother. He squatted and held himself tightly—trying to keep his tears in. He hit his forehead over and over and wiped snot from his nose. Mom and the stranger's last words echoed again and again inside of her head. She cried too.

Mom stumbled into the house, trying to be quiet, but she was too tipsy to enter like the mouse she hoped to be. She closed the door behind her and entered the kitchen, then a white flying object landed and burst on her forehead. Yellow yolk slid down her face as she screamed.

Carl came out of hiding and yelled, "Shut up."

"Boy, you must done lost your mind. I'm gonna beat the skin off you, throwing an egg at me."

"Shut up," he yelled again.

Mom stumbled closer to him. "You got one more time to tell me to shut…"

Carl walked closer to her too. She looked at his troubled face and bleeding hands. "I saw you tonight. Nasty, with nasty men."

"You ain't seen nothing but me saying good night to my new boyfriend," she said.

You make me sick, Mom.

Carl yelled in her face like Carmia wanted to. "No, I saw you in that Shack with Henry touching you all over."

"Watch your mouth," Laura said in anger.

Got the nerve to get mad.

Mom lied. Now, Carmia knew her mother had always told stories, but that night showed her what her mother regularly did— who she had always been.

"I was there, saw you with my own two eyes, and I just heard you with a different man," her brother cried.

Carmia was glad her mother was figuring it out. She finally realized he had seen her in the worst possible way.

So did I.

Mom's face looked so sad. Wrinkles formed in her chin. She shook her head and stepped back. Her shoulders hunched over like she never allowed them to do. She wiped her nose.

Probably thought of getting a fix.

She reached out to bring Carl close for a hug like so many times before.

Always needing comfort—wanting us to comfort her.

Carl moved away from her. Carmia now stood in the doorway connecting the kitchen and hallway. She subconsciously stepped back too.

Carl yelled at her, "Every time I been fighting, defending you was for nothing."

"I told you so," Carmia said, coming out of the doorway.

Mom reached out to hug her kids again. All Carmia could think of was her mother's male-musky body, liquor-soured breath and touch-tainted arms—everything Mother Johns had ever told her was confirmed.

They both backed away. Carl seemed to know like Carmia did, that they deserved better. The wind slammed the door and broke the window that Carmia had just been looking through.

Maybe Ma Evans is angry.

She said, "You need Mother Johns to help you before you can be our mother again."

Laura looked at them. "That fool woman done brainwashed y'all...I'm your mother. I gave birth to you. I ain't gonna let that old horse steal my kids."

Carmia and Carl walked away, hugging each other, and the cock crowed.

13

Mom Gives In

WEEKS LATER, CARMIA AND JOSEPH SAT IN MA EVANS' KITCHEN reading children's Bible stories.

I must seem dumb. Don't know any of these stories like him.

Carmia looked at a picture of a man inside of a whale. "Do you know what happened to him?"

Joseph smiled. "Of course I do. My grandma had me in church before I could walk."

She smiled and pushed her shoulder into his arm. "Well, teach me."

"Ain't that what I been doing?"

He held Carmia's hand and traced it with his right index finger. She stared at his white teeth and dimples.

Hope he don't walk his fingers up to my neck.

Mom walked into the kitchen during a commercial break from watching Oprah on TV. She pretended to ignore them as she got a

Coca-Cola from the refrigerator. Then, when she turned to leave, she sucked her teeth, looking down at the book of Bible stories. Finally, she eyeballed Joseph with her boobs swinging loose under her t-shirt. He smiled uncomfortably.

Carmia frowned. *Just leave us alone.*

Her mom hadn't even combed her hair. She burped right in his ear.

"What y'all supposed to be doing?"

"We studying the Bible," Joseph said.

"You believe that crap? Must think you really something—a nice boy hanging around here with my daughter and that Bible." She pushed his arm with her can.

He looked unsure about answering her or not. Carmia shook her head.

Mom sat at the table. "*Nice boy?* Your grandma know you coming around here?"

He was quiet. She laughed. "Not so nice after all, sneaking behind your grandma's back, hanging out at the heathen's house."

Carmia's face turned purple.

"Grandma Johns don't think Carmia's a heathen. She's helping her. We pray together for God to help you."

"You going to that devil about me?" her mom asked.

"My grandma ain't no devil," Joseph said.

Mom put her finger in his face. "*Shhhh.* Not talking to you. Get out of my house."

Carmia stood. "Mommy, why you got to be so mean?"

Joseph got up to leave.

"Why don't you just be a good mom like other people's mothers?"

Carmia slammed her hand on the table. "I hate you. You're the reason our lives are so bad. We'll never be accepted because of you." She grabbed her mother's can of soda and threw it. "I don't want to be like you. You got to break the curse. Do it for me." She was in tears, shaking.

Joseph hugged her.

Carmia had never said she hated her before. She didn't even feel bad about giving Grandma Evans' important papers to Mother Johns anymore.

Her mother seemed shaken. "Okay. Okay, baby. I'll try."

Carmia was still in a frenzy.

"It's okay now. Did you hear?" Joseph asked.

Mommy grabbed her into a rocking hug. "I'll do it. I'll go to church to get saved."

Joseph wiped her face. "Your prayers worked, Carmia. You did it."

Carmia settled down and looked into her mother's face. "Do you mean it?"

Mommy was fidgety, trembling as she said, "Yes, baby. I'll do it if it means that much to you. I just want us to be better—our family to be together again."

Carmia saw Carl watching through the window. He didn't appear to be moved, but Joseph seemed convinced, so she believed her mother too.

Laura sat in church on communion Sunday, feeling trapped in a net.

Shoot, I done let the fishers of men catch my wild, catfish, scavenger behind.

She grinned. She hated church and hated Mother Johns, but she wanted her children back. Carmia had pressured her for weeks to get her life right with God.

Brainwashed my child to believe in breaking a curse that was conjured up in Mother Johns'mind.

She huffed too loudly. Some parishioners looked at her.

Pastor Himley stood behind the podium and gave his Sunday morning message. After listening to him carry on hacking, huffing and puffing about Jesus for ninety minutes, she was done. He was so long-winded that Sunday, her mind drifted in and out of the service, although, for once in her life, she tried to ready herself to join the church while listening to him preach.

Following the sermon, Pastor Himley geared the congregation up for the altar call. Laura rubbed her nose and started fidgeting in her seat. She looked at her hemline, wondering if Ma would have approved of the length of her dress.

I know you watching.

Her children studied her every move, and she knew it, so she fake-smiled at every scripture shared, every word given and every action made.

I can't breathe.

Deacon Pitts walked across the front of the church, escorting Mother Givens to her seat. Laying eyes on him was a perfect escape, him being so strange and all.

These people got me itching. Can't join. Ha, *I'm allergic. I crack myself up.*

When Laura and Deacon Pitts were about fifteen, he told her, "Bishop King's Black Movements and speeches were false about the *continent* of Africa."

She chuckled. *Bishop calling Africa a country instead of a continent was a thorn in Deacon Pitts' flesh.*

He had also told her the continent Bishop and the others prided themselves in, but had never actually visited, would be better off if they went there and educated Africans about business or something.

Deacon Pitts is such a weird, lonely man, lonely even though married.

She pitied him and loathed him, too, because he was a hypocrite just like the rest. She knew he hated the protest crowds throwing up hands and yelling, "Save black blood," while discriminating against their own for having dark skin.

His crazy self got a point, though, about how some black men treat their women with no more respect than the white slave master, leaving them with babies to raise alone.

During altar call, Pastor Himley yelled, "Just like the lepers needing to be cleansed, you might feel like a leper today. Been keeping away from the church, feeling like you ain't worthy enough for God to touch you–t–t–to heal you–b–b–b–but I say that Jesus came to take your spiritual leprosy away." The organ had his back where the congregation had fallen silent. "Come as you are, children. We have all been a leper of one kind or another. Come to the Lord and let Him heal your disease."

The organ whined again in Pastor Himley's support, spurring the church mothers into action.

"Let Him heal your disease," the mothers spoke like a rehearsed chorus.

"C–C–Coooooome as you are," Himley almost sang.

"C-ooommme as you are." The mothers board backed him up along with the organist.

By now, Pastor Himley had worked himself into a fit that scared the newcomers but excited the regulars. Some comforted their visitors and reassured them they would go up front and stand with them while they got saved. One by one, a few people walked forward—trembling more in fear of Pastor Himley's heavy-handed touch, which had caused some people to fall more than the Jesus they had learned about and wanted to meet.

Laura wasn't going to be forced by anybody to serve a God she didn't believe in, but she joined First Baptist of All Holiness Church of God for her children's sake. She stood, trembling. Carmia took her hand.

First time in months she's even come close to me.

With her daughter at her side, she floated down the center aisle of the church then stood at the altar to receive salvation and membership. Joseph took Carmia's hand and stood proudly with them too. Mother Johns' face turned cold. Carl sat in a middle pew like he wanted to disappear. Laura knew Mother Johns was disturbed by the whole spectacle, and she was gonna enjoy it. Mother Johns called the rest of the mothers board forward to form a circle around Laura and the others.

"God, we ask you to save this sinner today..." Pastor Himley prayed.

"Yes, God," Mother Johns agreed and took over the prayer. She spoke her words to Laura and stared her down. "Deliver this Jezebel from filthy, riotous living. Staying out all hours of the night.

Hanging down at that devil's den called The Shack."

The congregation gasped. Carmia put her head down.

"Stop her from going home, greeting her kids with the smell of alcohol on her breath."

This witch don't care about my salvation, trying to shame me in front of the whole church.

To Laura's surprise many parishioners looked down or away, unwilling to witness her humiliation. They shrank inwardly every time Mother Johns turned their way. They were probably used to her public persecutions. One lady jumped in her seat because the wicked mother stared at her too long. Laura read the woman's lips. She prayed, "Please don't pull none of my bones out of the closet. Lord, let her pass me and I'll do better."

Whenever Laura met the gaze of some congregant, they quickly looked away, not wanting to cast their stone.

Each word of Mother Johns'prayer unveiled more of Laura's skeletons. The details made it easy for Laura to figure out that Carmia had betrayed her. She looked at her daughter.

Look like Mother Johns'betraying her too.

Carmia rubbed her palm in the way she always did when she was nervous or uncomfortable. Her facial expression pouted like she was saying, "Sorry."

Mother Johns continued about Laura being a harlot, addicted to drugs.

What the heck am I doing here? God gonna strike me dead for the thoughts in my head.

Carmia's betrayal was like poison. She felt a sharp pain in her chest and hunched over. The congregation praised God like deliverance was happening—like healing and salvation were happening.

These people get emotional over anything. I ought to roll on the floor and spit up.

Carmia was in tears, and with a mother's love, she smiled warmly at her. She didn't want to be angry and hurt. She tried to heal even though Mother Johns designed that moment for her humiliation. Laura grinned at Carmia and started pretending to dance in the spirit. The congregation roared in praise. Laura winked at her daughter and did it again. They laughed. Laura's forgiveness of Carmia had won her back—that and a little playing around in church.

Mother Johns frowned. "Stop your foolishness. Church, calm down."

She knew Ma was turning in her grave.

Carl smiled for the first time in weeks. He went to the front, grabbed his mother's hand and started spin-dancing too. "The whole family done caught the spirit," Pastor Himley yelled.

Mother Johns looked harshly at him. "Shut up, you old fool."

Laura was the happiest she'd been in years.

Maybe I am getting saved. Feels kind of good. Turned that old hag's plan around on her.

Pastor Himley stood, ready to say the prayer of salvation with her. Laura straddled between two opinions—one voice inside told her to beat Mother Johns' butt, but there was another voice inside.

Ma's telling me to be strong for my kids.

She sighed deeply, held her fast-beating heart and stopped herself from running away. She looked at her kids. Carmia nodded.

No matter how ridiculous it seems, if it will win my children back, I'll do it.

She submitted to receiving salvation by focusing on her children's faces.

"Repeat after me," Pastor Himley said. Laura shook her head in obedience. "I believe with my heart and confess with my mouth that Jesus is Lord."

Laura repeated his words. Carmia seemed to cry tears of joy. She smiled at her kids again as Pastor Himley continued.

"I acknowledge and agree to the church bylaws of First Baptist of All Holiness Church of God and do receive my membership."

"Yes," Laura vowed.

"I declare this day that you are our sister in Christ."

The congregation offered a faint clap as Pastor Himley, Deacon Barnes, Deacon Pitts and the mothers board gave Laura the right hand of fellowship. Mother Johns' hand was limp.

Carmia hugged her. "I'm sorry, Mom. They're supposed to clap loud, like the angels praising God whenever someone comes to the Lord."

Louder claps were given to the others when they received their handshake into the fellowship, so Carl booed.

"She ain't none of my sister," Mother Johns said to Mother Thompson as they returned to their seats but Laura ignored them.

She faced the congregation with a somewhat deceptive grin and the church house remained cold toward her.

She walked down the center aisle with her head up high, although she heard many gossiping.

Ma always said they had a form of godliness but denied the power.

She raised her eyes to heaven. *I know, Ma; I ain't gonna give up so easy. I'm trying.*

Laura walked home with all the dignity she could muster, both of her children by her side again.

14

For My Kids

IT WAS A HOT NIGHT. LAURA'S THIGHS RUBBED AND STUCK TO-
gether as she walked onto the porch and sat in Ma's rocking chair.
With thick thighs and an hourglass figure, her clothes hugged her
body, no matter what she wore. She was trying to live better, but
her neighbors wouldn't let her forget their familiarity with her.
Some men in the community sought her out, continuing to grope
themselves as she walked by.

She withdrew from nightlife and church, stopped using too.
Her heart broke, seeing Carl discovering street life just as she was
leaving it, and there wasn't much she could do about it. She was still
on the porch when he ran right past her.

"Carl, you come back in this house," she yelled.

At nearly fourteen, her son was tall now. He ignored her and ran
to meet his friends around the corner. She took off after him, but
when she reached the end of the road, he was nowhere in sight. She

bit her lip and sucked the blood.

She walked back to the porch, sat, and looked up to heaven, feeling that with all her effort to do better, her son was just getting worse.

"What am I supposed to do, God?"

Ma, you see me trying. Can you give me a hand with my kids? Man, I miss you.

Laura sat with her legs wide open; she rested her elbows on her knees. Her hair fell around her face like a mane as she held her head down and wrung her hands in frustration. She wanted to get high, but squeezed all the cravings for cocaine back down like swallowing her own vomit. Her stomach cramped, head ached continuously as she broke out in sweats. She kept her internal eyes focused on her children and endured all of her pain, even the voices inside that told her she was nothing. Then she heard the still whisper of her mother uttering from the grave: *That man hurt you. Stop hurting yourself. I done took care of it.*

I was a just child when she took care of it. Her boyfriend who touched me.

She couldn't erase it out of her mind. *I was little, hurting, but I didn't want him dead.*

Laura was twelve when she stood behind the door watching Ma fix her boyfriend's plate for breakfast. It was just like always, except Ma had a strange coldness to her he never noticed. Even as a child, she could tell he was too self-centered to have ever really paid attention to Ma, her moods, her hopes, her anger, her anything— the biggest mistake that abusive, arrogant men like him didn't have the good sense to figure out.

Ma's face seemed to say, "I'm done being a victim."

She'd had it. The coffee finished percolating. Laura watched Ma put drops of something in his cup—those drops made him fall dead after only two sips. The big, bad man who had pinned her to the bed so many times was now gone. Guilt gripped her. Love and hate for Ma entered her.

I don't fully know the type of woman Ma was, the type of woman I am—but we the type of women I hope Carmia will never be.

For Ma, it seemed his death was a show of love toward her daughter. But for Laura, it was the death of him, the death of something in Ma and in her too. Something inside of her had forever changed—pain, resentment, love and hate, all rolled up like one thing, one big confused, hurting thing.

"Mom?" Carmia shouted from within the house.

Her mother didn't answer her, so Carmia sashayed onto the porch, touched Mom's head and gently massaged it. Mom looked up at her daughter, revealing red eyes. Carmia stood in front of her, barefoot and robed.

How many times have I told her to put shoes on her feet before coming outside? She was too weak to fight that battle. *Be nice.* She looked at her daughter and smiled. *My girl's so beautiful.*

"Mom, I been looking all over for you. What you doing out here?" She rubbed her mother's face. "What's wrong?" She put one butt cheek on her mother's lap.

"Chasing after your brother." Laura repositioned her legs.

Carmia got up. "He went out in the streets with those bad boys again?"

"Yeah, baby. I don't know what I'm gonna do with him."

"Mom, let's go inside. It's cold out here."

"It might help if you kept shoes on your feet like I told you. Neither one of my kids pay me any mind."

So much for being nice. Couldn't help myself.

Carmia ran inside, followed by Laura. The screen door slammed closed behind them, and dust filled the air.

Dirty house. Don't feel like cleaning. Ain't been up to it for weeks.

Laura choked as she picked up shoes, socks and other clothes from the living room floor.

"Mom, do you believe God is real—for real?"

"Honestly, sometimes I do, and other times I don't."

What's going on in that head of hers? Carmia turned to leave. Laura watched her turn back, then turn away again. *Whew.* Carmia went to her room. *I don't know how to make her feel okay. She's always searching for something—God. Good husbands.* She looked up. *God, if you're there, help her find what she's looking for.* "It's time for another visit from Mother Givens," she mumbled.

Laura flopped onto the couch, letting the clothes fall to the floor. Her face writhed in pain. Her eyes filled with tears, but she didn't let out a sound. Laura held herself tightly and sobbed.

Carl's ways must be payback for the way I've lived. She heard her daughter talking in her room. *If she got that Joseph up in her room, so help me, God.*

She ran to Carmia's room and peeked into the door unnoticed. Her child was nearly thirteen, standing in front of the mirror admiring her budding breasts. Her daughter's womanly acts worried her. She watched the preteen pull her gown tightly against her body and raise it to give the appearance of a short dress.

She is becoming more beautiful. I can't stop it either.

Carmia placed her right foot on top of a shoebox, looked seductively into the mirror, and said, "Go ahead and kiss me," then she kissed her image.

That horrified Laura. "Carmia." The alarming command of her voice startled the girl; she belly-flopped to the floor. "What are you doing?"

"Nothing."

Laura rushed to Carmia, lifted her off the floor, and shook her, trying to stop what she thought was a repetition of her own undignified ways happening in her daughter.

"Baby, nice girls don't act like that." Laura held her stomach, made sick by the demons of her life visiting her kids.

They both sat on the bed. "Mom, what's wrong?"

"I'll be alright, baby. I just need a minute," Laura said. The burden she felt made her withdrawal from the powder sting even more.

Shoot, I need some coke.

She bit her nails and rocked herself.

Carmia was afraid. She rubbed her girl's hair gently.

"Mom, if you don't stop using drugs, you're gonna die too. Then who's gonna take care of Carl and me? Don't leave us."

She snapped, "Don't worry about that."

I don't want to leave them either.

She caught herself and lightened up. "We gonna be alright. I'm gonna ask Mother Givens to help us. You said she's the nice church mother, right?"

"I guess so. Mom?"

"Yeah, baby?"

Carmia looked her mother eye to eye. "I'm sorry for being mad at you, for listening to Mother Johns and…"

She stood and kissed Carmia on the forehead. "Baby, I know. Don't worry about that. I love you. Just glad I got my baby back. Now the truth is, I'm sorry too." She walked to the door, flipped the light switch off and shut the door.

Carmia woke up frightened; something was hitting against the house. She ran to her window about to scream but smiled instead. Joseph ran through leaves, sliding his feet across the dirt before he jumped and banged himself against the side of Carmia's house. Although he was aiming for the branches on the southern magnolia tree that spread extra-wide, north and south, like open arms outside of her window.

Don't wake up my mom.

He was revving up for the sixth time in a row trying to reach the branches outside of Carmia's window, and he still hadn't lost strength or determination.

He ain't never been in my room before.

She looked her room over, put her dirty clothes in the hamper, and brushed her fingers through her hair.

I wonder if having a boy in my room makes me a bad girl. Hmm, not a nice boy like Joseph.

Carmia rubbed peach lotion on her arms, then returned to her window and watched him again. She shook her head with each failed attempt.

This boy is crazy.

Joseph finally landed as his crotch straddled a branch that wavered and then settled again.

He actually made it this time.

He squirmed due to some hurt, leaned back, and panted, waiting for relief.

Good Lord. He nearly killed himself or woke up Mom, which is just the same.

He pulled himself up the tree like a baboon and jumped inside Carmia's window. His walk showed he was still injured.

He pulled balled-up daisies out of his pocket. "Hi, Carmia. You been okay?"

She looked at his dry, scaly hands. His fingernails were brown with dirt underneath them. He had pinkish torn skin on the sides of his fingers and hangnail cuticles.

She half-frowned and then smiled. "I'm okay, but you seem like you're trying to kill yourself or something."

"Or something," they both said with a grin.

"*Shhh.* Lower your voice. Mom left my room just an hour ago."

She'll skin us alive if she catches us.

He tried to straighten out the flowers, but they kept falling. "I'm just checking up on you. I miss you coming around church. I'll be going to high school next year, so I might not see you no more, only when the gang is walking to school, but it seems like you ignore me then too. Did I do something?" He handed the wilted flowers to her anyway.

She sat on the floor and placed the flowers next to her. "I'm not going to church no more, and if people see us talking on the way to school, it's just gonna get back to your mean old grandma." She picked one daisy from the group and twirled it between her index finger and thumb.

He sat on the floor too. "Grandma's prayer for your mom was too detailed, but she didn't mean it in a bad way," he said.

She stopped twirling the flower and pulled a petal, ignoring his words. "You like her." She drew another petal. "And she likes you." She laid the flower down with the others. "Mother Johns treats you different because you're her grandson. I'm not going back to that church."

He smiled extra wide. "Not even for me? It's lots of fun things to do at church if you don't listen to the old people," he said.

She grinned, tilted her head and squinted. "Like what?"

He smiled, then looked away. "Well, if you sit way in the back corner near where they store offering envelopes, there's creeping bugs that come out of the boxes…"

"Yuck," she said.

"I get sticks and poke a roly-poly with it. They roll into a tight ball, then I use them as my puck, and I knock them with a stick—a miniature-sized hockey game."

"Poor roly-poly," she said.

"When the roly-poly unfolds, I do it all over again until I make a goal knocking the bug near some lady's purse and hoping she sees it and screams."

"That's a silly old game and mean to the bug and the lady."

"Ain't no sillier than our June bug kites or when you sat on the playground balancing a pencil on the tip of your nose like a teeter-totter."

They laughed and looked at each other with goo-goo eyes, straight eyes, then crush eyes. Carmia batted her eyelids, accepting his adoration. She liked that something about her made him act so goofy. A prolonged stare brought her back to her senses.

Is he gonna kiss me? I want him to, and I don't want him to.

She shifted away from him. He was leaning so much into her, he nearly fell.

"I'm not going to that church anymore. Don't even know if God is real," she said.

His mouth dropped. "Why you saying fool things like that?"

He looked at her like she was a backsliding sinner he felt sorry for.

"I don't need to get saved by the likes of you or your grandma," she said.

Spend your compassion on somebody else.

"If God is real, why are so many bad things happening to my family?"

Joseph looked at her wide-eyed and said, "Has been a lot of bad following y'all, but that's more reason to come to church."

Carmia began to whimper, a low humming cry that eventually rolled into a full-blown ugly cry with snot and tears. Joseph didn't seem to know what to do. Her nose turned red; her body jerked with every hiccup.

"I'm sorry, Carmia. You don't have to come back to church if you don't want to. I'll come here to visit you like I did today," he said.

Carmia lifted her head and looked at him. She could barely speak, and when she did talk, her words came out jittery. Her head jerked with each breath. "That's not why I'm crying." She sighed intensely, followed by rapid sniffs. Seem like my whole family is falling apart." Her lower lip trembled; she hid her face.

I can't stop crying. Everything seemed louder to her—even her own heartbeat.

Joseph seemed to panic. He looked as if he wished he could take their whole conversation back. Tears filled his eyes. Carmia never wanted to be weak, but at that moment, he seemed to want to take her pain, and she let him.

He hugged her. "Don't cry, Carmia. I promise you, God is real."

She allowed herself to cry like a baby. "I ain't got nobody. My grandma is dead, my mom's sick from them darn drugs, and C–Carl is hanging out with bad boys."

"You got me, Carmia."

"You're just a kid, like me. What are you gonna do?"

He paused and opened his mouth but didn't let the words come out. He held his breath, then sighed. "I love you, Carmia," he said, exhaling.

Carmia wiped her face and looked at him. "You…really love me, Joseph?"

"From the first time I saw you when you were acting mean and angry about being here, and I always will love you." They stared at each other. "You gonna be my wife, remember?"

"Mother Johns won't allow it." He looked in her eyes with an authority that calmed her crying. "When we're older, she won't have no say-so about it."

She sighed—no more sniffs. Joseph put his arm around her shoulder. "I'm gonna marry you."

He tickled the back of her neck. She moved away. He kissed her cheek.

She wiped it off and pushed him away.

Don't know why I did that; I like him.

Carmia wiped her tears. "You promise, Joseph?"

"I promise," he said.

He took a Ring Pop out of his pocket and slid it onto Carmia's middle finger. She laughed and moved it to her ring finger. They each licked it.

"Carmia, you're the smartest, funniest, prettiest girl in the world. This is my ring to you until I give you a real one. When you're done eating the candy, will you please save the plastic base to remind you?"

She smiled and nodded yes. *Maybe this is where good husbands are found.*

Joseph leaned toward Carmia to place his lips softly on hers, but a light flashed in the hall. They jumped to their feet. They held their breath. The old wooden floors creaked as he tiptoed toward the window. Carmia dried her face and got under the covers. He climbed onto the window ledge.

Why am I nervous. I ain't done nothing like her?

Laura peeped in, and Carmia sat up. "Why are you still up?" her mother asked.

She was oddly bold, like she didn't care if her mother knew Joseph had been there. "Can't sleep, I guess." She watched Joseph climb down the branch outside.

"Go to sleep, baby." She closed the door, not seeming to notice anything wrong.

We almost kissed. Carmia lay smiling.

A year after Ma Evans' death, Carl was still driving Laura crazy. At fourteen, he couldn't seem to stay out of trouble. She parked her car across from the church, then she and Carmia hurried toward the police station. Carl had been an accomplice in a car theft. She looked around, not wanting anyone to see them entering the police station.

My son stealing cars when these policemen don't mind harassing black boys without a second thought.

She breathed heavily. Her forehead was covered with beads of sweat that reappeared just as soon as she wiped them off. They scurried in the station like roaches, not knowing in which direction to go. Dressed in their Sunday's best as they entered the place, everything else about them was disheveled.

Laura stood in front of a black officer seated at the front desk, but he never looked up. She cleared her throat, but he kept ignoring her. She cleared her throat again.

"Excuse me. I'm here about my son." She stared at his thick mustache, which looked itchy to her as he kept writing as if she weren't there. Her anger stirred, but she knew she had to stay cool.

Moments later, he lifted his head as if he were annoyed she was still standing there.

"Sign in, write your son's name down, then take a seat until called," he said. "It's written on the sign."

The police officer's attitude toward her made her self-conscious, as if she had done something wrong. Nevertheless, she did as she was told, fidgeting and pulling her skirt down over and over again as if it were short, but it was calf length.

He thinks he's better than me—the worst kind of black cop.

Laura took Carmia's hand, and they sat on a nearby bench. The black officer looked up at them from time to time, never smiling. She wanted to disappear. She was worried about Carl and pissed off because she had to go to the jailhouse to get him. She was also pissed off because she was tired of being treated like garbage.

Look at this Uncle Tom–looking flunky staring me down. He wants some of this like all the rest.

She looked herself over to make sure no flesh was showing. *I've seen you down at The Shack, too, Mr. High-and-Mighty.*

She tried to calm herself, but she and Carmia were fidgeting in their chairs. She wiped her sweat again. Finally, Laura sat up, perfectly poised, but the constant rub of her thumb on the gold clasp of her envelope purse gave away that she was nervous. She tried fake-smiling at the black police officer.

What's taking them so long to tell me something about my son?

She feared that they might not release Carl. She shook her head.

Ma must be turning over in her grave and blaming me.

Her gaze wandered, and she noticed how filthy the place was. There were newspaper pages here and there. She saw a headline about the Unabomber's arrest. Wastepaper baskets were filled to the brim with candy wrappers and soda cans. It was an otherwise decent station with honey-brown wooden furniture and lime-colored accents, but covered with crumbs and coffee stains. She checked out the large black officer still seated at the front desk. His butt hid his seat, which squeaked whenever he shifted.

So fat. Looks like a sumo wrestler.

Carmia was chewing gum to calm her nerves. *Smack, pop, pop, smack.*

"Girl, if you don't stop with that gum," Laura yelled.

A white police officer passed her, smiling, but she didn't know what to make of the smile.

Is he thinking I'm gonna lock your son up until he's forty or I'm gonna help you out? You and your son will be okay?

She watched him discussing something with the black officer. They read a piece of paper and looked back at Laura once or twice. Finally, she heard the black policeman say, "Okay, Chief."

Now, look at this wannabe, kissing that white man's butt—calling him Chief when he ain't even really the leader.

Black locals in Bovina saw black officers as sellouts of their race trying to get ahead personally, not minding how other blacks suffered around there. Still trying to calm her nerves, she picked up an older copy of *Time Magazine* off the seat next to them. It had Nelson Mandela on the cover.

Hmm, first black president of South Africa. I guess there's hope.

Two white police officers walked in and stood by the black one. They looked Laura's way and laughed.

Y'all lollygagging around here with my child still locked up.

Laura looked down at her skirt, pulled it down, clutched her blouse, and made sure that no cleavage was showing.

What in the world is going through his mind?

She turned to Carmia. "Give me a piece of that gum."

She sat, poised like a statue, trying to smile whenever it seemed appropriate—even at the Uncle Tom, who put his pen down whenever she looked his way.

Don't like your chubby, wind-up, rock 'em, sock 'em, sad excuse for an officer self.

She didn't believe he was doing anything to help her son, but she gave him a closed-lip smile anyway.

Carmia leaned on her mother's shoulder, ready for a nap. They both slumped—being proper was too much work. Carmia popped her gum, but Laura didn't care anymore. Her eyes settled on the floor stains as her mind drifted back to two hours ago when Mother Johns had called her about Carl's arrest.

Got her ears in everybody's gossip, calling me with joy in her voice.

Laura had been washing Carmia's hair when she grabbed the phone to answer it.

"Hello. Who is this?" Laura had asked.

"This is Mother Johns," she almost sang.

There was an eerie silence as she studied Mother Johns' pleasant voice. "*Ummm-hmmm.* What you want?" she asked.

"Thought you'd wanna know your boy been picked up by the police along with his thug friends," Mother Johns said.

She stopped breathing. "Wh–What for?"

"Stealing cars and such."

Laura hung up the phone and gasped, then she and Carmia rushed to get dressed. They pulled Carmia's hair back into a wet ponytail, suds and all. "That boy flames me to high heaven."

"What Carl do, Mom? What'd Carl do?" Carmia asked.

Laura swore to heaven and hell as she got dressed, but it was really her fear talking—her sense of failure as a mother. It must've frightened Carmia so much that she stopped with the questions and focused on getting dressed and into the car. "We'll never live this down. Why the heck did it have to be Mother Johns who called me?"

She looked up again and noticed the black officer jerk in his seat, caught off guard, staring, not expecting her to look at him just then. The grinning white officer kept smiling and walking in a hurry back and forth, so she kept smiling back at him, watching him go.

Maybe that smile is how he deals with his white guilt. She hoped for the best.

Whatever it takes.

Two-and-a-half hours had passed since Laura and Carmia had entered the station. Then, finally, the smiling white policeman walked into the waiting area with Carl.

"Carl." Laura hurried to hug him more tightly than ever before, with Carl's hands hanging lifelessly at his side.

I've messed my kids up. How did we ever get here? My momma's boy won't even hug me back.

"He was with a crowd, stole a car. It was his first offense, so I worked to get him released this time. Got to stay outta trouble though," the white cop said.

Carmia observed her brother's actions and didn't even try to embrace him; she gave him an awkward smile.

"What you gonna say to the nice officer?" Laura eyed Carl strong enough to laser his heart.

Carl raised his head, hardened his face, then strutted out of the place. He walked with a toughness that the policemen standing around didn't like.

Laura was worried and ashamed.

What am I gonna do with this boy? How is he going to grow into a man without a father?

The black police officer shook his head, looked at the white cops standing around, and said, "I told you so."

Laura heard Ma telling her to keep her head up. The three of them got in the car, and some of the shame melted away.

Just my luck.

Mother Johns and the church mothers were crossing the street on their way to the church. Mother Johns pointed at the family with a stern expression. The mothers board watched them sitting in their car, about to pull out of the police station.

Carl leaned forward and shoved his mother's shoulder.

"I'm ready to get out of here," he yelled into her ear.

Laura's humiliation rose, and she couldn't take his attitude anymore. She reached behind the seat and socked him in the arm. He blocked her second blow, so Laura turned her body completely around and began to punch his chest frantically. "I am still your mother…disrespecting me. I brought you into this world, and I'll…"

"Mom, Mom, stop," Carmia cried.

Carl got out of the car and ran away from them. The church mothers turned up their noses like Laura and her children were moles on their faces.

Hypocrites.

Laura had played "the queen" all day—trying to behave in a way the community found acceptable, but she was tired now. She took a deep breath and cried.

Carmia felt sorry for her. "You know what, Mom?"

"What now?"

"I hope those mean old mothers'faces stay that way."

Laura burst into laughter, imagining the old women stuck in their frowns. Carmia growled at Mother Johns, so Laura did too. *Feels good.*

Mother Givens laughed out loud and growled at the mean church mother. It infuriated Mother Johns.

"That's the nice old mother," Carmia said.

"Yeah, baby. She is nice."

Don't know how she tolerates them other old hags.

Laura drove off, and their tires splashed mud onto Mother Thompson and Mother Johns. They laughed themselves to tears. They saw Mother Johns raise her cane high and slam it to the ground with her mouth going on and on as if she was swearing at them. On the way home, Carmia said a prayer for Carl.

Laura was depressed because she had made an even bigger mess out of their lives since Ma had passed. She had tried the church way, had gotten saved a year ago, stopped using, and stopped going to The Shack. She tried to be the mother her kids needed, but Carl couldn't move past what he had seen that night at The Shack. He was never the same toward her again; it was as if she was dead to him. All of her iniquities were showing themselves in her kids'lives now, but it was bigger. Generational iniquities had been passed to her and now cast through her to her kids. Carl was out of control, like she had been, driven by his pain, like her. He ran out night after night against her will, and she was tired of the arguments and the insults he felt emboldened to use.

I'm a screwed-up parent, like he says.

She knew her behavior had pushed him away.

Laura paced in her room, wiping her tears after chasing Carl down the road in the middle of the night. She feared for him because he was young, because he was a hoodlum and because he was black. She rubbed her nose on the sleeve of her robe, then looked at her dresser, shook her head and paced again. Finally, she sat on the edge of her bed and squeezed her legs tight. Her whole body was shaking; she socked her left palm with her right hand, ran to her dresser, and pulled out a plastic bag full of white powder. Anxiously, Laura made a line on her handheld mirror and sniffed herself into a better place.

15

The Red Oak

LAURA APPRECIATED MOTHER GIVENS FOR SPREADING HER NUR-turing wings over the kids and her in Ma Evans' absence. Old Mother made weekly visits, sometimes armed with home-cooked meals. Most often, Laura and Carmia made tea and sugar cook-ies, the church mother's favorites. It was awkward when the older woman lost her thoughts. The two young ladies secretly laughed. Mother Givens would turn to prayer, which seemed to straighten her all out.

They shared stories of Ma Evans reminiscing about her jiggling belly or stern facial expressions. During one visit, Laura sent Carmia into the kitchen for more honey so she could speak to Old Mother in private.

"Mother Givens, Ma put a lot of faith in you, and I know she asked you to look after us when her health took a turn for the worse." Laura leaned in to whisper, "Now, I think I should do the same. I just feel so insecure about how things are going." She leaned back when she saw Carmia standing in the archway listening to her every word.

"Now, now, don't talk like that. We praying for you to be delivered from them drugs," the church mother said.

Carmia sat and passed the honey. Laura didn't try to hide the topic anymore. "I know I'm gonna do better...Just wanted you to know if anything ever happens to me, I want you to look after my kids; I already put it in my will."

Mother Givens nodded, careful about Carmia's presence, and gave Laura a gentle smile. "Now, no more talk about gloomy things." The church mother patted Carmia's leg and pinched her cheeks, noticing the girl's glossy eyes.

They drank tea again—didn't say much with words anymore. Instead, they seemed to ponder the idea of Laura passing each in their own way—communicating their fear by sipping tea with awkward smiles and silence.

In the winter of 1996, Carl dropped a bombshell on Carmia. Their house was freezing that night. Carmia ran to the clothes basket in the corner of her room, grabbed the heavy peach-and-green afghan, jumped back in bed, and covered herself, watching her breath become visible in the cold air until she drifted fast asleep. She tossed herself to the right of her bed because something poked her on the left.

"Carmia?" Carl called, nudging her again.

"What?" She sat straight up with her heart beating fast.

At fifteen, Carl seemed all grown up. He leaned toward her. "I'm leaving. Do you want to come?"

"Where you going?"

"I don't know, but I ain't gonna stick around here no more. Ain't the same since Grandma died," he said.

Carmia's heart was pounding. She was only fourteen. She couldn't leave home. "What about Mom? She don't have nobody else," she said.

He hit his baseball cap with his left hand. "She don't even care about us. She using again. Only a bad mother would choose drugs over her kids." He reached toward her. "You coming or not? I'm getting out of here tonight."

She put her head down and shook it over and over. "I can't. I can't leave Mom. I already hurt her because of Mother Johns." She thought about her mother being confused about missing money, too sick to figure out what happened. Her mom had mentioned something about the deed to the house and how those things were supposed to help them when she passed. Carmia figured Mother Johns must have taken some of the money, but she couldn't confess her actions to her brother or her sick mom. She sighed, feeling trapped.

Carl looked at his sister face to face. "Even she left Grandma when she was young."

Carmia looked away. "You gonna run with those bad boys in the streets, aren't you?"

How else you gonna take care of yourself?

She turned back toward him. "You just a boy, not a grown-up."

"I been grown up ever since Grandma died when Mom threw her life away at that Shack and stopped being our mother. You're grown too; you just don't know it yet. Ain't no parents around here for us."

Carmia took a deep breath. The air rustled out of her mouth with each word. "Everybody says you're selling drugs. You gonna get yourself shot by one of those white police, then I'm gonna be all alone."

Carl stood up sharp, looking like a man to her. "And what if I am? Ain't nobody's business but mine. I got to survive. I'm gonna save up and move away from these crazy people." He looked her in the eyes, then at the floor. "I love you, Carmia. You can come, but I'm leaving now."

Carmia panicked. "Please don't leave, Carl. I'm afraid."

Her cries made him shake his leg fast then he stopped. "I'm leaving. Are you coming?"

"No. I can't leave Mom like this."

"Well, bye, Carmia. I've got to get outta here."

She followed him to the doorway. "Where you going, so I can find you?"

"I don't know yet."

Her chest was pounding; she panted like she had run a mile. "If you hear that something bad happened to us, will you come back?"

He took a deep breath. "I can't come back to this house with Mom like she is."

"If you hear of anything—if I need you—will you meet me at the red oak, our family tree?"

Carl frowned, then pondered a while. The anticipation of more passed loved ones appeared to turn the tree's ghosts back into respected ancestors in his mind. Carmia had come to love the tree, too, ever since Ma Evans had passed.

She could tell he felt sorry for her. "Yes. That's where we'll meet." She grabbed his arm, then hugged him. "Promise, Carl?"

"Yeah, I promise."

She held him tightly as if squeezing him might make him stay. "I love you, Carl."

"Me, too." Then he left.

Mom was a mess. They searched everywhere for three weeks; even the local boys didn't know where Carl was. Carmia tried to care for Mom—make her eat, somehow make her happy. But Mom sunk so low, she didn't seem to care about anything. Men from The Shack were boldly hanging around the house. The place Grandma Evans had bought in tribute to the sacrifices made by their dead relatives—their ancestors—was now nothing more than a drug house.

It broke Carmia's heart the way it seemed her mother would do anything for a fix. Nevertheless, she stayed loyal to Mom, although she didn't like her anymore. She sometimes wished she had left with Carl.

Nonetheless, considering all of her mother's problems, even as a drug addict, Mom was still a better person than Mother Johns. Life had been teaching Carmia that everyone had their strengths and their weaknesses. So many arguments had happened between

Grandma Evans and Mom and between Mom and Carmia that it caused her to figure out some things about women, people and pain. Her mom was weak when it came to drugs and past hurts that kept her trapped. Carmia understood her mother wanted to be better, tried to be better, but in her mind, there was no excuse for Mother Johns' kind of meanness. She was beginning to piece together hard things about life, but not in a way that would keep her safe from it all. Painful, wrenching thoughts filled her mind as she remembered the day Mom found out about her betrayal…

Mom stormed into the living room. "Carmia," she yelled with a screeching voice.

She panicked. "What, Mom?" she said, wide-eyed, looking up at her. "What's the matter?" She could tell by Mom's face that it was severe.

Mom's chest was pounding, her head shaking from side to side; she could barely speak. "You been telling that Johns woman about more than I realized that day in church. You shared our family secrets and my whereabouts at night. Even what time I come home, if I have a drink or what friends I hang out with?"

"N–N–N—" Carmia started, but Mom wouldn't let her get the word no out, refusing to be lied to.

Mom had found evidence. "I read it in your diary."

Carmia couldn't see her mother's violation in reading her diary because her betrayal was greater—she had chosen a stranger over family. Carmia broke into a hyperventilating cry, but Mom and Carl didn't seem moved. Her mother burned the diary in the living room fireplace, shunned Carmia as she tried to hug her, and left the room. Carl stood near the sofa, watching his sister cry her heart out. She wailed so long and hard that he finally tried to soothe her with a hug.

She thought of these things and couldn't forgive herself for siding with Mother Johns.

A couple of months passed, death hanging over Grandma Evans' house like bad spirits the mothers board tried to cast out of people. Carmia was just fourteen years old when she had to brace herself for the worst. Mom didn't even look like herself anymore, and she never had an appetite. All she seemed to want was something to make her high. Her mother had been hospitalized so many times for nearly overdosing that even Carmia was getting numb to the scare. The teen was embarrassed that she sometimes hoped she'd succeed. She loved her mother and wanted her to stay with her forever if she got better. It was hard to care when it didn't seem like her mother did.

Carmia stood at her mother's bedside in the hospital. The mothers board was sitting around, touching and agreeing about Mom's situation being something she brought on herself.

I hate them for saying it, even if it is true.

A stench filled the room that Carmia had smelled before—the smell of sickness and death like when Grandma Evans died. She felt sorry for her mother because she had dealt with fake church charity day after day as an invalid, unable to protect herself. She had overdosed again, but it didn't look like she would pull through this time. The mothers came daily; all but Mother Givens began to resent her for not dying and delivering them from their duty.

If Mother Johns hadn't tricked her into joining the church, y'all wouldn't have to be here pretending to care for your so-called sister-in-Christ.

The women began to sing "Savior, Do Not Pass Me By" in a mournful tone. Mother Thompson shook Mom to try to wake her. "You best try to get right with God. You done lived a whoring, sinful life." Mother Johns twisted her lips as if she wanted mom to bust hell wide open.

Mother Givens looked like she wanted to slap both of them with the back of her hand. "Tread softly now, mothers, here in her daughter's presence. I won't have you being so mean at a person's deathbed," she said.

Mom couldn't talk, but her eyes welled with tears as she tried to communicate with her daughter.

"I love you, Mom," Carmia said.

Her mother nodded, but that gesture took all she had.

Carmia lowered her gaze. *I hate this whole town.*

In her last moment, Laura looked at Carmia and gave a weak smile.

These people's hate for Mom killed her. She looked into her mother's eyes before they closed. They were hopeful, as if they were reminding her, *Remember Grandma Evan's words: Everything you need is already on the inside of you.* Then Mom turned away from her daughter's young eyes to die.

You're better than them.

"Mom, I'm glad I'm your daughter," Carmia said.

She turned away from her mother's bed and began to shoo the

mothers out of the room.

"She's not the devil. You're the devil."

"Look like thangs repeating itself," Mother Thompson said to Mother Johns.

Mother Johns nodded. "Told you so." She jerked once as though the Spirit had hit her.

Carmia sat at her mother's bedside, begging her to come back. After a while, she thought of the faces of her family in the bark of the red oak tree and how Grandma Evans must have joined them even though she had some skeletons—problems from the past that seemed to hurt Mom. She thought her mother's drug issue had something to do with that past pain. She remembered more of Grandma Evans' words: "When your loved ones die, they're on the other side helping you—generations of family rooting for you, trying to accomplish generational dreams through you that they once hoped and prayed for—dreams they want to see happen through you, their fruit."

I guess now Mom is one of those ancestors with Ma Evans. They'll be in heaven, helping Carl and me from the other side.

Mother Givens rubbed her back and prayed silently.

Pastor Himley took Carmia by the hand and gently led her away, saying, "Your mom is gone now. You got to let her go, child. You got to let her go."

Carmia kicked Pastor Himley and looked at them all intently. "Y'all killed my mom with your hate, and I hate y'all with that very same hate."

"Her mother asked me to care for them children, and that's what I'm gonna do, if it kills me. I ain't gonna let this child be alone in the world," Mother Givens said.

"That don't mean nothing. Ain't got your right mind, talking about caring for children." Mother Johns said.

"Come here, baby," Mother Givens said to Carmia.

Mother Johns stood in Carmia's way.

"I ain't said my last word on this yet. I'm supposed to take care of this child. Now get out the way," Mother Givens insisted.

Mother Johns didn't move. Carmia ran, screaming out of the hospital. She passed Deacon Pitts, who shook his head. She screamed like her soul was leaving her body. Some tried to grab her, hold her until she calmed herself.

"Don't touch me. Don't none of y'all touch me never again." she wailed.

She heard Ester say, "That poor child done lost her mind."

She growled at them all and kept on running until she was clear out of town. Her stomach was tight with cramps. She went straight to the red oak tree, longing for Carl to meet her there. She cried herself sick. Her head hurt, and she was dizzy. She slouched over a stump of the tree's roots and laid her head on it. It was somewhat comforting thinking that, in some way, her family was there.

She looked for Ma Evans' and Mom's faces in the bark but couldn't find them. She stayed and prayed for Carl to come. It was all she had—the last promise from her only living family member. She studied the lines and specks in the tree and assigned each color in it to one of her family members. Grandma Evans was given gold for her wisdom, Mom black for her passion, brown for Carl because of his physical strength, and white she gave to herself because of her hope for purity and better days. The tree, like her family, was flawed, but it was secure. It had weathered the test of time. Beat up, but it still existed. She further relaxed on it and took a little consolation from its time-tested strength.

The sun went down and rose again three times with her still at the tree. She had watched the townsfolk search for her at Grandma Evans' house, but she was glad it never seemed to occur to them to look for her at the red oak. Carl never came. She finally went to Grandma Evans' house, but someone had locked every door.

I'm hungry. Where are you, Carl?

Filled with sorrow, she headed to town. When she got to the middle of Walking Town Road, she spotted Joseph.

"Carmia," he yelled, smiling. "I been looking all over for you."

She shuddered and looked in his direction but didn't say a word. Her appearance was haggard, but she didn't care. He moved close to her. She shrugged away; he grabbed her for a hug anyway. She broke into a muffled cry against his chest.

"You're gonna be okay now," he said. Along the way to town, Joseph picked an apple from a tree, rubbed it on his shirt, and gave it to her to eat. She wiped her face and ate.

He took her hand and led the way.

"Where was she buried?" she finally spoke.

"Next to your Grandma Evans." He turned to go another way. "Come on. I'll take you. Mother Givens made sure to bury her just like she wanted," he said.

"Have you seen my brother?"

"No. I thought maybe you had run away with him."

"I wish. I'm alone now," she said.

"You ain't never gonna be alone. You always gonna have me."

"Maybe Carl didn't hear that Mom passed yet. I gotta come check here every day."

"And I'll come with you," he said.

When Carmia reached her mother's grave, she didn't cry. Instead, she touched the grave where there should have been a stone memorializing her life. She held her hand there for a few minutes, then walked away. They reached town in the middle of a mild April rain. It was muggy, and her clothes stuck to her everywhere. She was tired. Dark circles had formed around her eyes, and her lips were white. Carmia balled her fists as she approached the town with a strength that shocked them. She looked at her neighbors eye to eye and walked with a surety they had not seen in her before.

"We should have searched longer for her," Mother Farrell said to Mother Thompson as Carmia passed by them.

"Yeah. She seems a little different-like," Mother Thompson said, "and not for the better."

Carmia was silent. Her presence appeared to scatter them from her path. Ester stepped back, then Deacon and Sister Pitts. Sal moved away like the girl was the plague. Ducky saw her coming his way, and he joined Sal. Mrs. Davine seemed to want to hug her, but she put her head down as she passed. Mother Johns stood in her way and looked her eye to eye.

I'm gonna do worst to them than my mom did.

Carmia growled and bit at her, so the mean church mother jolted aside. Mother Givens handed her a ham sandwich. Carmia wanted to hug her, but before she did, the mother stumbled as if she were dizzy, and Pastor Himley caught her.

Carmia looked around at them all, and none of them made her feel safe. She wept, running back to her mother's grave with Joseph following her. He watched and listened as she released a shrilling scream and threw herself on top of her mother's grave. She remained in that position for nearly an hour with Joseph patiently waiting. Finally, just before sundown, she got up, and they sauntered back to Grandma Evans' house.

"I'll break the window for you to get in if I have to," Joseph promised. Carmia was too sad and weak to respond to him. She mostly wanted Carl now.

Joseph grabbed her hand tightly. "Don't you worry. I told you when you moved here that I'll look out for you."

Carmia looked at him, "Mother Johns don't want us to be close and I hate everything about her now."

I'm gonna do the opposite of everything she wants. He looked at her expressionless.

She held his hand more tightly. He touched the plastic Ring Pop base still on her finger, stood taller, and smiled while leading her toward home. But something about him seemed uncertain. Maybe Joseph wondered how he would bring his grandma and Carmia together now that there was so much division between them.

16

Greed

EIGHT DAYS AFTER MOM DIED, PASTOR HIMLEY CALLED A church meeting to decide what to do with Carmia. She wore itchy tights that Mother Johns insisted she wear, even though it was a warm day. She shifted and sighed with her head down. The area under her eyes was still dark, her complexion dull.

Joseph sat directly across the pew from her, trying to get her attention. She noticed his gaze but rarely looked up. He kept his eyes on Carmia as if looking at her could strengthen her.

He's just a boy. What can he do?

She looked at Mother Johns with hate in her eyes because the old woman had denied her mother's instructions for her children to be cared for by Mother Givens.

Pastor Himley stood at the podium to get the meeting started. "Now, we are gathered here to decide what's to become of the child, ah, Carmia."

"We know the girl's name. Don't want to waste no more time on this than we have to, so get on with it," Mother Johns said.

Sal stood with hands on her hips. "She oughtta be a ward of the state. Ain't none of our problem."

Carmia sat quietly, dazed, while the congregation discussed her future.

Don't want to be here, no way.

"I'll take her in. I can do it. It's what her mother wanted anyway," Mother Givens said, putting her arm around Carmia.

She the only one who cares.

She looked to Pastor Himley and Mother Johns, trying to gauge what they were thinking.

Why don't they let me stay with her?

Carmia couldn't help herself and broke the silence. "I'll behave. I'll listen to Mother Givens. I'll behave."

Pastor Himley moved close to them and put a hand on each of their shoulders.

"Now, Mother, we appreciate your offer, but you gotta consider your health condition. You can't take on a fifteen-year-old girl."

"You ain't gone worry me, Pastor. I say I can." Mother Givens seemed confused with an unfocused anger. "I said I want to help this child."

"I know I didn't behave well in the past, but I'll do better," Carmia pleaded further.

The church began to hum with whispered discussions. Carmia hoped some were touched by her words and believed she should live with Mother Givens. She fake-smiled like her mother had done so many times before, trying to soften their hearts, but Mother

Johns was stone-faced, scanning the congregation to see who would dare disagree with her.

Mother Johns struck her cane on the floor and silenced the place with a single raised eyebrow. "The devil will say anything to find a new home. Beware," she said.

Carmia sat hunched over, elbows on knees. More than an hour passed, and still, no one Mother Johns would approve of had agreed to take her in. Then Mother Thompson came running into the meeting. She held her aching heart and breathed out a screeching sound, *"Haaaaaah!"*

She had run too fast for her large frame and weak, wobbly knees. After adjusting her huge breasts back into proper position inside her bra, she held the only relatively tapered part of her body—her waist—with her left hand. She placed her right hand on her chest, still trying to catch her breath.

Mother Thompson peered over her glasses, waiting to see who would be sensitive enough to her need to provide a glass of water. Finding no hand extending this kindness to her, she shifted all of her weight onto her right leg, hand on hip—a sign she would not speak until someone got wisdom from above to provide water to satisfy her thirst.

Deacon Barnes moved as quickly as he could to meet her request. *He sure is one ugly man.*

He was sixty-nine years old but looked every bit of ninety. He had a physical appearance of something broken, with deep, mournful lines surrounding his mouth. Barnes wouldn't have been so disgusting to look at if he didn't also have the stained rumor of pedophilia on his reputation—and if he didn't still display actions that seemed to confirm it. Carmia shook all over at the thought of him touching her or any other child.

Can't stand to look at that man.

Sadness covered her face as she gazed at him. She turned away. His presence caused past hurts to resurface in Carmia's mind.

Deacon Barnes needed to be perfectly groomed just to appear human in her eyes. Still, he allowed himself to go unwashed—crusty mucus seemed to reside in the corners of his eyes, along with dried saliva in the corners of his mouth. Only Mother Thompson wanted him anywhere near her. Carmia knew they were more than just the friends they pretended to be.

She watched Deacon Barnes stretch his long flabby, sixty-nine-year-old arm in front of Mother Thompson. She grabbed the glass of water quickly before his fingers failed him. She gulped the entire glass down in just a few seconds. Carmia's stomach turned as water mingled with her slob and leaked from each side of her mouth. Deacon Barnes and his fragile hands appeared again in front of Mother Thompson's face and took hold of the empty glass with better steadiness. She gave him a lover's wink, and he returned a broad smile that revealed a single tobacco-stained tooth surrounded by darkness.

With her need met, Mother Thompson stood straight and cleared her throat to speak. When she opened her mouth, they moved to the edges of their seats. She taunted them, enjoying her rare position of power—pursed her lips until she had rid the congregation of their patience.

The mean church mother banged her cane on the floor again. "Enough already now. Speak your mind, or take your seat," Mother

Johns ordered at the end of her tolerance.

Mother Thompson glared unappreciatively but yielded all the same. "As y'all know, I am a former librarian, well-educated, skilled with books and finding information, so I took it upon myself to go down to the hall of records, and it's done come to my attention that we had a modern-day scrooge living amongst us. While many of us lived our lives scraping the bottom of the barrel for enough food to feed our babies, there was a nearby neighbor who could have eased our load—if she had the heart to do it."

Carmia smacked her lips. *Just talking gets this old hag outta breath.*

"This person was our late Ma Evans; God bless her stingy soul. She was richer than we ever thought." She pointed at Carmia. "This here child and her brother be the sole beneficiaries of all her money."

Everything went silent; all eyes fell on the teen. Carmia sat quietly, not fully understanding what was going on.

"Holy moly. That child is filthy rich," Sal said before thinking.

Mother Johns settled her eyes on Sal, stayed there for a while and silenced her out-of-line ways.

"We'll take her in." Ducky couldn't help himself. Both ladies hushed him with their eyes.

"E–Exactly h–how much is she worth?" Mother Farrell asked.

"Don't know exactly. Think it be more than four hundred thousand dollars goin'to this child," Mother Thompson answered.

"My Lord." Pastor Himley praised. He clapped in jubilation as if he was in the middle of preaching a sermon. Mother Givens raised herself, standing still until the entire church was silent. She tilted her head to the side and sucked the front of her dentures to moisten her mouth. Whiskers had regrown above her lip in complement to her long salt-and-pepper eyelashes. She looked gentle as if she might purr, yet her spirit was feisty. The whiskers on her face peeked between the wrinkles that framed her mouth whenever she moved her lips. Her dignity and grace arrested the congregation whenever she managed to be in her right mind.

Mother Givens spoke as if she were Yoda, the *Star Wars* alien.

"We are a people brought together for God's purpose, but where is our love? When is the last time we healed the brokenhearted or set the captives free? Everything is always about money. Calm down, Pastor. Ain't fitting for no pastor to behave so about money."

They thought long and hard about her words. Then, a buzz filled the church, with several groups whispering about the state of the church funds.

Mother Johns flapped her arms, sucked the insides of her cheeks, then twisted her lips like she had a terrible taste in her mouth. "Order, order. I say order in the house of the Lord. What's done got into y'all? The love of money be the root of all evil. Don't let the devil blind you about what we dealing with. This here child got to be delivered. Nothing to play with, demons in her genes."

Mother Johns looked at Carmia. Her words brought the congregation back to sober thinking, and their energy rejected the teen. Mother Johns wiped the sweat from her forehead and leaned on the podium.

"Now, it be our Christian duty to look after orphans, reach out to lost souls and such. Can't remove her from our community just yet. This being an issue attached to money, the burden falls to me— church treasurer, chair of our boys' outreach and the overseer of our future girls' home. I'll go see about guardianship over this child. In the meanwhile, I'll deal with the devil and take her in."

Carmia sobbed silently. Joseph handed her a tissue he had been readily holding during the whole meeting in case she needed it.

Mother Givens stood and yelled, "I object. I object."

Mother Johns laughed at Mother Givens like she was crazy. "You might be heard if this was a court of law. This be my court; I make the law around here. Now sit yourself down."

Mother Givens flinched and seemed confused, like she was trying to remember something important. She looked around. No one stood with her, and no one else contested the mean mother's decision. Even the girl didn't mention her mother's will.

"Remember, congregation, it was her mother's fault and not her own that she was born into such a life of sin, and it's now our duty to save her soul," Pastor Himley said.

Mother Johns walked into the pulpit and declared, "We are God's people, and He has given us power to trample over serpents and scorpions, and we are going to cast the devil out from around us and save this poor child from his grip."

All the people said, "Amen."

A chill filled the room as they began to exit the church.

Hell ain't no other place but here.

Carmia wrapped her arms around herself and moved away from Joseph as he approached her.

Carmia learned the pattern of Mother Johns' stride well, always a stomp after a step as she hit her marble bottom cane to the floor.

But, noticeably, it was a very different sound from the step and drag that Grandma Evans' walk made.

I don't care no more what they do with me. I just don't want to be around her no more.

Mother Johns entered her guest room, which was temporarily Carmia's room. She looked around as if she had expected to find someone else there. Carmia looked up at the church mother, wondering what she wanted.

"I been to the courthouse many a day on the count of you and your brother. I finally got everything figured out about what to do with you. I'm gonna ask you one more time to tell me where your brother is."

"I told you already. I don't know. He left me."

"*Hmmm.* When I find him, he'll go along with you at the Pittses' house. Since y'all don't know the whereabouts of your father's side of the family, it's been left to our community to see about you. Ought to be grateful for our charity, gal. Do yo'best to be obedient. I got custody over you, but with Noah and Joseph living with me... Well, it ain't fitting to have you living in the same house with my grandsons. I'm paying the Pittses to take you in, you understand?"

"Yeah, whatever," Carmia mumbled.

Mother Johns' lips quivered. "Ungrateful child. Don't appreciate what's been done for you." The girl stared blankly. "Well, I'll see about correcting this wayward behavior. Count it my responsibility to uproot it out of you, you hear?"

"Yes."

"Come on here."

Carmia put her doll with the missing arm, the plastic base of the Ring Pop, and her mother's perfume—all she had left that reminded her of home—into a plastic bag, then followed Mother Johns. Carmia got into the back seat of her mother's car, finding Mother Thompson in the passenger seat.

Already stole Mom's car.

They drove through unfamiliar bumpy trails to Brook Haven Road. "I originally wanted to put her into a girls' orphanage but ain't none close by," she heard Mother Johns say to Mother Thompson. She watched yellow, white, and spotted butterflies in a cluster hover over wild daisies. "I gained guardianship, so it wouldn't be right to have her too far away," she continued.

"How'd you get guardianship?" Mother Thompson asked.

Mother Johns swatted her flunky's arm. "Shush up."

She looked at Carmia in the rearview mirror to see if she heard them. The girl was hunched over, chin on the back of her hand, looking out the window. The church mothers thought she wasn't listening, but she was. "I went to see Fibbs, got the papers changed. Don't know why nobody would want Mother Givens' senile self to handle important business no way."

"You just got custody? Nothing else?" Mother Thompson pried on dangerous ground.

"What I told you is all you need to know. Gonna finally open a local girls' home too." Mother Johns ended the conversation by focusing on the road.

I need my brother.

Mother Thompson looked back at Carmia.

"Would've been perfect if you had already opened the girls' home. You wouldn't have to worry about paying nobody."

"Won't be long now. We got property to use for it down at Evans' former house."

She couldn't stand to hear Mother Johns' plans and hear her stories about how she went out of her way to care for her. She plugged her ears the rest of the drive.

As far as Carmia could tell, the Pittses were a couple in their mid-forties brought together for all the wrong reasons. It was clear their marriage had problems, and they were just starting a family. She remembered her mother describing Deacon Pitts as a nerd. He had beautiful, kind eyes with soft crow's feet at each corner. Soft gray hairs sprouted from both his temples, giving him a distinguished look. Although he was good-looking, his large glasses, thick facial hair, and square demeanor hid his attractiveness. He had a pleasant personality and confidence but was also a little unsure. Even when people surrounded him, he seemed lonely. Carmia could relate to that part of him. Sister Pitts was an amazon beauty with straight, sharp facial features. She was curvy but muscular. Her pregnancy hid some of her girly shape.

Carmia sat at the dinner table. The two adults were mostly quiet, so she was too. Sister Pitts watched Deacon Pitts watching Carmia from the corner of his eye. He paid attention to her every move. She wanted to shrink, didn't want any trouble, and tried not to move.

"What's done become of your brother?" Sister Pitts asked.

She didn't like talking about Carl and how he disappeared, but it was better than the loud silence. "I don't know where he is."

Sister Pitts shifted in her seat, rubbing her stomach. "I reckon when you find him, you gonna want to be where he is."

She smiled. "Yes, ma'am."

Sister Pitts seemed to like her—feel sorry for her. In some ways, she began to treat her like a daughter, even French braided her hair, but Deacon Pitts kept giving her reason to grow jealous with his wandering eyes. Sister Pitts seemed to fight the urge to go there, but being pregnant had finally gotten the best of her. She was slowly changing. Carmia just wanted to be accepted—tried to gain both of their approval. She did everything she could to help the expecting couple in hopes that she might become a part of their family. She held her family in her heart, but she rarely went to the red oak anymore.

A few days later, Carmia longed for home and made the trip back to Ma Evans' house. The community had boarded and nailed the house closed. She walked around the porch like an abandoned cat, then went to sit by the red oak. She searched for her matriarchs' faces, but the bark was just a blur caused by her present tears. She couldn't make out any of their faces. Carmia hugged the tree anyway, trying to absorb some degree of strength from it to help her endure living with the Pittses and dealing with Mother Johns' hatred of her. She hoped to someday pay Mother Johns back for all the wrong she did to her family. She touched the tree as if it was her only friend and headed back to the Pittses' place. She held on to the idea that in some way her family was still with her.

16

Curse Breaker

LAURA'S DEATH MADE THE TOWN A BIT MORE SETTLED IN Mother John's view. It was free from Laura's loose, sinful behavior, which most other females in town disapproved of. Mother Johns relished her absence, but to her, their community wasn't going to be whole again until she had dealt with Carmia too. She despised everything and anyone who had anything to do with Ma Evans' bloodline. Mother Johns would not be at peace until she had destroyed them all. But with Carmia, she was patient, plotting and planning for her life to be as miserable as her own.

Just three months after Laura's death, Mother Johns stood in the shadows of the curved alley between the grocery store and the gas station. It was unlike her to be there on such an important day—she had organized a day of charity that shut down Brook Haven Road for the whole day. She was in the dark instead of the spotlight, waiting on Ducky. He and another man she didn't know but heard Ducky calling Big Man approached her. Big Man handed her a bag. She looked at Ducky like he should've been the one she was dealing with. She opened it and pulled out a wad of money wrapped in a rubber band.

"Don't seem like all I was expecting," she said to Ducky.

"It's all there." Ducky nodded.

She looked Big Man up and down; her eyes didn't like him. "You tell Mosley to get my money right."

"Yes, ma'am," Big Man said, unmoved by her bite.

Ducky and Big Man turned and disappeared into the alley.

She stepped into the light and smiled.

It's a good day.

She stepped, then stomped, paused, stepped, stomped, and stepped again. Then there was a prolonged silence as she checked all her pockets. Finally, she pulled a large silver cross out of her left dress pocket and kissed it.

Need this later to cast the devil out our midst.

She went over a checklist in her mind as she checked more pockets.

Got anointed oil at church. Um-huh.

The street looked something like a fair. Mother Johns walked on proudly, admiring what she wanted to believe was her work. But she knew it was really the work of volunteers, done for those in need within the Bovina community. On that day, the air was unusually hot and humid; she needed a drink of water.

Somebody ought to hand me a bottle of water.

Mother Johns took out her fan.

They see me fanning myself. I carries a heavy load caring for all them—not one looks after me.

Mother Johns walked farther down Brook Haven Road, closing out the noise of the busy path with her thoughts. The area was humming with people giving and receiving help. Kids were playing hide-and-seek, hopscotch, and jump rope in the middle of the street. She smiled at the festival. This annual day of charity was put on by the church, but it was her brainchild. There were booths and tables all over, even the sale of raffle tickets. The mothers board donated their older hats and baked goods to the cause—no winners ever selected their fascinators, but it was fine by them.

There were two large tents on opposite ends of the street where people could get bags of food and other necessities like toothbrushes, blankets, first aid, and all sorts of support for the disabled. The large blue tent kept inflating and swaying in the wind, like a big blowfish swelling up to float away. They were nervous every time it lifted a few inches off the ground.

Why in the heck ain't nobody dismantling it before it dismantles us?

The people watched Mother Johns as she examined them, wanting her nod of approval. Stomp, step, nod. Stomp, step, nod. Stomp, step, almost a nod.

She approached a table laden with food. Carol had given generously from her restaurant, compared to Ester's paltry offering.

Ester ought to be ashamed, sending out biscuits and gravy, Carol outshining her with baskets of fried chicken.

She picked up a chicken leg and took a bite.

Mighty good too.

She withheld her nod to Ester, but smiled and nodded at Carol, then walked on. Ester rolled her eyes a little too soon for Mother

Johns to miss it. She turned back.

"Business not so good lately, Ester?"

"Business been alright," she said.

"I would think so. Everybody around here avoiding Carol's in support of you, just 'cause you're black. Nearly driving that poor woman out of business." Ester seemed to boil. "I noticed her chicken taste mighty good. Maybe we ought to support her instead, with her giving heart and all."

Ester gave a half-smile-nod. Mother Johns walked on, nodding and smiling to others as a sign of her approval. She breathed deeply, enjoying the scent of her control.

She started sweating, looked around for a chair. *This day was supposed to be more cooling. Surges of heat in my lungs. Can't breathe.*

"What does an elder got to do for a drink of water in the sizzling heat of July?" she asked, slamming her cane.

Four men ran to her from four directions with bottled water. Pastor Himley reached her first, simply because he was closest to her. She frowned as she watched him remove himself from a nearby bench that had a bucket of bottled water on ice next to it.

Can't get you to do nothing. Drinking up the water from them that need it.

She snatched the bottle from his hand.

Mother Johns sat, observing them all. No other day caused her pride more than the annual day of charity. The congregation and community partners had outdone themselves, tending to the needs of those members who suffered from physical disabilities. They provided hearing aids, wheelchairs, service dogs, and food to those who needed it.

Mother Johns' grandson Noah was one who needed this kind of help; he was the real inspiration for her charity. She smiled, watching the blind teen bond with a service dog as Joseph helped him. Sal had already been watching her sons from across the street. She joined her mother and sat on the chair next to her. Sal wiped the sweat from her brow and attempted to use the same cloth for her mother.

Mother Johns shooed her away in scorn. "You know better than to touch me with that filthy cloth."

Passing off your sweat like it be anointed oil.

"Mama, you a piece of work." They laughed.

Mother Johns grinned at Sal. "Look like the festival done turned out well again."

"Sure did, Mama. You always make the annual charity day a day to remember."

"Been four years now I been puttin' it on." She looked around, took it all in, and her gaze fell on Noah again. "My Noah, poor thing. My eldest grandson touches me so. I'll never understand why the good Lord see fit to let people like us who serve Him bear disease and disabilities, same as sinners." Mother Johns dabbed the corners of her eyes. "I done prayed so hard for his healing and nothing." A few tears got away—wet her bosom.

"Well, it's a successful day, Mama. I appreciate all you've done for my boys and me. I don't know how I would've raised 'em without you. Look how the community has come together."

Mother Johns patted Sal on the head and then shooed her away. "Go on. Time to wrap things up." She watched the other members of the mothers board, who were busy directing the church's younger members in passing out food bags. Then, she sat with a group of boys and had Noah, her eighteen-year-old grandson, sit next to her.

"There you go, my boy. Grandma's gonna always be here to help you. Don't you worry."

She watched Noah trying to find his new service dog and pat his head. When he couldn't locate the dog's head right away, she helped him with glossy eyes.

"You black boys are special, you hear? It seems like society wants to forget you, but not Mother Johns. Y'all won't go without so long as I have breath in my body."

Squeaky and some other mothers sat with the boys, too, and overhead Mother Johns' words to her grandson and the others.

"Thank you, Mother Johns. Don't know what we'd do without you."

Buckeye Belinda wasn't going to let Squeaky out praise her where Mother Johns was concerned.

"You one of the few leaders trying to keep our black boys out of the hands of the police."

Mother Johns sat proudly, accepting their adoration.

Mother Farrell had heard the whole exchange. Got her feathers in a fluff, seeing Mother Johns soaking in all the glory while they were doing all of the work.

"You ain't did it alone, though," she said in a rare challenge to Mother Johns. The other mothers walked over and caught the tail end of Mother Farrell's comment. They nodded in agreement amongst themselves—neglected workers in need of a union. Mother Johns checked out their discontent, stood and gestured for the young women to gather their sons and head home, then she addressed the old flock.

"We don't do charity to be seen by men. What we do is unto the Lord."

Mother Givens stood next to Mother Johns and spoke to the mothers board too. She had been developing a sharper tongue ever since Mother Johns blocked her from caring for Carmia.

"In-ter-resting how she give this speech after all the praise done been bestowed on her."

Mother Johns wasn't going to speak her mind with her praisers near. She stood and stretched her arms wide.

"Thank you, everyone, for your help today. The 1997 Annual Day of Charity was a success. We sincerely hope you got some needed assistance…time to clear out now. We got other business to attend to now."

She shooed them, and they began to clear from the churchyard and all down Brook Haven Road. Carmia was sitting alone on the steps of the church waiting for Mother Johns as she was told.

Gonna cast that Evans devil out of you today. She smiled.

It seemed the mood of the day had changed. The hot wind whisked dust into the children's mouths; they cried for water as they walked away. She looked at the elderly mothers and observed their weary faces.

"Let's go inside the church, mothers." They grumbled but followed. "The First Baptist of All Holiness Church of God is a light in dark times, and today, we gonna break that generational curse from off Ma Evans' seed."

Whenever they had curse-breaking ceremonies, the large white doors of the church were kept wide open, so the demons could run out. All lights were on as the mothers board marched around inside and outside the church, laying hands on pews, doors and windows. The smell of olive oil saturated the air, and oil-based handprints covered the furniture—they had smeared it everywhere, on every item and themselves, but mainly on Carmia. Her face shined with greasy radiance from anointing oil, which didn't stop them from applying more. They prayed and praised, sang worship hymns then prayed more with unusually commanding voices. It was their time of special intercession to set the girl free. Mother Givens stood next to Carmia, praying in tongues, yielding to the Holy Spirit. Acting as though she was trying to cast the devil out of Mother Johns.

Mother Johns looked at her as though she wanted to pray rebellion out of Mother Givens too. The other mothers moaned and groaned in such a way that their prayers were no longer distinguishable.

Carmia quivered in fear. She shook herself, trying to break free from the event that seemed to be devouring her. Mother Johns looked at her with loathing eyes. She looked back at the mean mother with equally despising eyes. The church mothers continued to march around her. Then the girl doubted.

All the bad stuff happening to my family; what if she's right?

She sobbed as the mothers marched around the building and periodically circled her.

Wonder if they do have magic. She just wanted to be made pure again.

God, help me.

The mothers were breathing heavily and grunting. Carmia

looked up at Mother Givens and decided to focus on her to get her through it. Mother Givens smiled at her with a reassurance that whispered to her heart, "Everything is gonna be okay."

The other mothers circled her again and said, "I decree the curse is broken."

Pastor Himley's shaking hands took the bottle of olive oil from the pulpit, poured some into the palm of his left hand, and took his right index finger to draw a cross on his balding head. Then, he smeared a spot of anointing oil in the middle of Carmia's forehead.

A tear rolled down her face.

Lord, if there's some kind of evil in me, take it out.

She thought about her family's problems and wondered if it was because of a curse. She could hear Grandma Evans saying, "It's better to be safe than sorry. When in doubt, make the decision that covers both sides."

She took a deep breath and began to repeat what she'd heard the mothers chanting all around her. "I break the generational curse of sexual i-m-morality."

She cried so hard, it turned into a groan. Mother Givens hugged her tightly. Pastor Himley heard her and backed away—went to the pulpit. He sat in his pastoral chair, shaking like a wet dog in winter and prayed in a low voice. He looked up from time to time with unusually large eyes, watching the mothers board perform their curse-breaking ceremony. Mother Johns finally approached the girl and looked around for their man of God. When her eyes locked on Pastor Himley, he quickly put his head down. The mean mother shook her head like she thought he was a sad excuse for a pastor.

Mother Johns took on the job herself. "Confess your sins, gal," she demanded from the child.

"I–I'm a sinner," the girl said.

"Name your sins and reveal the demons residing in you."

Carmia sat silently, not knowing what to say. She looked to Mother Givens, who shook her head. The girl's silence was taken as rebellion.

Mother Johns leaned into her face. "You got sexually immoral thoughts, don't you?"

She looked to Mother Givens again, but she was praying so hard she had her eyes closed. "*Ummm.* I–I g–guess so."

"Well, I know so. Confess after me: 'I have sexually immoral thoughts.'"

"I have sexually i-m-moral thoughts."

Mother Johns looked her in the eyes. "The sins of your mother been passed to you. Now you got to close every door to the devil." She squeezed Carmia's legs closed tight. "Say it."

The front of Carmia's dress became wet as big drops of tears began to roll down her cheeks. "I close every door to the devil."

Mother Farrell's heart was touched; something didn't seem to feel right. She began to cry, too, as she took a seat next to Mother Givens.

Mother Johns directed her scorn to them now. "Weak-minded old women with no backbone. Many are called but few chosen." She moved closer to Carmia, who had thrown herself onto the floor in tears. She held her stomach. It was cramping from crying; the veins at her temples bulged.

"Lawd, we thank you for the blood of Jesus, and we break this curse off this child," Mother Johns said.

When Mother Johns touched her back, Carmia screamed at the top of her lungs. Strings of slob fell from her mouth and trickled onto the floor. Carmia focused on Mother Givens again, needing some hope that everything was going to be alright.

"The blood of Jesus is against you, devil." Mother Thompson stayed in agreement with Mother Johns.

"Devil, we rebuke you," Mother Johns continued.

"Devil, we rebuke you," both mothers chanted.

"We break this curse," Mother Farrell whispered, still confused until Mother Givens gave her a sharp look.

Mother Givens was stirring in her seat, trying to get her mind together—she couldn't take no more. "Mother Johns, the spirit you operating from ain't right," she said.

Carmia kept looking into Mother Givens' eyes; she seemed to have received strength from God to rise out of her seat and stand at the girl's side. She yelled at Mother Johns with a boldness, "You going too far."

Mother Johns tried to move Mother Givens away from Carmia, but the old woman defended the child. "Now hold on, Janice, before I give you a piece of my mind. I might not be fully well in my thoughts, but I ain't no fool, and I will fight you about this child." She poked her chest out. "Oh, help my mind, Jesus."

"'Help my mind, Jesus,'" Mother Johns mocked.

Mother Givens looked like she might be calling on all her faith and strength when she turned toward Mother Johns and spoke with great conviction. Her face was peaceful, but her words were sharp.

"Now, Mother, don't go too far. She ain't actually the devil. Y'all the ones actin' like devils around here."

"Sit down, Mother, meddling where you don't belong...not in your right mind," Mother Johns said.

"I'm here now, clothed in my right mind." She hit her bosom. "And I'm watching you."

Mother Givens cried out then preached, "You have a form of godliness but denying its power."

The others gasped. Mother Johns shook with anger. "You done loosed a sharp, bitter tongue today. Usually can't form a comprehensible phrase. Now that you do, you gonna come up against me this way?"

"You always pushing everybody around with your big voice and big personality, but where is the big God in you?"

Those near Mother Givens moved back as Mother Johns charged in her direction.

"You questioning me? You dare question my godliness? I do more for this community than..."

"God gives us the ability to help others. What you always bragging for?" Mother Givens said.

The other mothers seemed to agree. Carmia had settled down; Pastor Himley helped her off the floor to a nearby pew. They sat and watched the ladies argue, their heads turning from mother to mother as they spoke.

Mother Johns was now indignant. "I'm not bragging. Y'all jealous behind what I do for the less fortunate—peoples disfigured or blind like my grandson," she said.

"A worthy charity, Mother Johns, but your spirit ain't right the way you obsessed about taking the credit for it. And where is your charity for this here child? You do a lot for black boys because you love your grandsons, but what about our black girls?" Mother Givens rebuked.

Mother Johns pointed at Carmia. "This child come from a family of women that's harmed our community. Laura stole my Sal's fiancé and left her abandoned with two children, one blind. She stole Sal's man away and didn't even stay with him—married some other loser."

This information lodged a new pain in Carmia's heart.

The mean mother continued, "My Sal and her kids was alone in the world until Ducky come along to help her...I won't mention what Ma Evans did to me."

"This child ain't the blame," Mother Givens said.

"I won't have her kind ruining our town, disturbing a new generation." She clenched her teeth.

"I rebuke your wicked, mean spirit, Mother Johns."

Mother Johns was livid. She looked as if she might levitate. "I rebuke your ignorant, weak mind...Get thee behind me, Satan."

"Satan ain't nowhere but in you, and I rebuke you," Mother Givens said.

"Mothers, ain't y'all rebuking the wrong thang? Now, focus. We got to finish," Mother Farrell interrupted.

Carmia seemed comforted by Mother Givens'defense.

The church mothers had calmed themselves but circled the teen again. Their emotion returned as they rebuked the devil, but she was less frightened. They declared their power over the enemy and began to stomp while shouting, "The devil is under our feet."

Mother Thompson grabbed Carmia by the hand, pulled her out of the chair the mothers had been circling and told her to stomp the devil under her feet. Carmia obeyed. Her eyes were red; her nose began to run—she appeared to be having a fit. She began to cough, her throat dry from yelling. The mothers silenced themselves. Mother Johns rushed to get a tissue and gave it to Carmia; she coughed up green mucus. The mothers frowned as they watched, but victory twinkled in their eyes.

"Hallelujah," they praised God.

Pastor Himley rose from the pew and shouted, "The Lord done purged her and set her free." Carmia finished coughing.

Mother Givens handed her a bottle of water. "The so-called curse is broken. Moving right along. Now, leave this girl alone."

Carmia smiled and shouted, "Thank you, Jesus" over and over as the mothers urged her on. They hugged each other in victory, and Carmia hugged them, too, sighing in relief.

Mother Johns walked over to Carmia with a box of tissue. "Wipe your face clean."

When Carmia finished, she opened her arms to hug Mother Johns, too, but the old woman turned away.

18

Lonely

CARMIA JOG-WALKED AROUND THE PITTSES' HOUSE—COOKING, cleaning, serving—jumping to Sister Pitts' every beck and call. It was September. She had just turned fifteen and had lived with them for a few months now. Sister Pitts had become undone over Deacon Pitts' attention to the girl.

I ain't telling your husband to look at me.

She never knew when Sister Pitts would be kind or pissed with her. She just wanted to disappear whenever the Pittses were in a fighting mood.

Sister Pitts seemed to enjoy telling Carmia about her background in the armed forces and how it had prepared her for all sorts of battle on the water. Discussing her military memories was the only time they seemed to have peace. But all the girl could see was how her service days had not prepared her to overcome her insecurities.

Carmia's hands were gray and wrinkled from long hours in soapy water. She kneeled on the tile floors on all fours and scrubbed the grout with little success. Sister Pitts sat with a smirk, watching like she knew Carmia's labor was in vain. Deacon Pitts puckered his forehead, disappointed by his wife's actions. "Let the girl rest."

Sister Pitts threw her napkin in his face. "I only agreed to let her stay because of the help. Did you have other plans?"

"Don't start today." He turned away from her and looked at Carmia. His eyes fell on the girl pleasingly. He looked at his wife, back at Carmia, then socked the table.

"Jealousy used to be beneath you. I don't find it attractive," he said to his wife.

"You ain't nothing but a low-life racist. How could I be so stupid marrying you? You're the worst kind of racist, the kind that's done deceived himself when everybody else got you figured out, just a bigot acting like he ain't."

"Shut your doggone mouth."

"Or what? You gon' whip me? I thought you married me because you like black women and knew I was smart and successful."

"I was fooled by you," he said.

She moved to strike him, but he caught her hand. Carmia trembled in disbelief.

"The way you look at this girl proves you just lust after black flesh—preaching in the church about how people need to die to their fleshly desires. Looking down on black men like you got better control than them."

He looked as if he wanted to choke her, and that just made her elevate her insults.

"You a pink-faced devil wanting to rape black women like your forefathers."

He still had the impulse to strike her in his eyes. "I ought to whip you. Not because you're black, but because you're stupid," he yelled.

"I'm pregnant with your child. It's done made me so sick, and you treat me like this." She leaned into his face. "I don't find your constant staring at that girl attractive. Ought to go to the mothers board."

Deacon Pitts moved close to her right ear. "I wish you would." He threw the napkin back at her. "My God, woman, have you no confidence at all? Didn't I marry you?" He walked to the garage.

She followed him, and so did the teen.

"Really? You're taking out your gun? You don't intimidate me. I know how to use a gun too."

Sister Pitts struggled to breathe. The seriousness of their conversation caused Carmia to stand in the garage doorway. He had unlocked his tool drawer and began to clean his pistol.

Seem like he ain't right in his mind. What's wrong?

He chuckled like maybe he wasn't thinking anything bad, but his first look—the crazy one—never left her mind.

"This ain't no threat. Can't I clean my gun, woman? You'll know when I'm threatening you," he said.

Sister Pitts held her stomach. "A real prize you turned out to be."

"If I use it, it won't be on no woman," he said.

Carmia started cleaning again.

Brother Pitts don't seem happy with her or himself.

He seemed a bit scary. She tried even harder to prove herself to

Sister Pitts. She wanted to be saved from so much confusion and pain all around her. She wanted to belong somewhere and to feel safe.

Sure wish Joseph was here; he probably don't care about me no more.

She looked down at the plastic Ring Pop on her finger and squeezed her fingers so tightly together they turned pink.

She felt tears rising but stopped them. She was tired of crying. Deacon Pitts yelled at Sister Pitts about something she didn't understand, then he stormed out of the house.

Carmia had noticed black people didn't quite know how to take Deacon Pitts, but they respected him because of his teller position at the local bank.

Must hurt, with his own race hating him for marrying a black woman and blacks not fully trusting him because he's white.

She watched Sister Pitts to learn how to deal with Deacon Pitts and his angry behavior. She knew when Sister Pitts was unhappy with him. But when he came home upset about work, she kept quiet, so Carmia did too.

She was clearing the table, and with him gone, Sister Pitts freely followed her into the kitchen.

Shoot, I ain't did nothing.

"I know you just got settled in living here, but don't get comfortable. I'm gonna see you leave my house—and soon. My husband won't agree, but I got God on my side. You see, you're Hagar. I'm Sarah. Ain't gonna be no Ishmaels around here, girl," she said, referring to the Bible story.

Sister Pitts grunted, startling the girl. The woman held her stomach, doubled over in pain, then raised herself slowly. Carmia tried to help, but Sister Pitts pushed her away and slapped her face with a rolled-up newspaper.

"Read this, heifer. Your brother ain't coming for you, and you still gonna get out of here."

Carmia was too stunned to read the paper, but Sister Pitts' transfixed eyes made her. She unrolled the paper and read it until her mouth fell open. Sister Pitts chuckled out loud. She reread it, couldn't believe it. She stared at a picture of Carl in handcuffs. The headline read, *Sixteen-Year-Old Car Thief Gets Three Years*. She held her tears—didn't want to satisfy Sister Pitts, who stood smirking, then walked away.

She read that the law in Arkansas had notified local authorities about Carl being found guilty of theft and locked him up there. The Bovina police had shared the news with the local paper.

Those bad boys he hung around must've put him up to it.

She felt hot and dizzy, and with Sister Pitts no longer there, she wept—quick rustles of breath made her head jerk. She had heard bad stories about jail and couldn't imagine what her brother must've been going through. She wondered if prison might change him.

We'll be together again one day. Got to stick together like Mom always said.

She wasn't saddened just for Carl; she would continue to be lonely without him.

Sister Pitts' moaning and groaning increased, but she had less compassion for her. She tried to ignore her, but she screamed so loudly, it interrupted her own tears. She went into the hallway.

If I try to help, she'll just push me away. Let her suffer then.

Carmia slid down the wall where she stood, eyes wide open. She bent her legs and held her knees close to her chest. She listened to Sister Pitts' every sound and thought about how she needed Sister Pitts, how they needed each other. The Pittses were the only family she had now. She squeezed herself tight and eventually gave in to sleep.

Carmia woke up in the arms of Deacon Pitts. He lifted her from in front of his bedroom door. Frightened at first, she tensed up as he carried her toward her room. He never said a word, just placed her on the bed, then looked her over. For the most part, Deacon Pitts was a kind man, she thought. She kind of liked the attention and was afraid too. It had been comforting to have her head on his chest. The smell of his aftershave lingered on her. She was lonely, and he had given her an unexpected ease. She wanted to be close up and far away from him—so confused.

He kept looking at her, so she moved close to him for a hug. This surprised him. He trembled.

Gonna push me away?

He hugged her.

Maybe he feels comforted next to me too.

Deacon Pitts sniffed around her neck. He straightened his back, raised his chest, and she felt his heartbeat speed up, as though his blood was rushing all through his body.

Maybe Sister Pitts and him don't feel this kind of good together no more.

He squeezed her tightly against himself.

Sister Pitts coughed in the next room, breaking their silent affection, causing Deacon Pitts to let her go. He turned to remove himself from her room, then looked back. She smiled, let her hair loose from a ponytail, and shook all of her glory before him. She giggled as if they had been playing a game.

He got a crush… What's he thinking about?

He looked like he couldn't make up his mind. She smiled like a girl, then tilted her head like a woman. Then she wrapped herself in her sheets, acting unaware of what had happened, what she had done to him. Deacon Pitts held himself below and shut the door.

I got a secret power over him. She smiled.

19

Friends

CARMIA DIDN'T SLEEP THE WHOLE NIGHT THROUGH. SHE WAS sluggish when morning came, but she got out of bed anyway. She went to the kitchen for a bowl of cereal. After a while, she nodded as she watched a mouse run from the south side of the kitchen floor to the north, carrying something Carmia's sleepy eyes couldn't identify. It seemed confused by the lines in the tile, which resembled the jagged lines in turquoise.

Those lines trapping that mouse like a cage. Mom was like that. Now I'm caught too.

She knew her mother hadn't always done the good in her heart she had intended to do. The mouse stopped running in circles. It moved back and forth, outsmarting the trap Deacon Pitts had laid to steal his freedom and life.

She looked around the dirty kitchen and didn't care. Sister Pitts wasn't around to torture her; she had been rushed to the hospital two days before. They were going to keep her for the last two months of her pregnancy. She was enjoying her freedom from housework, but now she didn't know how to spend her time. She dozed, bobbed her head a few times, then jolted when she heard loud laughter—the noise of kids playing outside even though it was cold. She walked over to the small window on the side of the house. Hopscotch. She moved into the living room for a clearer view and gazed through the large picture window at giggling little girls.

One foot, one foot, one foot, two, one, two, then one. She counted their hops. *I wish I could play.*

She wasn't wanted, so she tried to convince herself hopscotch was for babies. Slightly older girls that she recognized from school were rocking, twisting, jumping in and out of two ropes on the west of the Pittses' house. She mouthed along as they sang, then hummed: "Ice cream soda, cherry on top. Who's your boyfriend? Let's find out. A-B-C-D. David, David, do you like Bearlissa? Yes, no, maybe so…"

Those girls were Carmia's age and level of development, so she couldn't rely on her games are for babies' arguments with this group.

They never liked me since I came here.

They had her same qualities—trapped between girlhood and womanhood. They had shortened their skirts and loved wearing halter tops underneath their coats. They had all of the appearances of young women but were still children. Their hair was a museum of colorful beads in braided hairstyles instead of jewels on a queen's crown. These caterpillars were still wrapped in the cocoon without sufficient strength to break free from the mummy-like wrap that housed them. They wanted Daisy Dukes shorts and miniskirts for Christmas and dreamt of becoming mothers—they wanted someone to love and for someone to love them back. She was just like them, but she experienced it alone.

Day after day, she watched the others play. She swayed herself as the other girls rocked before jumping into the rope.

One day as she combed her hair and got dressed, she decided to try to make friends with the girls.

When Mom was a girl, she would of walked out there and made them let her play.

Her mother didn't deal well with rejection; if people were going to refuse her, she wouldn't make it easy for them. Carmia pinned her hair up, leaving two thin curls hanging on each side of her face. She rehearsed popular things to talk about, but all that thinking just made her nervous, so she went ahead and burst out of the front door, smiling at everyone, waving with an openness to friendship.

She eased over to them with her head down.

Put your head up, girl.

She heard her matriarchs' voices. A few more steps, and she found her head down again. She bit her fingernail on her left index finger and said, "C–Can I jump rope too?"

Bearl had her back turned when she approached them, but she recognized the voice. She seemed to freeze in shock, then she turned around.

Please don't remember the fight we had at school over a ribbon.

Bearl looked at her and smiled.

Don't trust it.

Bearl walked toward her with a girlish kind of power—her stride was slow and playfully wicked. Bearl stuck her toe out and rolled her foot back to the heel, flat on the ground with each step. She tilted her head like a princess and twisted some strands of her crimp-ironed hair, showing off that she now had pretty ribbons, too, the same style as the one she'd yanked out of Carmia's hair five years ago.

Bearl grinned at the other girls.

"Carmia, I was wondering when you might come out of that house and join us. We see your eyeballs staring every day, kind of scary like a stalker," Bearl said.

The other girls whispered and giggled. All of her senses told her not to trust them, but desperation brought her walls down. Bearl took the ropes from Sarah and handed them to Carmia.

"Will you help turn the rope for us?"

"Yes." She took the ropes. After laughing with them and turning the ropes for others, Bearl signaled it was Carmia's turn to jump. She began to rock her body in the rhythmic movements of Double Dutch jumping and leaped in successfully. She twisted, jumped, jerked, and smiled—hopped in and out. She closed her eyes and imagined she was a bird flying. She was a natural. Some of the other girls smiled, admiring her abilities. She felt happy because they seemed to like her.

Bearl looked at her smile and seemed to hate the sight, so she yanked the ropes straight. Carmia fell a short distance to the ground, but it felt forever long. So many thoughts filled her mind; the fall seemed in slow motion. She heard Grandma Evans' voice talking about strength passing from one generation to the next and talking about her own transformation from vengeful to forgiveness.

I knew better than to trust her smile. Should've listened to myself.

Everybody staring at me now like I'm a fool.

She hit the ground, knee first. Her whole body bounced a bit and throbbed with pain; she couldn't tell if the fall had made her feel that way or the embarrassment. She bit her bottom lip and held her bloody knee. It felt like a giant bee sting and made her hot with anger. Bearl laughed, then the laughter spread. She thought of her mother telling her to beat the crap outta anybody who laid hands on her first—Bearl had laid hands on her through those ropes.

Bearl seemed to have tolerated her joy as long as she could.

"Did you really think you're good enough to hang out with us? Pretty clothes can't make you one of us."

Bearl wasn't going to let her friends enjoy Carmia and form friendships with her. She looked sternly at the other girls, offended by their silence. Her facial expression communicated they had better back her up.

"Them are my church clothes from last year you wearing anyways. Why you wearing them today? It ain't Sunday, stupid," Sarah teased.

Tears began to well up in Carmia's eyes. "Leave me alone."

Bearl teased, "Leave me alone," and pushed her. "My mama said you're trashy just like your mama was."

Carmia wanted to cry and run away. She felt like one of those filthy rags she had heard about in Pastor Himley's sermon. Remembering all her mother had faced in this community wouldn't let her just stand and take it.

If I'm dirty to them, I may as well be dirty then.

Her legs wouldn't follow her brain's command to listen to Grandma Evans' wisdom rather than her mother's rage. She grabbed the ropes from the ground and began to swing them violently—whipping all who stood near. Red whip marks slashed across Bearl's legs. Other girls got anointed with thumps on the arms and head. They cried, and the girls scattered each to their own house and into their mother's arms.

Carmia's fingers had grown numb, frozen into a solid grip where her hands balled tightly around the ends of the rope. Her blood had stopped flowing. With some difficulty, she peeled her fingers from around the cords. When her hands regained movement, she dropped the ropes and started in the direction of the Pittses' house. She could feel how wrinkled her forehead was. She blew in and out between her teeth, feeling her cheeks repeatedly puffing and deflating. The tears in her eyes refused to fall. She pressed through the path made difficult by the other girls' mothers who had begun to congregate. Even Squeaky had left the laundry because of the ruckus.

What they looking at?

The other girls' mothers had lined up to loathe her, their lips tight and arms folded. Squeaky turned her head as if nothing had happened when Bearl hacked and spat on Carmia's dress as she passed.

At first, Carmia was going to let the thing go, but open wounds turned her around. She was tired of people bullying her. She growled, then she laughed, remembering she and her mother doing the same to Mother Johns years ago. She kicked in mid-air, then moved close to kick Bearl. She bit her, grunted and jumped all over Bearl, landing a punch to her eye. She etched scratches all over her rival's face. Bearl socked her in the stomach and tried to trip her to the ground, but it didn't work. All it did was piss off Carmia. She could still hear her mother saying, "Beat her butt."

I'm gonna beat you so bad you'll never mess with me again.

It was as if her mother was standing on the side with all the other mothers watching. She felt like her mom was cheering her on. In a matter of moments, Bearl's face had become different shades of berries—purple under her left eye, burgundy on her left cheekbone and bright pink on the right side of her forehead. Carmia felt her elbow hit something soft. It had landed inside of a small, soft place during the tussle.

It wasn't until later that she realized Squeaky had gotten a black eye from her elbow while trying to break them up. She screamed at the crowd, "I just wanted to play. I just wanted a friend."

Mother Johns and Mother Givens walked in a hurry, heading for her. They wore colorful flowered and polka-dot maxi dresses and dusters that blew in the wind like capes, but all Carmia saw was black. Mother Givens carried her Bible and balanced her lemonade, trying not to spill it.

I wish they would speak all that Bible talk today. Not today, old people.

Mother Johns had determination written on her face. She walked with a steady stride that made the sole of her stacked heel shoes thump on the ground just as loudly as the stomp of her cane.

Mother Johns got to Carmia first and spoke with a slow, piercing tone. "Didn't I tell you to stay inside the Pittses' house and not to bother these girls?"

Carmia had mixed reactions to the mother. She wanted to cuss her out and bite her, too, but she trembled inside. She was exhausted, tired of crying, tired of yelling and fighting. She was out of breath, and this community wouldn't let her rest.

Mother Givens finally caught up, and when she laid eyes on Carmia, she sighed in relief. She looked around at all the angry faces staring at her and refused to join them. She smiled and winked at Carmia instead.

That's what Mom would do.

Mother Johns stood over Carmia, waving her cane at her. "I'm done being gentle with you. You ain't gonna do right unless you get a switch taken to your ungrateful tail." She looked around for a switch. Mother Givens lifted her index finger toward Mother Johns, twitching with each word. "No such a thing, Mother. I won't stand for you touching one hair on her head, lessen I notify the law. Mind your words and mind you don't hurt her feelings neither..."

Too late for that. These people don't do nothing but hurt me.

"So hateful. Can't you see this girl is lonely?" Mother Givens said.

Mother Johns pointed her cane at Mother Givens. "She's always making trouble, even after we broke the curse."

"You are the curse." Carmia yelled.

Sadie eased up to Mother Johns in support of Squeaky.

"That girl is just like her mother. Look at what she done to Bearl, even done give Squeaky a black eye."

The others mumbled in agreement.

Mother Givens groaned in deep grief. "That poor girl ain't cursed, just lonely and sad. I don't understand why y'all don't have no heart."

"Hush up, Givens." Mother Johns yelled, thrashing out her Spanish-style fan, trying to cool down.

Surrounded by them, Carmia breathed deeply, on alert. She had stayed secure, wearing her inheritance of strength with no tears. But their hate stares continued. Though Mother Givens had tried, their hearts weren't moved to compassion. Her shoulders fell while a waterfall of tears covered her face.

I ain't got the kind of strength like Grandma Evans.

Mother Johns threw another dart. "I'm gonna see to it that you don't leave that house but for school and church."

She stood staring at Mother Johns, expressionless and motionless.

They continued to stare at her without concern until Sarah said, "We shouldn't be so mean to her. I feel sorry for her."

Sadie pinched Sarah's ear. "Shut up. Look at the way she whipped you."

"But we started it," Sarah continued.

"Shut up, I said," Sadie yelled, noticing the other mothers' disapproving stares.

Carmia ran back into the Pittses' house and slammed the door behind her. "Why do you hate me, God?"

She walked to her room and threw her Bible into the mirror.

"Didn't no curse-breaking ceremony set me free," she said, looking into the cracked mirror.

The mothers board, Pastor Himley and all that stupid congregation don't have no power from God.

She felt crazy for yelling at the devil and using her own words to join the wicked mothers' curses against her.

"I hate Bovina, and I hate my mother for bringing me here. I wish I had never met none of them. Wish I had never been born."

20

Desperation

CARMIA WATCHED JOSEPH AS HE STOOD IN FRONT OF THE Pittses' house, probably trying to convince himself to go to the door and knock.

Please visit me.

He was sixteen now, very tall and lanky. His arms stretched far past the cuff of his corduroy jacket. His khakis didn't touch his long, skinny legs anywhere, like his physique was lost inside of them. He rubbed his hands together and blew inside of them as though he were trying to warm them up. She gently tapped her window as a signal she wanted him to visit, but he didn't hear it. She couldn't be louder or Deacon Pitts would hear her. She tapped again. He still didn't hear. She wiped the side of her mouth with the back of her hand, pulled her hair more tightly into a ponytail, and quickly dressed.

Please go to the door and knock. I miss you, Joseph.

Joseph jumped, lightweight on his toes, and shook his head to crack his neck, then he hurried to the porch and started knocking on the Pittses' door for what seemed like hours to her.

Why don't Deacon Pitts answer?

He turned to leave.

Joseph, come back.

Carmia was about to exit her room and go to the door when she heard the deacon open it. She stood in the hallway so she could watch and listen.

He sounded irritated. "Who is it?"

When he saw Joseph was leaving, he tried to close the door quickly, but Joseph turned back and ran to him.

"You're a persistent son of a gun, knocking on my door like this early in the morning. Can I help you?" Deacon Pitts asked.

"Hi, Deacon P–P–Pitts, sir. I came to see about Carmia."

Stop looking at him like he's a terrorist and let him in.

Joseph stood straight, shifted his weight from side to side and smiled to one corner of his lips, which he kept licking. The deacon made him stand on the porch way too long, staring at him, trying to make him uncomfortable.

Doggone, Deacon Pitts. Why don't you leave him alone?

"I wonder if Mother Johns knows you snooping around here," he said, opening the door more widely.

Joseph shrugged and smiled. The deacon was probably thinking about what it meant if he was rude to him. He decided he'd better lighten up.

"Come on in," he said.

Finally, Carmia sighed. She moved closer to the living room so she could see them better.

Joseph entered the house and sat in Deacon Pitts' favorite chair, unaware of his crime. Deacon Pitts grunted in disapproval. Mother Johns' grandson or not, he wasn't gonna give up his chair. She heard the squeaky noises of Joseph moving from the chair to the couch.

"Carmia, somebody's here to see you," Deacon Pitts yelled and took his chair.

She heard him but didn't want to come out too soon.

"Carmia," he yelled again.

"Who is it?" She entered the room, acting barely awake.

"Hi, Carmia," Joseph said, smiling.

He looking at me the way he used to when we first met.

"Hi, Joseph." She half-smiled, then half-frowned.

What took you so long to visit?

He stood like his body was light and warm inside by just laying eyes on her. She smiled at Joseph again. He seemed so happy to see her, waving his long arms aimlessly by his sides. She was filled with happiness too. They sat, and he told Carmia how his grandma had threatened to send him away to her sister if he tried to see her.

Joseph took out a piece of paper with the police station's address on it.

"This is a surprise for you. I know how much you want to find your brother, so I got this information so we can get his address and try to write to him."

Her face shined with happiness. "Thank you. I been worried sick about Carl." She took the paper and rubbed his hand. "This is the nicest thing anybody ever did for me." She smiled.

He winked at her.

Deacon Pitts watched, peering over his newspaper the whole time. They sat on the brown-and-peach plaid couch that made Carmia's soft skin itch and tried not to do anything that would make the deacon angry.

Joseph moved a little closer. "How have you been?" he whispered.

"My whole life is bad," she said, covering her mouth, unsure of her breath.

"Yeah, I heard. Everybody is talking about the way you beat Bearl. You still a strong woman, just like the day I met you."

They chuckled.

"Well, she deserved it, but I'm sure they blame me."

"I don't know. I think a lot of people been secretly waiting for somebody to whip Bearl's butt. I know I was."

He laughed again. Carmia smiled again.

She began to sob in a muffled whimper, not wanting Deacon Pitts to know she was crying. Joseph hugged her as she rested her head on his shoulder. She sighed and relaxed on his chest; he relaxed too.

I still like him; wish he would never leave.

The deacon shifted in his chair, looking at Joseph with envy. Joseph scowled at him as though he didn't like a grown man acting so interested in them.

He watching the way bad men do.

Carmia leaned on Joseph all the more.

Joseph put her hand on his knee and traced the outlines of it. "Do you remember our promise?"

She tensed for some reason. He tickled her.

Always tickling me when I'm nervous.

She relaxed a bit but barely got her words out. "Y–Yes, I–I do."

He pulled back a little and looked at her. "Why you so nervous? You only stutter when you're nervous."

She shrugged.

Someone pounded on the door. Deacon Pitts grumbled under his breath, "I guess the whole town is coming to my house this morning."

He opened the door to find Mother Johns fuming with a switch in her hand.

"Is my grandson here?"

The deacon grinned and gestured in Joseph's direction. He and Carmia were still cozy on the couch.

Mother Johns pulled Joseph up by his right ear. "Didn't I tell you to stay away from this girl?"

He held on to Carmia.

"I told you I couldn't do that, Grandma."

Mother Johns twisted her lips and tightened her grip on his ear. *Why don't everybody just leave us alone?*

Carmia breathed heavily and frowned, imagining Joseph's pain.

"Oh, you can't, huh? You will when I get done beating you with this switch," Mother Johns continued.

"I won't stop seeing her, Grandma. Can't you see how lonely she is? I'm all she's got...and...well, I love her."

Mother Johns' nostrils flared. Her mouth protruded like she was sucking on a boiled egg.

"Oh, you love her, huh? Against my will."

"You love her?" Deacon Pitts echoed.

His response caused them all to pause. Mother Johns held her head to the side and looked Deacon Pitts over. Joseph looked at him, squinting. Carmia furrowed her forehead.

"Yeah, I love her," Joseph said again.

"Well, then I guess you can't stop yourself from coming over here," Mother Johns sarcastically agreed.

The deacon looked confused. Carmia hugged Joseph more tightly.

Mother Johns was repulsed by their affection. "After all I've done for you, you go chasing after the likes of her."

Mother Johns looked harshly at the two of them snuggled together. "All right then. You think you gonna defy my authority, huh? Not so long as there's breath in my body. I'm sending you to that all-boys boarding school over in Hyde Park directly."

"No," he yelled.

"No," Carmia echoed.

Joseph cried in defeat, already knowing Mother Johns would have her way.

The church mother moved close to Carmia.

"This is all your fault, gal. Take your hands off him."

"I won't go." Joseph yelled.

Mother Johns tried to pull them apart, but they would not be separated—they held each other more tightly. Mother Johns looked at Deacon Pitts as she struggled, to no avail. "You can't even control a little girl…Help me."

Deacon Pitts grabbed Joseph by the waist and lifted him away from Carmia, kicking and screaming. Unfortunately, the deacon misjudged his size; they almost fell. Carmia reached out to Joseph as Mother Johns stood in her way.

"I love you, Carmia. I'm gonna marry you. Remember our promise," he said.

Carmia stood silent, making him fight more to be free from Deacon Pitts' hold.

I can't lose you.

"Don't listen to them trying to break us apart. Remember our promise." Joseph yelled as he was carried to the porch by Deacon Pitts. "Answer me, Carmia."

Carmia looked as though she had been underwater and was coming up for air when she said, "I will remember. I remember our promise. I love you, too, Joseph."

Mother Johns shoved Joseph away from the Pittses' house, thrashing her switch across his legs as they headed home. Carmia wanted to run out behind them, but Deacon Pitts blocked the doorway.

"Where do you think you're going?"

She backed away. "Nowhere, I guess."

My heart hurts. She turned toward her room.

Christmas was over; it was near the end of winter break from school. Deacon Pitts had become Carmia's only friend. He insisted she call him Georgie. He brought gifts home for her almost every day.

Daddy used to bring me stuff too. Maybe I shouldn't take Georgie's stuff. It seemed like she was his only friend also. He didn't seem very happy even though Sister Pitts had given him a daughter—

premature but a pretty one. They were both still too weak from a lot of blood loss and infection—they had to be hospitalized for a few more weeks. That left Carmia and Georgie alone a lot, and she didn't think he was angry like when his wife was home. But over time, their suspicious smiles and questionable hugs had stirred up things between them she knew were grown-up things. She kinda liked it, though. And she liked how as soon as he got home, he listened to her, talking about anything. It was like she was the most crucial person in the whole world to him. She felt like a real princess. Not the way she felt when her father used to call her that.

Will I still be a princess when Sister Pitts comes back?

She cooked him baked chicken for dinner and had just placed it on the table when he walked in. She was trying to be grown-up but didn't fully understand what that meant.

I wonder if I'm a woman to him.

She stood where he could look her over.

He says I'm a good girl.

"Georgie, do you think I'm pretty?" He was no longer Deacon Pitts to her.

"You put on her clothes and make-up again? You don't need that stuff." He laughed. Carmia put her head down.

"You're the prettiest girl I know…Any of them boys been talking to you?"

"Joseph is gone," she said.

"There's other boys." He sat silently, staring at her. "You look so innocent when you flip your hair around…Do it for me."

He's nice.

A strange, pleasing feeling ran through her body. She walked close to the deacon and whispered in his ear, "Am I pretty like a woman?"

He didn't answer. She sat on his lap; being close to him was satisfying in ways she didn't fully understand. She rubbed her nose against his playfully.

"You'll be attractive like a woman one day," Deacon Pitts answered.

"You're lying, Georgie. You think I'm attractive right now. I could see your heart beating and hear your blood rushing that night you picked me up. Don't that mean I'm pretty the way women are?"

Deacon Pitts pushed himself as far as he could against the back of the chair. It seemed his heart was starting again. Finally, he stood and moved away from her.

Probably thinking of his wife and how she struggled giving birth.

Carmia looked at him from head to toe as he turned to leave the room. "See, you do think I'm attractive."

Deacon Pitts trembled as he closed the door.

Mother Johns ordered Pastor Himley to cancel Wednesday night's Bible Study, saying the church officials had more important business to attend to. They had convened right outside of The Pittses' house, but she had already been on the porch peeping inside. The deacon's cell phone rang, and he answered right away.

"Me and the mothers board want to speak to you about your declining church attendance," Mother Johns said, watching him through the window.

Deacon Pitts took a deep breath. "*Ummm.* Well, I don't know about…"

She was smiling inside, flexing her motherly muscles. "No, no, no, it weren't no question."

Ought to know me better than to think I would suffer an old fool's excuses.

"*Hmmm,* well, *ah,* okay. I'll be on my way to the church…" he said.

"No need. I'm at your door now…"

Mother Johns let herself in and started her inspection straight away. Carmia and Deacon Pitts were both sitting on the couch. Her eyes darted back and forth; their eyes darted too. The view of them in the living room wasn't odd, but their reaction to her struck her with brow-raising suspicion. The rest of the mothers board pushed their way through the door, followed by Pastor Himley, who sat down in Deacon Pitts' chair, trying to make small talk. His butt was so massive he dropped down into the chair to preserve his back and knees from holding his weight too long as he squatted to sit. The deacon bit his bottom lip.

Mother Johns wore the discernment of something being out of order on her face.

She sighed and squinted at Deacon Pitts as though looking through him, not at him.

I'm on to you.

He sat like he was constipated.

"We sure do miss you down at the church, Deacon Pitts," Pastor Himley said, giving him some relief.

The deacon spoke to Pastor Himley but kept his eyes on Mother

Johns because she kept her eyes on him. "*Uh-huh.* I miss y'all too. Can't wait until the Mrs. is doing better so we can all attend church regularly again. She's been struggling ever since the premature birth."

Pastor Himley lowered his head. "So sad indeed. We praying for her and the baby's strength." He smiled. "We sure did miss Sister Pitts at the bake sale last week. Can't nobody make peach cobbler the way she can."

He licked his lips like he could taste it on his tongue. "Yeah, her peach cobbler is special," the deacon said, still eyeing the mothers.

Mother Johns watched Carmia sitting quietly. *Stiff as a statue, a regular angel.* Hmmm, *ain't no truth to that.*

Mother Johns circled back to Deacon Pitts. "Speaking of your wife, that's why we made this visit. We just came from the hospital. She say you ain't been by today."

The mothers board drew near, watching his response—even Mother Givens.

"Yeah, well, I was gonna head by there after a while. Been working all day, keeping up the house in her absence too; somebody has to tend to this child here."

Disbelief filled the room; the mothers eyed each other about his words.

He continued, "Made sure the girl had her breakfast this morning."

She looked down on Carmia, still wearing an apron.

The mothers board, unsatisfied with his excuses, snooped more boldly. "If it weren't for the hospital threatening to release her each day, I woulda moved this child till she come home," Mother Johns said.

"*Ummm-hmmm,* that seems right," he said.

Mother Givens ended her espionage and smiled at the teen while handing her a bag of gummy bears; then, she sat next to Carmia, took her hand, and prayed silently. Although rarely in agreement, Mother Johns could tell Mother Givens had discerned a problem too—she wouldn't look at Deacon Pitts very long.

Hmmm, not challenging my discernment today.

Pastor Himley, in his blatantly unaware manner, had been the perfect decoy to accompany the mothers board on their visit.

That fool don't know when he's in the enemy's territory.

He sat playing spiritual father, blabbing, trying endlessly to fill the pews. Mother Johns picked up the mail and thumbed through it.

Congregation ain't grown in ten years, trying to catch fish already been caught.

She noticed Sister Pitts' makeup on the kitchen table and frowned. Next, she inspected Carmia's face: no makeup, but her lips were faintly red.

"What you been putting on your lips, gal?"

"Nothing," Carmia said.

"Looks like lipstick. Don't lie."

"Don't have no lipstick. Probably Kool-Aid stains." Carmia shifted and rubbed her palm.

The church mother raised her brow, settling her eyes on the girl for a while.

Think I was born this morning.

She hadn't put her finger on it, but there was something different about Carmia that she didn't trust. Her appearance was calm, polite, and peaceful, but such perfection was a dead giveaway that deception was present. Mother Givens was still holding the girl's hand and praying for her, but she was tense. Mother Johns saw Mother Givens peering at Carmia with worry. The two mothers eyed each other and didn't say another word to Deacon Pitts. Mother Johns looked at M.T., who peered at Mother Farrell, who gazed at the old mother. Then, in unison, like a flock of birds in strict formation, they wrapped themselves in their shawls and left the Pittses' house with perfect parting courtesies: "Blessings on you, Deacon Pitts—Carmia."

Deacon Pitts uneasily rose from his seat to see them out. He smiled, saying nothing in return. Mother Johns watched Pastor Himley from the porch, exercising his formalities.

"Lord be with you until we meet again, brother."

The deacon, unconcerned with their meaningless traditions, nodded.

"Until we meet again, Pastor."

Pastor Himley smiled at Carmia and had begun pastoral good-byes when he heard Mother Johns' voice calling from the porch, "Himley. We're waiting on you." He quickly patted Carmia on the head and rushed away to the demanding cry of the mothers board in waiting. Mother Johns watched Deacon Pitts close the door behind them. She could see him through the window as he walked past Carmia, like she wasn't there, although she seemed to want to be seen.

I'm gonna skin that cat yet.

21

Mother and Child

AFTER TUSSLING FOR HOURS DURING THE FREEZING NIGHT, Carmia fell into a deep sleep, but a faint sound that escalated into the noise of someone pounding on the door woke her.

Might be Joseph.

She wrapped herself in her robe and ran to the door. She bumped her head on the door as she approached it. "Who is it?"

"Me. Let me in my house." It was Sister Pitts possessing all the anger and pain of a woman scorned and neglected, held in the hospital weeks after giving birth.

Carmia quickly unlocked the door and opened it. Sister Pitts seemed to flame with anger all over, yet her demeanor was cold. She held her one-month-old crying baby in her arms and had a box and suitcase on the porch. Her hair hung like Rastafarian dreadlocks— her eyes were torches housed in pits. She shook with vexation as she spoke between her teeth.

"What you staring at me for? Get my stuff off the porch."

Carmia could hardly complete Sister Pitts' first command before the woman demanded further aid. "Hurry up and get the diapers off the steps too."

"Okay," Carmia said.

I'm a slave again.

"Where is my husband?"

"I–I don't know, Sister Pitts," the girl whispered.

"Don't call me Sister. You ain't none of my sister, by blood or spirit."

Carmia shivered from Sister Pitts' voice. "He might be asleep. I'll go see."

It seemed Sister Pitts' face turned burgundy at the thought of Carmia viewing her husband in his bedclothes. She pushed Carmia out of the way with her hips and said, "I'll do it myself."

The girl stumbled to the side, making the hallway clear. Sister Pitts' bags were still in her hands. The woman irritated her. She glared in her direction. Sister Pitts marched down the hall like a wounded soldier abandoned by her army. Carmia's anger toward her was interrupted by a rising smile on her face.

That's why you been embarrassing yourself out in public that way.

She had noticed a red stain on the back of Sister Pitts' skirt. Carmia giggled, not finding the strength to contain herself until she heard Sister Pitts swearing in the distance. The newest member of the Pittses' family continued to wail.

Carmia sat on the suitcase and began to bite her fingernails, something her mother would have scolded her for, but the reality of her present life was causing her mother's voice to fade farther and farther away. The face of the woman she called Mom was a foggy memory. Her grandmother's face was waning, too, just as the lives themselves had already done.

"Ouch," the girl said. She held her bleeding index finger with the nail ripped away too high.

Carmia heard the Pittses arguing. Georgie stormed past Carmia, then out of the house. She sauntered to their room and peeped in. Sister Pitts looked like the lady Pastor Himley had preached about years ago in Ezekiel.

She struggling in her own blood, barely alive, needing God to cover her with His wings and make her whole again.

She was weak—sweating so much her clothes were wet. Carmia stood quietly in the Pittses' bedroom doorway, still waiting to see if Sister Pitts was going to want her help. She bit her nails again. Sister Pitts kept rocking her baby up high toward her breast, and eventually, her arms fell to her lap. The baby was hollering, face red and frowned up—lips quivering with each cry.

Cute little angry thing.

Sister Pitts looked at her like she was a roach. She wanted to stomp out of her life. She tried to hush the baby again, but she was too weak. Her arms fell again. She looked dizzy, like she might faint. She had made it clear that she didn't want the girl's help, but she needed it.

Gonna have to trust me. Ain't got no choice.

The girl just stood there waiting.

Carmia smiled to reassure her and said, "Do you want me to hold the baby so you can rest?"

Sister Pitts just shifted in bed with her baby still hollering.

She making my ears ring. She thought the baby had to be getting on her mom's nerves.

"Sister Pitts, what's your baby's name?"

The woman rolled her eyes. "That ain't none of your business," she said and pointed to the bottle of milk. "I just fed her. Don't know why she's so upset."

Carmia handed her the bottle.

Grandma used to say children take on the mood of their parents, but I won't dare say it.

"Newborn babies just like to cry. Ain't use to this world yet," she said.

Unfortunately, she's got a whole lot of crying to do being a girl in this world and in this family.

Sweat rolled down Sister Pitts' face so that it got into her eyes. Carmia went into the bathroom, wet a face towel, and handed it to her. Sister Pitts hesitated at first. Carmia could tell she didn't want to put her baby in her arms, but she gave in and surrendered her child to the girl's careful embrace. Sister Pitts wiped her face, then collapsed into a hunched-over position on her bed.

The kind of whole-again touch she needs is for inside and out.

Carmia trembled, looking at the baby. It felt good and scary to hold such a tiny, innocent person.

I want to be pure like this baby. Seems like that's what we all want.

"Hush, little baby." Carmia sat on the floor with glossy eyes and fed the baby until there was no more milk. The baby cried again in a low whimper.

It wasn't much milk. The baby was still hungry. *This baby crying for something this house can't give, something I want too—love.*

She and the child were both hungry, and the sun rose on them that way.

The next night, Carmia waited up for Deacon Pitts, pretending to be asleep on the couch. He entered the living room and found her there. He shook her, but she didn't move. He lifted her and carried her into the hallway toward her room as he had before.

He smells sour like Mom did.

Her weight and his poor judgment in balancing the two of them caused him to stumble.

He's drunk. I should wait. But he doesn't pay me any attention anymore.

Carmia opened her eyes and kissed his lips as they entered her room. She wondered if he had been with a woman down at the Shack.

If he has, I hate him.

She kissed him, trying to be seen again, wanting what they had before the mothers board had visited and before Sister Pitts had come home.

He squeezed Carmia, held her close to his chest, and kissed her back. Then he stopped, looked at her, and moved away. He trembled and cried.

It's okay. Love me, Georgie.

He sighed like a weight had lifted. He seemed to have finally made up his mind. He licked his chapped lips. Carmia was proud to be so beautiful that he couldn't resist her. She relaxed further in his arms. She wanted to replace Sister Pitts in his life.

She's a mean woman.

Carmia hugged him, enjoying his sensitivity to the softness of her skin.

He seemed bound to her, couldn't let her go now. She felt loved. She lay in bed, trembling but yearning for his affection. She had laid in bed, thinking of him so many times. Her eyes filled with tears, but she didn't know if it meant joy or fear.

She kind of hated herself for wanting him, needing his touch. She forgot how much she wanted to be pure. The wedding gowns she admired as a girl flashed through her mind. But she couldn't stop herself.

I'm just like my mother now.

She imagined that was how her mother felt about the men she was with—men were a temporary fix for a high they were seeking that could never be reached.

She wanted to be loved. "Georgie?" He ignored her, frowning like her voice irritated the moment. "Georgie," she said again.

"Huh?"

"Do you love me?"

He froze like he didn't know how to answer.

Why don't you say it?

"Yeah, I love you," he mumbled. He closed the door and locked it as he gave in to his desire for her.

Several minutes later, the deacon exited her room with only a sheet around his waist and stood in the doorway. Tired. The kind of weariness of the soul that needed to be taken to Jesus for rest. Then he looked back at Carmia blankly, as though he didn't seem to be wrestling inside anymore. Carmia looked into his eyes, and tears began to form in them.

What's wrong? A deeper understanding of their act was unfolding in her mind. She panted as her body shook.

I'm dirty. He hates me now.

"Georgie, what's wrong?" He didn't speak. "Tell me."

They were both in tears. He gazed back at Carmia as though it were the first time he had really seen her pain. Carmia was naked, her soul exposed. Her eyes longed for something he wasn't prepared to give. She had given herself to him as a sacrifice for love and warmth in return. She looked at him, somehow aware that her beauty had faded in his eyes.

She reached for him—reaching for what he couldn't give, for what she remembered this house was unprepared to give her and the baby.

Why doesn't it feel right anymore? Why don't I feel loved anymore? Mom, help me. I feel like I'm dying.

She bawled uncontrollably; he trembled in tears. He looked at her as if he could feel her hurt, see her desperation—the desperation of generations of hurting women in her family. Carmia felt this weight too. He seemed to gaze at her like he could see again that she was just a girl, not a woman. Then she remembered him teaching in church about God helping him to live a spotless life. Holy and consecrated, he had called himself. He was proud because of it. It was as though preaching was one of the few times he ever appeared truly happy. Now his face looked tortured.

Maybe he feels soiled now, dirty like me.

She couldn't stop this flood of pain that had entered the room. "I'm sorry, Carmia," he said.

Then it occurred to her that maybe what they had done was too much for a man of God to bear. She could hear the mothers' voices attacking him—attacking her too. She panicked and started shaking her fingers like they were on fire. She wanted Grandma Evans and was ashamed to want her too.

He ran from her doorway into the garage, unlocked his tool drawer, and pulled out his pistol. With a trembling hand, the deacon placed the gun in his mouth and pulled the trigger. The explosion startled Carmia, who ran into the garage, wearing her thin, pink robe. Georgie's face was unrecognizable. Blood and tiny particles of his flesh were everywhere. She couldn't move. The gunshot had awakened Sister Pitts and the baby. She grabbed her fussy child and followed the sound in horror. She looked at Carmia and back at her husband—bloody on the garage floor, wrapped in the girl's flower printed sheet. Terrified, she looked at Carmia with blame and slapped her right cheek. The baby cried louder. Carmia screamed and raced into the street. She bumped into Pastor Himley, who had run out of his house because of the gunshot.

"What's wrong, child?"

Carmia shook, her eyes big and puffy, slobber hanging from her mouth. She panted and convulsed, pointing toward the Pittses' house. Pastor Himley trembled too. He was all shook up seeing her, hearing gunshots, and so much ruckus. He threw his heavier robe to her and ran in his pajamas toward the Pittses' house, huffing and puffing. More neighbors came out of their homes, hurrying and scurrying to follow Pastor Himley to the Pittses' home. But not Mother Johns; she seemed to walk in slow motion toward the house. She stopped beside Carmia, who remained on the curb with the pastor's robe on, and gazed at her. It was as if the mother looked into the depth of her soul, observing generations of Ma Evans' bloodline. The old woman pulled the robe more closely around the girl's body, patted her on the head, then gestured for her hand. Carmia took the mother's hand, and together they walked to the dead man's house, where all the commotion continued—the girl limp as though she might faint. The mother left her on the porch shivering as she entered the place.

Minutes later, Mother Johns emerged from the Pittses' home with Pastor Himley, the rest of the mother's board, and a few others from the community. She looked at Carmia and shook her head. "I'm anointed to deal with peoples like her. I'm gonna have this child stay with me for a spell, 'til I know better what to do with her."

"Amen." Mother Thompson said. While Mother Givens put her head down as though in prayer.

Pastor Himley looked at Mother Johns and said, "You's the salt of the earth for this, the salt of the earth." Mother Johns smiled like a good mother should.

She took a few steps and yanked the girl's hand. Now they walked at a brisk pace, in tempo, as if in a separate eerie universe all of their own. Finally, when they were out of earshot, Mother Johns faced the girl, a smug smile on her lips. "I can sense when new life is conceived. You just been a little monkey in heat, ain't you?" Carmia looked up in fear. Relishing the fright she instilled in the girl, Mother Johns said, "I'm gonna train you the way I never did get to school your grandma and Laura. You gone learn 'bout the consequences of spreading your legs to married men. I'm gonna choke the sin out of this cursed bloodline yet, so help me, God. You gone pay the price they all should've paid —a family of Jezebels." Tears welled up in the girl's eyes. She shivered, not from the night air, but from Mother Johns' cold presence. As she followed the mean church mother down the street, Carmia realized she was trapped. Even though she was leaving behind a life of abuse and betrayal, she was heading toward a more horrific fate with Mother Johns.

Will Carmia ever free herself from Mother Johns' control?

Can the voices of Carmia's matriarchs guide her to wholeness?

Will more family secrets be revealed as Mother Johns attempts to break Carmia?

When the Bovina community learns that Carmia was sexually assaulted by Deacon Pitts, will they comfort her or condemn her?

Will Carmia and Carl ever be together again?

What type of punishment does Mother Johns have in store for Carmia?

Will Joseph turn his back on Carmia and their childhood promise?

Author's Note

GIRLS IN SEARCH OF COVER IS A GRIPPING STORY, WHICH CONfronts the tragic reality that some sexually abused children and adults face daily. While Carmia Pullens is a black fictional character who is abused as a child while living in lower-to middle-class communities, childhood abuse happens at every social-economic level, across ethnic and cultural lines, within all religions and at all levels of education. Importantly, 95% of abuse is preventable through education and awareness. (Child Molestation Research and Prevention Institute). This book is written to draw attention to this devastating epidemic. Carmia's psychological journey was carefully drawn to demonstrate the crippling emotional and mental torment that may lead many victims to have very poor self-esteem and even suicidal thoughts, which can manifest outwardly in destructive behaviors. Emotional damage is more severe when a child is sexually abused before the age of six for a lasting period of time. Child and teen victims of sexual abuse together represent a 42% increased chance of suicidal thoughts during adolescence. (American Counseling Association). My hope in writing this book is to encourage any sexually abused persons reading it to gain the strength to seek help and support. If you or someone you know are or have been a victim of sexual abuse and need help, please call the RAINN (Rape, Abuse, & Incest National Network) Hotline at (800) 656-HOPE (4673).

I have listed other staggering statistics below for your awareness:

- There are more than 42 million survivors of sexual abuse in the United States of America. (National Association of Adult Survivors of Child Abuse)
- One in three girls is sexually abused before age 18. (The Advocacy Center)
- One in five boys is sexually abused before age 18. (The Advocacy Center)
- One in five children is solicited sexually while on the internet before age 18. (National Children's Alliance: Nationwide Child Abuse Statistics)
- 90% of childhood sexual abuse victims know their perpetrator in some way. (U. S. Department of Justice)
- Approximately 20% of the victims of sexual abuse are under age eight. (Broward County)
- There are nearly half a million registered sex offenders in the U.S.–80, 000 to 100, 000 of them are missing. (The National Center for Missing and Exploited Children)
- "A typical pedophile will commit 117 sexual crimes in a lifetime." (National Sex Offenders Registry)

I do not know firsthand what it is like to experience the exact same situations that Carmia faced in this novel, but I do know what it is like to be sexually abused by an adult when I was a child.

I also know the crippling effect it has on one's emotional well-being. I know personally how sexual abuse can rob an individual of self-worth and how this trauma spills over to negatively interfere with nearly every other facet of a one's life without him or her ever realizing it. If this sounds like you or someone you love, please see the support resources listed above and seek help.

Acknowledgments

I GIVE THANKS TO MY HEAVENLY FATHER, WHO INSPIRED ME TO write this novel as an act to help myself, and hopefully others, receive some degree of healing from sexual abuse. Lord, I have come to appreciate the journey, although difficult, because you've taught me how to rise above the pain and then reach out to help other hurting people. It is my prayer that sexually abused people might see themselves in my characters' actions or psychological journey and receive inner healing from their own hands as well as through help from others around them.

To my lovely daughter, Mariva, you have always been the reason I flew, even with broken wings and believed until I could soar as an eagle. You are such a gift from God to me and my greatest blessing. I could not desire a better daughter who is supportive, sensitive and as caring as you. From day one, we became a team, in which one couldn't fall because of support from the other. I didn't know so many years ago that I would give birth to my best friend. Let's keep traveling the world and conquering it together along the way.

Mommy Patricia, my longest love. You are God's wings in the

flesh forever covering me. I could have no other mother but you. No one else could play the role of mothering me from birth until now as gracefully as you have. I would not be the person I am today without your unwavering love, guidance and spiritual wisdom. I am thankful for your caring heart and I grow in greater understanding of your unconditional love daily. I am overwhelmed by it. These words are another way that I seek to give you your flowers, Proverbs 31 woman of God. I call you blessed (with overtures of Kevin's voice too).

To the best brother ever, Kevin D. May. I miss you dearly but I am thankful that I had a brother like you for as long as I did. Some siblings will never know the unconditional love between brother and sister that caused so many strangers and those who knew us well to wonder how we became so close. Thank you for always making me feel accepted and protected in the midst of my many insecurities. You were my steady place and continue to be. I know you're on the other side still rooting for me to win the race given to me. I sense you cheering me on still. Thank you for your last physical words repeated to me three times, "I love you." I love you back, big brother.

To my prayer partner and aunt, Linda Spotville, thanks for always believing in me on a level that wouldn't let me forget that which I'm capable of achieving because you see my gifting (spiritually and naturally) more clearly than I.

Thank you to the rest of my closely knit family members: Brenda Thomas, Ricky Spotville, Mr. and Mrs. James Spotville, Mr. and Mrs. George Spotville, Shaun Ná Erwin, James Reeves, TraVell Erwin, Angela May, Bria May, Aisha May, and the Mshana family in Tanzania, Africa. Because of all of you, I know that someone always has my back. We always come together when one of us is in need and sometimes just in want. We have modeled the concept of a family that prays together, stays together.

To all of my supportive friends, I am so grateful that you do not let me walk through life's journey without chosen family: Joyce Lee, Toni Ann Johnson, Jo Duer, Dani Rasshan, Raquel Watts, Dr. Betty R. Price, Cheryl Price, Shandria Richmond-Roberts, Stephanie Joseph, Robbyn Stafford, Lori Paley, Sherry Young and Stephanie Baker.

To my awesome writing coaches and first readers: Kate Maruyama and Robert Harders (coaches), Linda Spotville, Dani Rasshan, Mariva Mshana-Dawes, Nicole Smith-Moshari, Meg Harders, Lori Paley, Stephanie Joseph, Jen and Nicole De Anda, Sherry Young, Toni Ann Johnson, Dr. Betty R. Price and Regina Porter. Your collective and candid feedback has been invaluable to the development of my novel and overall process. I know the time you took from your busy schedules to read this novel and provide meaningful and impactful insight was a true labor of love.

To Dr. Betty R. Price and Toni Ann Johnson, I truly appreciate your kind words provided to express your support of me and my work.

To my wonderful editors, production team and mentors: Nicole Sconiers (content editor), Chandra Splond (copy editor), Olivier Darbonville (interior designer), Lita P. Ward (consultant), Laura Duffy (cover designer and graphics), and Robert Harders, Toni Ann Johnson and Kimberla Lawson Roby (mentors). You all applied your expertise and advice to help my novel shine and I wouldn't have accomplished this publication without your time and support. God bless you all and grant you a hundred-fold return for giving your time, advice and love!

Heartfelt,

Dr. Pamela Mariva Mshana

About the Author

PAMELA MSHANA, PHD IS AN ACCOMPLISHED PLAYWRIGHT, author and educator with work produced at Playwrights Horizons, Off-Broadway theater in New York City. While she is already a published playwright, *girls in search of cover* marks her debut novel. Dr. Mshana earned a Bachelor of Fine Arts (BFA) degree in dramatic writing from New York University (Tisch School of the Arts); a master's degree in education from Azusa Pacific University and a PhD in urban leadership from Claremont Graduate University, (both located in Southern California). Dr. Mshana has been an educator for more than 20 years, serving in multiple roles from teaching to administration. She was born and raised in the Inland Empire. Dr. Mshana is the proud mother of Mariva Mshana-Dawes and honored daughter of Patricia Hughes-Caraway. She loves to travel, both nationally and internationally, and has visited 23 countries on four continents. Her wealth of diverse life experiences greatly informs her creativity and wisdom as an author.

Made in the USA
Columbia, SC
22 May 2022

60731125R00174